Review Quotes for Beneath the Mask

By V—

...This tale has many twists and turns that ramp up the tension in believable ways. A regency romance to remember.

By J—

...Even if you're not sure if this is your kind of book, if you read the description and feel called to read more, do so. You won't regret it.

By D—

Awesome Regency Romance! ...was pleasantly surprised to be sucked into the story and taken for a wild romping good time!

Other Works by
Margaret McGaffey Fisk

UNCOMMON LORDS AND LADIES
(SWEET REGENCY ROMANCES)

A Country Masquerade
An Innocent Secret

THE STEAMSHIP CHRONICLES
(STEAMPUNK ADVENTURE)

Safe Haven
Secrets
Threats
Gifts
Life and Law
Steam and Shadows

FOSTER'S WAY
(SWEET CONTEMPORARY ROMANCE)

Becoming Home

SEEDS AMONG THE STARS
(SCIENCE FICTION ADVENTURE)

Shafter
Trainee
The Captain's Chair (Indie Traders Novelette)
Apprentice

SHORT STORIES (eBook only)

When the Shoe Won't Fit
Forged
War Child
Curve of Her Claw (illustrated by Star Olsen)

*Visit margaretmcgaffeyfisk.com for more information
about these and other titles.*

Beneath the Mask

UNCOMMON LORDS AND LADIES

BOOK ONE

Margaret McGaffey Fisk

TTO
PUBLISHING

Cover Art by Margaret McGaffey Fisk

Background illustration is the Interior of Theatre Royal, Drury Lane. Circa 1808 published as Plate 32 of Microcosm of London (1808)

TTO Publishing logo design by Blue Harvest Creative
www.blueharvestcreative.com

Beneath the Mask

Published by
TTO Publishing

ISBN-10: 1-63139-026-0
ISBN-13: 978-1-63139-026-5

First Print Edition

Visit the author at:

Website: margaretmcgaffeyfisk.com
Twitter: @Marfisk
Google Plus: +MargaretMcGaffeyFiskAuthor
Facebook: MargaretMcGaffeyFisk

Prologue

Monsieur Henre watched his favorite pupil twirl, her arms curved into a perfect oval above her head. "I've been practicing," she said, spinning to a stop in front of the dance instructor. "Don't you see, Monsieur Henre?"

He offered an indulgent smile. The teaching contracts helped fund his true love: dance theater. In Lady Daphne, though, he'd found a star. A pity her talents would be wasted. "You know I see how hard you work. You have the grace of a swan. Lord Scarborough will be proud."

She frowned. "My father doesn't care what I do." Her lower lip jutted out past her chin, making her look much younger than her seventeen years.

With a laugh, Monsieur Henre finished packing his things back into the carpet bag he used. "He cares enough to recognize you love to dance. Most fathers would have stopped your practice sessions with me long ago. Most only want their daughters to glide across the dance floor so they can catch the eye of some rich nobleman."

Her pout vanished as the young woman spun again, this time ending with her arms wrapped around her budding body. "He gives me this, you're right. My sister is the one to marry well. She's prettier and the eldest. All I want to do is dance."

"And dance you do, with a skill that rivals some of the professionals I work with. It's good that your father lets you have this luxury." Monsieur Henre picked up his bag and walked to the door, believing the conversation over.

A slim hand clutched his arm, halting him. "Then let me come with you. If I'm so good, let me dance for a true audience. I would make you proud."

He looked down into her pleading face and saw only what trouble such a gift would cause. "Lady Daphne, your father indulges you only so far. Think of the scandal if one of your position would dance for all comers. The Earl, your father, would never stand for it."

She laughed, the bitter tinge obvious to her teacher. "I don't care about scandal. And my position's a joke. Our title's old, granted, but we live like paupers. My father should be proud that I want to help support the family."

Monsieur Henre put out a hand to stop her outburst, shaking his head. "But we both know he would not. You'll need to tend to your other studies if you want to help the family coffers. Become a governess. That's a worthy occupation for one of your standing. You know nothing of true poverty if you think fine houses and dance instructors mark a pauper's life."

Daphne twisted her toe against the thick carpet. "I don't want to be a governess. I want to dance." She glared at him, ignoring his caution, her slender body trembling with the force of her passion.

"You would have made a magnificent dancer with all that fire," he murmured to himself. "You'll find happiness easier if you let this go," he said in a stronger voice. "It is something you can never have, and you'll break your heart in crying after it."

"I won't give it up," she said fiercely. "I won't give it up for anything."

He reached out and patted her cheek to calm her. "Lady Daphne, I just hope you never have to." Sweeping a low bow, he opened the door and moved through it, leaving her troubles behind as his own rose to take their place. The dance hall failed to bring in enough of an audience again the previous night. Their contract would be cancelled if he couldn't provide the bored nobles and tradesfolk with something new, something extraordinary.

Chapter One

So? Which one is it?"

Jasper turned toward his friend and shot Aubrey a heated look. "I think Baker's boy has the best whip hand I've seen for a while. Thatcher, though, can take corners with no regard for the innocent traffic. That alone will shave minutes from his time."

Aubrey jerked the monocle out of Jasper's hand. "You know full well that's not what I'm talking about. Your mother gave you a month to choose a bride, and today's your last day. Who have you chosen?"

Pushing to his feet, Jasper tossed down enough to cover their light lunch, suddenly having lost interest in seeing the end of the cart race. "What does it matter? They're all much the same. Not a single real thought to spare among them. The same teachers, the same dressmakers…they are block prints on the fabric of my life."

Aubrey wisely kept silent as they strode through the streets of London, passing the places frequented by their mothers and heading for those where they'd best not be identified by any of the female persuasion.

Finally, Jasper stopped outside a pub catering mostly to sailors fresh off the naval boats. "I couldn't choose," he said, the irritation clear in his voice. "I couldn't debase myself further by actually considering any of them."

"You're letting your mother choose a wife?" Aubrey asked, horrified. "This is the woman you'll spend the rest of your life with. Can't you find the slightest interest?"

Jasper reached out to clasp his friend's shoulder. "If I do this to please my mother, let her be pleased. If I chose one of them and she turned out to be a hag, I'd have no one to blame but myself."

A surprised laugh burst from Aubrey as he shook his head. "You're an original, Jasper. Never would have thought it out that way, but you're right. She turns out horrible, and you'll be able to wind your mother around your little pinkie. I can see you now, 'I did it all for you, Mother, and see what I'm left with?'"

Pivoting Aubrey so he could push his friend through the door, Jasper grinned. "It's not like I'll see much of her anyway. I'll just whelp a child or two on her and spend my days here in London while she lords over one of my grand properties. We may not have the fancy titles, but my family is loaded."

"A caution, my friend. Your mother's like as not to choose some impoverished earl or duke to bind to the family. I can see her now, going over huge lists to find the candidates who have more title than coin. Oh, and don't forget, those without male line entitlements. If she can't raise her own standing or yours, she'll be sure to raise that of your get. Just imagine when your lady's father passes away and your oldest son outranks you."

Jasper signaled the barkeep. "Two porter, my good man," he called before answering Aubrey. "Does it matter? Her title means nothing once she's my wife. I will have charge of her and all her doings. She'll stay in the country as I will it, and the children with her."

Aubrey looked dubious, but said nothing further as their tankards arrived.

"Just think," Jasper added, laughter gleaming in his eyes, "You're next for the marriage bed. I'm sure your mum could happily find some chit to slip between your sheets."

Choking on his stout, Aubrey glared at Jasper. "I'll do the choosing," he finally gasped out. "I'm not leaving my future to chance as you seem willing to do."

Jasper took a long draw of his beer then wiped the foam from his upper lip. "At least you have a year or two before your mission is proved foolhardy. I tell you, there are no women among that gaggle of girls. Enjoy what time you have of freedom."

The door slammed open and a group of seamen staggered through the entrance, this obviously not the first stop in their day's revelry.

"Come, let's go find a more hospitable location to take our rest." Jasper strolled to the bar to pay his bill, unwilling to keep a tab at every place he went like most of his class. The smell of sea salt only brought back memories of what he could have been had either of his brothers survived to sire an heir. He'd been promised the Royal Navy since he wore short pants, but fate had a way of changing things.

"There's a dance troupe not far from here," Aubrey offered. "I've heard they're solid if not exciting."

Jasper forced his mouth to smile. "Solid describes much of my sorry life now. I might as well add another to the mix. It'll give us something to pass the time until we head to White's to check the results and collect my winnings."

Aubrey punched Jasper in the shoulder. "You're so sure of winning?"

"I always do."

A wave of his hand and a hackney pulled up next to them. "Give him the directions, Aubrey, and we'll go see these solid dancers of yours."

"He's from a good family with a title even if you'll bring in a stronger one. Lord Pendleton is a baron, not some tradesman buying his way into nobility."

Daphne slipped into the sitting room, wondering how to ask her mother to let her dance. She'd waited for the best moment to raise it, but Monsieur Henre was due back this very day, and she wanted to be able to tell him so. At least they seemed happy now with the question of Grace's marriage resolved.

"And money, dear, don't forget his family properties are exceedingly well managed. The boy goes wherever he likes just so the men can badger him about husbandry and farming. I'll be taking him around our properties myself."

Their mother laughed, gently stroking Grace's arm. "She doesn't care about husbandry, my love. She cares about the husband she'll spend the rest of her life with."

"And titles make the man?" their father asked in a gruff voice.

Rising from the settee, Lady Scarborough wrapped her arm through his. "Of course, my love. Titles are the icing on a delicious snack cake. If you hadn't a title to speak of, my parents would never have let me meet you, much less marry, and see how that turned out."

He patted her on the cheek, his smile so full of love, Daphne almost envied them, but she had more important things to do with her life than marry well.

"Exactly my point, dearest. We have to make sure the boy meets our criteria and then love will come in time."

"He's a man, not a boy," Grace muttered, her gaze modestly entangled with her twisting fingers.

Both parents turned to stare at their eldest daughter, surprise painted on their faces.

"How would you know?" her mother asked.

Grace looked up, her smile a fragile thing to see. "I've seen him at the Mackeley's ball. He didn't seem all that interested in any of us. I wonder that he wants to marry at all."

"Oh posh, no young man wants to be married. They don't understand just how wonderful it is until they experience the bliss themselves. Don't give it a second thought." Mother came to sit next to Grace again, pulling her eldest daughter's hands into her lap. "They see all they'll lose and none of what comes to them. Even my Thomas was reluctant at first, and see what we've become." She sent their father a look.

Daphne felt the tension between them as easily as she'd felt the love. Grace worried them. So much depended on her sister marrying well, but they wanted her to be happy.

Her request no longer seemed favored, so Daphne rose, trying to slip out of the room while they hadn't yet noticed her.

"Daphne?"

She froze as her father called her name.

"I hadn't seen you there. Do you have something to tell us?" Her father tugged out his gold pocket watch and checked the time before looking toward her again.

Daphne squirmed a little, trying to come up with something else she could say instead of begging to be allowed to dance professionally.

Father laughed. "Out with it, my girl. Ask any boon you want on this day. With Grace's future secure, there's little I'd withhold."

She moved to her father's side, pulling him into a hug. "You are the best father in the world," she whispered, meaning every word.

He put his hands on her shoulders and pushed her far enough away so he could meet her gaze. "Now I know something important is dancing around in your little head. Come on and tell your dear father. I never did like to wait on surprises."

Daphne took a deep breath before speaking, dragging her courage about her. "Dancing is right. Monsieur Henre says I'm really good I'm better than any of his other pupils." The words burst out of her in a rush, then she paused, waiting to see their effect.

Her father mussed her hair and smiled. "As it should be when you do something you love. I'm glad you enjoy dancing so much, but you have to remember there's more to life than just that."

"Not for me," she said, shaking her head. "I want to dance for always." She twirled in a circle, showing them a bit of the routine she'd been practicing.

Catching her outstretched hand, her father moved her through the complicated steps of a line dance until they both sank into chairs, exhausted.

"She definitely gets the dancing from you, Thomas. I've never had quite the balance to pull it off."

Too tired to move, he waved to Mother with a limp hand. "You have grace in other ways that make up for the dancing."

"I had Grace some nineteen years ago. And now I'm planning to let her grow up."

They all laughed at the wordplay as Grace rose to ring the servant's bell for drinks.

Only when they'd sipped lemon tea and nibbled on cucumber sandwiches did Daphne remember her purpose in coming to this room. "Father," she said, catching his attention. "I really am a fine dancer."

He smiled. "I'm sure you are. As your mother said, you come by it honestly."

"I could do so much more than be graceful at my sister's wedding," Daphne said, unsure how to ask.

"Oh, dear." Lady Scarborough put down her cup and rushed across the room. "You don't think we won't take care of you as well, do you? I know it's all been about Grace this season, but you're growing up also. Don't think we haven't noticed. Once Grace is settled, she and I will give you the best coming out ever seen. Won't we, Grace?"

Her sister nodded, fingers tense around the handle of her teacup. "I'll do whatever I can," she murmured.

"There. You see? Nothing to worry about. You just keep up with your lessons, and we'll find a man worthy of your love as soon as Grace is settled."

Daphne clenched her fists, angry at their preoccupation. "I don't want to marry," she declared. "I want to perform."

The room fell silent. Even Grace seemed stunned by her pronouncement.

Daphne wished the words unsaid, ashamed not of their content but of how she'd offered them. "Monsieur Henre says I'm good enough. He says I'm as good if not better than the dancers in his troupe."

She leapt out of her chair and went down on her knees before her father. "If you would just give your blessing, I could dance for real. I could become famous."

"Get up off the floor," her mother demanded. "More like infamous. What do you think the ton would say if my daughter joined the performers?" The way she said the last word made it sound dirty.

Daphne got up, but only to round on her mother. "They're nothing more than hardworking artists. You wouldn't condemn a poet for living for his art. Why keep me from mine?"

"Daphne Louise, you will respect your mother and honor her word. You are not to make a spectacle of yourself in front of strangers. It's not fitting."

She quailed a bit under her father's firm stare, but tried to stand her ground.

"I had no idea what foolish ideas that Frenchman instilled in her, Thomas. I'll not have him in this house again."

Daphne turned to face her mother, horrified. "You can't," she wailed. "I'll do anything."

Her father took hold of Daphne's shoulders and turned her back to face him. "You are a young woman now. Another year and your mind will be filled with thoughts of a husband and children. I take full responsibility for letting it go this far, but with delaying your coming out for Grace, and your mother being so busy, it seemed a fair exchange at the time. I should have paid more attention when I knew you mastered the formal dances, along with your other studies, long ago." He sighed and shook his head. "It's time to grow up, my dear. To take on adult interests. I know it seems harsh now, but you'll come to understand once you're out in society. Some things are just never done."

She raised trembling fingers to her mouth, water gathering in her eyes as her world tore apart. "I'll never understand," she cried. "Never."

Daphne pulled free of her father's hold and raced through their townhouse until she reached the nursery that had been her home every time they'd come up to London. She threw herself down onto her bed and stared blind-eyed at the ceiling. Never before had she felt so angry, so lost.

Chapter Two

Daphne did not know how much time passed as she lay there, but at some point her mind started churning once again. It offered up possibilities at first so wild she could hardly countenance them then more sober reflection brought hope. He'd been surprised, shocked even, but her father never stayed cross for long. She'd done much worse than wish for something he did not approve of when younger, and he always forgave her.

Daphne drew strength from the knowledge then used that confidence to calm herself. Crying would not serve her cause, but a reasoned argument might.

She had only to convince him to retain Monsieur Henre's services, and she'd give up any further dreams of performing. The power of a real audience, bringing pleasure and amazement to others, drew her, but after all, she'd never had those things beyond in her imagination. She could be satisfied with the teacher who gave her feelings life in the form of dance.

Waiting only long enough for the red marks in her eyes to fade, she ventured down the stairs once again, this time a controlled young woman.

"Father?"

He had retired to his study as she'd expected, his head bent over a letter as he put the final touches to it before sanding.

Lord Scarborough glanced up and frowned to see her, not the reaction Daphne had hoped for, but one she'd expected.

"I'm sorry, Father. I didn't mean to upset you earlier. Monsieur Henre is not to blame, only a young girl's fancy. He never once suggested anything beyond noting my skill. Please, I'll let it go, forget I ever had such a thought, if you'll only let him continue to teach me."

He settled back into his chair, the wood creaking with his familiar weight. "Daphne, the deed is done. It's time for you to turn your mind to other pleasures and prepare for your adult life. You cannot stay in the nursery forever."

Her confidence faltered at his words. "You dismissed him already?"

Lord Scarborough shook the excess sand from the letter he'd been writing. "I have his dismissal right here and will deliver it as soon as the monsieur arrives for today's lesson. Your mother and I have spoken on this. With Grace's future arranged, there's no cause to keep you back any longer. Lady Scarborough is off to secure the indulgence of an audience with the Prince Regent as we speak. It's well past time for it this year, but your schooling is long completed, and you need the distraction," he said, casting a stern look in her direction.

Daphne smothered her gasp with one hand even as she reached with the other to snatch up the dismissal notice from her father's loose grip. "I don't want to come out, not this season or any. I'll tear the notice to shreds so you can't do this to me."

He shook his head and put a hand out palm up. "Even were it not beyond the pale, obsession is not a pretty trait in a young lady. I accept the fault is my own. I let you run a little wild as a young thing, despite your mother's warnings, and the dance seemed a way to help you gain control. I never suspected it would harm."

Though he clearly intended her to return the notice, Daphne ignored the silent command. She rolled the paper and thrust it under her bodice. Stray sand tickled and itched against her skin, but she didn't care. "You'll not dismiss him."

Lord Scarborough made no attempt to reclaim the paper. Instead, he simply reached for a new sheet. "It makes no difference. You cannot change my mind in this. Go up to your room and wait until your mother returns."

Just then, the longcase clock standing in the front hall gave out its deep, booming chimes to count off the hour. Daphne gathered her skirts in one hand and raced from the room before her father could stop her, determined to speak to Monsieur Henre who would be just arriving.

The scrape of wood against wood gave warning that Lord Scarborough understood her purpose though, and despite her efforts, his long strides carried him past her to where Thomas was just opening the door to admit Monsieur Henre.

"Lord Scarborough would see you in his study."

The words had barely been spoken before her father moved to block the door from her sight. "I'll see you here," he announced. "You are no longer welcome under my roof. I've learned of the nonsense you've been putting in my daughter's head, and I will not have it in my household."

"My lord," Monsieur Henre said, but he never had the chance to finish his protest.

Daphne saw her father jerk a purse from his belt and thrust it at the dance instructor. "Take this as your severance. It's more than generous. If I see your face around here another time, I'll put out the word, and no one of significance will let you anywhere near their daughters again."

She heard no response to Lord Scarborough's threat, and even as she moved forward to say her own goodbyes, sure her father would allow her that at least, the front door swung closed with a thud.

Daphne turned and marched back to her room rather than chance what words would come from her mouth should she speak to her father.

Once there, she pulled out the dismissal notice and smoothed its pages. The vile thing served as her last remaining connection to the one teacher of all of them she counted a favorite. His Drury Lane address, carefully penned in her father's hand, only reminded Daphne of what she could never have.

The last bits of sand absorbed most of the liquid from her tear, keeping the address readable for all the good it would do her.

"Please, Daphne. I have no one else. You've been up here for a week, barely touched your food, and won't speak to our parents. You know they'd agree to anything you wanted to do."

Daphne rolled over, surprising a passionate look on her normally dutiful sister. "Why do you care so much about going shopping?" Daphne asked, intrigued by something for the first time since Father made his pronouncement.

Red tinged Grace's cheeks, and she looked down at her hands, mumbling an answer Daphne couldn't hear.

"What?"

Grace dropped to the bed next to Daphne, drawing one leg up under her. "Do you have to know? Can't you just help me? I've helped you often enough."

Daphne sat up and stared at her sister for a long time before nodding. "You have at that, but you've never asked before. I don't understand what's so special about this shopping trip that you need to hide from Mother and Father. But—" She held up a hand to silence her sister. "I'll do it. Whatever you're up to can't be half as bad as my scrapes."

She thought longingly of those simpler days when she'd sneak out to try Father's strongest horse, coming back all covered in twigs from where she rode through trees trying to duck the people who knew her family. Grace had always been there to usher her through the servant quarters and clean her up before their tutors arrived. If not for her and Willem, now their coachman, Daphne would have been in endless trouble.

Her sister pulled her into a tight hug, surprising Daphne out of her musings. "Thank you so much, Daphne. I'll never forget it. Never."

Daphne watched, mystified, as Grace leapt up and raced out the door to request the carriage at a pace very different from her normal decorous walk.

Finding the energy to prepare came harder for Daphne. She'd given up everything for dance and now she'd lost the only teacher she'd ever had. A wave of despair crashed over her and she sank back onto the bed, the effort too much.

"Come on, Daphne, you promised."

Grace pulled her arm until Daphne had to rise.

"I've got Willem bringing the coach round. Mother was delighted that you expressed interest. It took forever to convince her not to come with us. She'll probably be watching you from the front room to make sure you're all right."

While she talked, Grace pulled off Daphne's nightgown and tugged a faun-colored walking gown over her head. She pulled the side laces tight and threw a shawl over Daphne's shoulders.

"You'll need a bonnet. We haven't time to fix the mess you've made of your hair," she scolded, suiting actions to words as she pulled a flowered bonnet over Daphne's head and tied the strings snug under her chin.

Grace stepped back to survey the results of her labor. She looked Daphne up and down, then tugged a bit on the bodice. "You're going to need some new clothes soon. But for now, you should do."

Daphne hunched her shoulders and tucked the shawl across her chest. "Are we going or are we not?" she asked, hearing the pout in her voice. Somehow, the thought of getting outside had started to grow on her.

Their mother waved from the doorway of the front parlor, her strained face making Daphne feel guilty for a moment before she remembered why. Again, her loss threatened to overwhelm her.

Deliberately using an awkward gait as if losing her dancing instructor destroyed her balance, she marched the last bit and pulled the door open, not even acknowledging her mother with a word.

Behind her, she heard Grace give a quick goodbye before her sister followed her down the steps.

"Good afternoon, my ladies. Let me help you into the carriage."

"Good afternoon to you, too, Willem," Daphne said with a slight curtsy that failed to mask her grin. He'd been a friend and ally too many times in their childhood for her to be taken in by his elegant uniform.

He smiled and doffed his cap. "Thank you, Lady Daphne," he said, handing her up onto the seat. "And where will we be going this fine day?"

She waved at Grace, paying little notice to the directions. Shopping couldn't hold her attention, and now that the preparations were complete, even this trip seemed a drain on her meager energy.

Staring out the window, Daphne gave the passing scenery scant focus. If her father hadn't fired Monsieur Henre, she'd be dancing right now. She'd be learning something new, or practicing the steps she already enjoyed.

She sighed, the air whooshing out of her as her hand trailed along the carriage strap.

Grace jumped. "Must you do that?" her sister snapped.

"I can't help it. I've lost everything," Daphne said, sighing again.

Her sister stared out the window for a long moment, then turned to Daphne. "I need you to keep a secret," she said in a rush.

Daphne looked at Grace, shocked by the signs of agitation, the red blush marking her cheeks, eyes glittering as if fevered, and her hands clenched. "Do you feel all right? You don't look well."

Grace smiled, the expression giving a different meaning to her anxiety. "I'm fine. I'm more than fine. I just need you to listen, and listen quickly."

Pushing back her preoccupation, Daphne took one of Grace's hands between her own, chafing the chill from them. "Whatever it is, just tell me."

Grace shook her head, rejecting the offer. "What you don't know, you can't tell. Only promise me this. I will step down when we pass Grosvenor Square. You're to continue on. Buy some ribbon, a new bonnet, or whatever catches your eye. I'll pay for it from my allowance, I promise." She pushed some of her calling cards into Daphne's hand. "Just give them these and have the bill sent home."

"But, Grace," Daphne protested, tension binding her gut.

Grace reached out and tapped on the wall separating them from Willem. "Here's fine, Willem," she called. "I'll be here when you come back. Just pick me up as if we went together and I'll be in your debt. Say you'll do it, Daphne, please."

Daphne stared into her sister's pleading face and could not see fit to deny her. "But what of Willem?"

Her sister laughed. "He won't tell. He never has before, and he won't start now."

The carriage came to a halt with a short, jerky motion then rolled backwards a bit. "Here we are, Lady Grace," Willem called.

"Thank you, Daphne. I won't forget this."

Grace opened the door and slipped out before Daphne could respond or agree. She sat there, hands lax in her lap, staring at the now closed door.

Who was this person who had replaced her dutiful sister? And what trouble had she gotten involved in?

"Shall we go on, my lady?" Willem asked, leaning around the side.

Daphne stared out at the park, half tempted to find her sister and drag her back, but she had promised, or at least not disagreed. She sighed again, this time not because of her own troubles. "Carry on, Willem. I have to have something to show for the outing or Mother will question."

Chapter Three

The shopping trip held as little interest for her as she'd expected until her gaze fell on a book displayed in the window of a bookshop. She stepped inside and waited as an older gentleman finished his purchase, reminding herself that Grace had not planned for Daphne to spend a large sum.

"Can I help you, young lady?" the shopkeeper asked, his eyes glittering with amusement.

Daphne blushed, knowing her eagerness had been too obvious. "That book in the window. The Life of a Dancer. Can I see it?"

The man laughed. "Ladies always seem so curious about the other half. Not sure I should show it to you though. Is your mother here?"

She drew herself up to her full, if moderate, height and frowned. "I'm old enough to choose my own reading material, sir, and I thank you to show me the book I asked for or I will take my business elsewhere."

"All right, young lady. No offense intended."

Daphne released her breath when he turned to get the book, smothering a laugh. She'd practiced that imitation of her mother in a snit many times but never had the chance to use it until now.

"Here you go then. It's a memoir, or so the authoress claims."

She took the book, smoothing her fingers over the precise leather binding and admiring the gold-leaf letters. Beneath the title said only: a dancer. "How much?" she asked, not sure she wanted to hear the answer.

The price he named to borrow the tale was well beyond what her sister could have dreamed of her spending, but she had to have it.

The little book called to her, as if it would reveal a secret answer to her problems. Promising herself she'd use some of her allowance to cover it, Daphne signed the bill, relieved to see the slip only said "book."

She glanced up at the clock above his head and gasped. "I had no idea it had gotten so late. Send the bill to this address," she said, handing the man one of her sister's calling cards. "I have to go."

He glanced down and froze for a moment before giving her a curious stare. "Yes, my lady. I'll have it sent right up. Would you like the book delivered as well?"

Daphne tightened her hands around the leather binding, instinctively protecting it. "No, I'll carry this with me." She didn't want to imagine the talk with her mother if they knew she had a book about a professional dancer, not after Mother had equated them with street-walkers.

He gave her a stiff bow, and she walked quickly from the store.

Daphne scanned the street for her carriage and crossed to it, clutching her two bundles and the precious book. By the time they drew up next to the park, the sun had already started to sink, making long shadows out of the trees. Grace stepped from behind one of them, showing no sign of upset that they were so late. She turned back just before opening the carriage door and waved.

Daphne stared into the shadow, trying to see whom her sister could have met with, but she could only make out a darker spot that might have been anything. She waited until Willem pulled away, taking them back home, before turning to her sister.

"Who were you visiting?" she asked, watching her sister closely for a reaction.

Grace blushed and looked at her hand as it pulled on the carriage strap. "I can't tell you. I can't tell anyone." She turned to face Daphne, her expression suddenly intense. "You won't give me away will you? You can't. Say you won't, Daphne."

Surprised at her sister's agitation, Daphne put a hand on Grace's shoulder. "Of course I wouldn't. I'm curious, but I'd never give you away."

Grace settled back into her seat, a long sigh of relief coming from her. "It feels so much better now that you know. I've been bottling this inside for so long."

Daphne shrugged. "I don't really know anything," she said.

"You know enough to be my help. I need you to keep me company often enough so Mother doesn't suspect a thing."

Wondering just what Mother shouldn't suspect, Daphne eyed her sister. What double life could Grace be living? Had she made friends with a young lady of disrepute? Was she helping the alley children? Whatever it might be, her sister was staying tight lipped about it.

"So show me what you got," Grace said, reaching for the packages.

Daphne snatched the book out of the way and pushed the hair ribbons toward her sister.

"I'm more interested in what you're hiding," Grace said, laughing. She lunged across the carriage, rocking it back and forth but returning victorious.

"Give it back." Daphne didn't care that her voice was low and intense. "I kept your secret. Give me back mine."

"Now Daphne. I wouldn't tell on you," Grace murmured, shaking her head. "But if it's so important to you, here it is."

Chastened, Daphne took the book, smoothing her fingers over its cover. "It's a book about dancing," she said. "The life of a dancer." She tensed, waiting for her sister's reaction.

Grace just shook her head. "Our parents will not be pleased. They want you to give up on this dream of dancing. It's not seemly."

Daphne frowned, staring at the book in her hands. "You've always known what you're supposed to do, to be. That's dancing for me. I've never had anything before. Just taking away my teacher doesn't make it go away. Dance is in my heart and soul."

Her sister looked a little taken aback by the declaration but then her face softened. "I won't tell them about the book. Just be careful. Sometimes following your heart can hurt the ones you love and sometimes it can tear you apart."

Grace looked so wounded that Daphne wanted to give her a hug, but her sister turned away, staring out the carriage window, her back rigid and uninviting.

Daphne gathered up the packages, tucking the spilled ribbons back inside, trying to ignore the hurt she felt at being shut out.

They didn't speak until the carriage rolled to a halt before the house and then only a hurried, "Give me one of the packages and put that book down your bodice," from Grace.

Once they entered the house, they were called to the parlor where Grace endured a light scold from Lady Scarborough for the long shopping trip, kept short only because their mother seemed to expect Daphne to faint away from the strain. As it was, Daphne had to be told several times to sit up straight because she hunched her shoulders in an attempt to mask the book tucked into her dress.

Grace drew out the ribbons as if she'd been the one to choose the colors, displaying each one for their mother's approval. Again, Mother looked to Daphne to see if she showed the least bit of interest, and Daphne tried her best, but really couldn't wait until she had a private moment to delve between the covers of her book.

Finally, she smothered a yawn, using her mother's concern as an excuse when the discussion of dresses seemed to take forever.

"Oh my dear, you must be quite tired, and here we are keeping you up and about. Why don't you run along to the nursery? I'll have cook send up something to tease your appetite in a bit." Her mother brushed aside the ribbons and helped Daphne to her feet as if she'd become a frail invalid.

Trying to appear docile, Daphne allowed the assistance, unaware of the risk until her mother's arm brushed against the hidden book.

Her mother stopped ushering Daphne toward the door and held her daughter at arm's length, staring down at her bosom. Daphne's breath caught in her throat as she waited for her mother to demand to see the book.

"You are growing up, aren't you?" her mother said instead. "That gown is a might bit tight on you. Only hussies wear their clothing that way. You have much more to offer than a nightwalker." She tsked while she turned Daphne one direction and then the other. "We'll have to arrange a fitting. You'll be making your coming out soon enough and you'll be present at several balls before then as we handle your sister's wedding, out or not. It just won't do having you bursting from your clothing."

She pinched Daphne's cheek gently. "You are becoming a young lady right in front of our eyes. You've been so busy with…" She waved a vague hand, unwilling even to say the word. "Well, you've been so busy that we've neglected you. That's all going to change from this moment on."

Daphne stifled a moan, staring down at her hands as if she expected them to burst into flame.

Her mother laughed. "Don't you worry about that right now. Go rest. Such a long trip must have been exhausting. Grace should have been more careful on your first outing."

Daphne shrugged, knowing she was as much to blame, but unwilling to reveal the cause.

"I hope she stopped at least to take you to afternoon tea? You must have been famished."

Nodding, Daphne mumbled something that could have sounded like agreement as she slipped out from under her mother's arm, heading for the stairs.

"Rest up, dear. We have so much to do for you," her mother called, the dreaded words following to the second floor.

Daphne fled along the hallway until she reached the nursery, burst through the door, and collapsed onto her bed, knees against her chest and arms wrapped about them.

"But I don't want more dresses. I don't want to come out," she cried here where no one could hear her and chastise. Daphne saw her future stretched out before her, the lovely Grace's bland sister who everyone invited out of pity. After a season or two, her mother would find some appropriate gentleman and tie her to him, never to know the freedom her heart craved.

SHE WOKE SOME TIME LATER, a tray with congealed soup and cold bread next to her bed. A blanket lay over her, and when she wiggled her toes, she found her shoes had been pulled off, just as if she were still only a child.

Memory returned in a flash and Daphne's hands pressed against her front, the panic only draining when she felt an edge. She pulled the book out, caressing its warm cover. Somehow, she already felt a strong bond with the woman in this book, truth or not.

Climbing out of bed, Daphne absentmindedly grabbed the bread and chewed on it while she lit a candle, unable to read in the evening light. She took the candle to her desk then brought the book over as well, wrapping her blanket around her to keep warm.

The room grew dark, the cold seeped in around her windows and the candle flickered in an errant breeze, but nothing could distract Daphne from the words on the page. The rough hand and raw language further supported this as a biographical effort, but the story pulled Daphne in as she followed the heroine through a troubled childhood in the home of a wealthy merchant.

When Daphne read the scene where the heroine ran away from her home, chancing starvation and other disasters to achieve her dream, she paused and stared at the wax dripping from her candle, barely aware it had almost burnt down to the brass candlestick supporting it.

She felt an overwhelming uselessness. Did she have it in her to follow her dream that far? Could she abandon her sister, her parents? Could she give up the only life she'd known?

Pulling another candle from the desk drawer, she lit it on the stub of the first. Her empty stomach rumbled, but she ignored it in favor of finding out what happened next in this dancer's life and soon enough felt the minor discomfort of her hunger nothing in comparison to what this woman suffered.

Enthralled, Daphne went through two more candles before exhaustion drew her back to her bed. She tucked the book beneath her pillow and curled under the covers, still wearing her walking dress.

Even as she slept, her dreams stayed trapped in the story, only she stood on the stage in a silence so complete she could hear the tinder strike as the stage lights were lit. Her lips curled into a gentle smile as she moved to the silent song in her heart.

Chapter Four

aphne faced the next morning with a greater sense of purpose than she'd felt since watching her father turn Monsieur Henre away. For the first time since that day, the thought pulled a smile across her face.

She leapt up, stripped to just her muslin underdress, and reveled in the freedom of movement. Without a second thought, her body moved gracefully through the first steps. Daphne thought she'd remembered everything and even kept her form, but couldn't be sure without the mirrors her father had installed in the small ballroom for her.

Light streamed in her windows, showing it to be early in the morning. The servants would be awake, but her mother and father tended to sleep a bit later. Daphne splashed her face in the water bowl, dried it quickly, and pulled on a simple shift. She didn't want to waste any time.

On the way to the door, she hesitated before going back for her book. Somehow, it seemed right to keep the book with her until she made her dreams into reality. She'd never have conceived of the idea without reading the dancer's life. She had a much easier path in comparison. Though her father would probably disown her if he ever found out, she could be careful. At least she already knew a dance troupe where the manager wanted her. Thanks to the dismissal notice she'd stolen, she even had the address of his theater.

Daphne slipped through the empty halls, stopping to twirl in her delight. The servants' stair took her closer to the ballroom, though it carried some risk of discovery. She could always say she'd come looking for early breakfast snacks what with missing dinner the night before.

The excuse almost became true as she passed the entrance to the kitchen. Fresh baked rolls sent their delicious smells winding out to the corridor, and Daphne could hear breakfast meat sizzling. She hesitated, her grumbling stomach declaring its choice.

Her arm slipped just then, and the book jabbed into her side, feeling almost like a cramp from hunger. Daphne remembered what the dancer, who never said her name, had suffered. She'd gone days without food, until the hunger stopped even calling on her. Daphne could suffer an extra hour or two in favor of completing her practice before her parents woke up.

Steeling herself, she marched past the kitchen and right into Willem.

"Now, you should be watching where you're walking, my lady," he said, his eyes twinkling with the humor that never seemed far from his face.

Daphne put a hand over her heart, feeling it flutter against her fingers. "You startled me," she accused.

He smiled, reaching out as if to touch her face before his hand dropped away. "I'm thinking it's the other way round. What are you doing down in these passages?"

She blushed, staring up into his handsome face and wondering if he'd still do whatever she asked of him. He had only a few years on her, but those years had made him wiser. And yet, she'd never make this work without someone's help.

"If I tell you, you can't tell anyone, not even Grace."

His happy expression fell away for a heartbeat before he smiled. "So you have a sweetheart as well," he whispered, his fingers twisting against the leather of his belt. It wasn't a question, but Daphne couldn't bear the thought so spoke out anyway.

"Of course not. Why would I? And if I did, I'd no more bring him through the back door than I would bring in a dog." She stamped her foot at him, angry that he could think so little of her.

He swept into a low bow that hid his face for a moment. "Then if not some lucky fellow, what brings you down here past the kitchen?"

"Dance." Even as she whispered the word, she expected it to sound frivolous, but it didn't. The single syllable held within it her hopes, her dreams, and her determination to make it happen.

Stepping aside, he put a hand to his forehead in salute. "I knew the master's command wouldn't keep you from it. I should have guessed where you were headed myself." He grinned at her and waited for her to pass him as if watching a parade.

Daphne startled something odd in his eyes as she moved past but she dismissed it, her thoughts turned forward to her practice.

The room seemed empty somehow with only her in it, but Daphne concentrated on doing the stretch patterns Monsieur Henre had taught her before going through the easiest step of her last routine. She felt untutored, her movements clumsy and uncoordinated.

She stopped, staring into the mirror as if it would find the answer to her problems. Instead, she only saw her sweat-slicked face and the doubt in her own eyes. Could she do this? Had her tutor meant what he said? Did she have the strength of the dancer in her book?

No confidence flickered in her eyes. Her mouth turned down and she looked away, unwilling to face the disappointment and failure there. Without dance, she had nothing. It and it alone made her special, unique. Otherwise, she was just another girl with noble blood, pretty, but not beautiful, destined to marry a frivolous, uncaring dandy.

Water gathered in her eyes, self-pity overwhelming her. "It has to work." Her voice held all the determination and command she could muster. That other life wasn't right for her.

"You'd do better with a beat to follow."

Daphne jerked toward the door, her heart beating furiously, sure her father had discovered her.

Willem slipped the rest of the way through the entrance and bowed to her, a smile on his face. "Your old master used the pianoforte. I'm no talented musician like he was, but I thought I'd offer my services."

Taking a deep breath to calm herself, Daphne sent Willem a dubious look, unsure whether to chastise him for watching her or take him up on the offer. "And how will you help?" she asked, a touch of arrogance in her tone. "Plunking one key would do little but make my head ache."

He shook his head back and forth, reproving her for her condescension. "I have but a servant's instrument, but a bit of a talent for it." He drew out a simple wooden flute, the like of which she'd seen old men whittling in the fields of their country home.

"You think you can keep a tune with that?" she asked, stepping closer as curiosity pulled her.

Willem grinned, raising the flute to his lips. "I've been told I play many a pretty tune, but you'll have to judge for yourself."

She nodded, giving him permission then sending a nervous glance to the door.

Willem had closed it behind him. The music wouldn't attract attention she couldn't afford.

The first note hung on the air, its solemn, almost mournful sound picking up on her emotion. Then he sent a trill of quick, high notes after, twisting around the first until she heard recovery, whether just wishful thinking or Willem's intent, she couldn't tell.

He played and played, pausing only to draw in deep breaths between tunes. At first, Daphne only listened, drawn by the sometimes sorry, sometimes joyful music. Then she started to feel the pattern lying under them and her foot began to move.

She closed her eyes, listening with her senses, allowing the music to draw her in and capture again that place where dance held all of her. The first step came almost as a surprise, but she moved swiftly to the next and the next, completing her basic forms with none of the hesitation that had caused her earlier doubt.

Soon, eyes open though only partially aware, Daphne danced across the hall, her body and soul tied into the movements. Deep in her heart, she felt the confidence and satisfaction sprout and grow until it spread throughout her.

Silence surprised her when it fell, leaving only the sounds of her indrawn breath and the scrape of her slippers against the hardwood floor. Daphne finished the motion, allowing her body to collapse against the floor, arms stretched forward and legs curled within the protection of her skirts.

She lay there until her heartbeat settled and her breathing eased.

"Lady Daphne?" Willem's soft voice barely broke the silence.

Daphne rolled to her feet, graceful even with exhaustion threatening to make her limbs tremble. "Thank you for that, Willem. You play beautifully." She smiled up at him and surprised a flush coloring his cheeks.

He touched his forehead, hiding his features. "At your service, Lady Daphne," he murmured. "Whenever you need me."

Deep inside the house, the longcase clock struck the hour of eleven, much later than she could have imagined. "Oh," she said, worry coloring her tone. "We've been here three hours."

A smile pulled up one side of Willem's face. "I told the upstairs maid you didn't want to be disturbed. No one will come looking for you for some time yet."

"But Father…"

"Has eaten and gone, I imagine. You've not been about much in these past days. Your absence won't be noted."

Daphne turned to the chair where she'd placed her proper shoes, unsure whether to be grateful or upset. Did she have so little a place in this household that she could vanish and none would question? And if she still wanted to carry out her plan, she'd have to continue as if devastated so no one would have expectations of her.

"My duties are light in the morning hours, Lady Daphne."

She turned to look at Willem, shocked. "I didn't think. Should you have taken my father to the House of Lords? Have I made you neglect your duties?" Suddenly, she imagined their house without Willem and hated the picture. She'd taken him for granted but always knew he'd be there when she needed an ally.

He laughed, waving a hand to dismiss her concern. "I'm coachman it's true, but the earl goes with another in the morning so they can talk freely on the way. Lord Michaels' coachman takes this leg while I go to get them at the end of the day."

Daphne tied her laces slowly, thinking about what he'd said. "Then you're free in the mornings?" she asked, a plan just starting to form.

"As long as you or Lady Grace has no need of me. The Lady Scarborough is unlikely to travel before noon." Willem gave her an intent look, as if waiting for her to say something, as if he expected her next words.

She'd thought to make a command of them, but her words, when she spoke, came out soft and gentle. "Would you meet me here then? At eight each morning? I'd like your flute to practice to."

He swept into a low bow, his grin visible from the side. "Of course, my lady. As you desire."

Her stomach rumbled before she could answer, making them both laugh.

"Morning will come again soon enough," he said, his tone filled with understanding. "You should go eat now, before the breakfast offering has all gone cold, fit only for dogs."

She nodded, her throat tight with emotion. With his help, she had a chance. She could really make this happen.

Lady Scarborough greeted Daphne with a nod, no longer showing any surprise at her daughter rising so late. Daphne slid into her chair and accepted the bowl of steaming porridge a maid put in front of her, the butter on top just starting to melt.

"I was thinking to go to my dresser's today, Daphne. Would you like to join me?"

Looking up, Daphne sighed inwardly at the hesitation in her mother's tone. She smiled, keeping back the intense joy she felt from her practice in favor of a subtler expression. "If it pleases you," she murmured, knowing she'd have to relent sometime.

Mother looked shocked for just a heartbeat before her face changed to show her delight. "It would. It would indeed. With the late morning hours you're keeping now, you'd think you already spent the night out at gala after gala. I think it's fine time to outfit you for a few small events."

Daphne nodded, hiding her grimace behind a spoon of the cereal. She'd be hard pressed to keep with her rigorous training schedule if she stayed up into the wee hours of the morning pretending interest in the gawking boys who were after her father's title. Even the dancing there held little of the passion and grace of true dance, not that she'd be allowed on the floor anyway.

Her mother continued speaking, planning which event would be best to make a quiet debut. Not a full coming out, but just an introduction, so she said. Daphne soon stopped listening, knowing well enough she need make no suggestions and that the plans would progress well enough without her support and even fine if she chose to express any objections.

She let her mother carry on, but Daphne had her own plans. The memory of her latest training drew a smile across her face, Willem's flute and her graceful form creating a powerful combination.

"Now I hadn't thought you cared much for Penelope. She'd be the perfect companion as you embark on this next step. Her parents are planning her coming out next spring. You could launch officially together."

Daphne stared dumbly at her mother for a long moment before she realized Lady Scarborough must have connected the smile to whatever she'd been saying at that time. "Penelope seems a nice enough girl," she managed, again filling her mouth to prevent an error.

Mother shook her head, waving to the maid to take Daphne's bowl. "You've had enough of that. For someone who will make her full debut in spring, you have to start being conscious of these things. Bring her some fruits and cheese, won't you, Mary?"

Smothering her protests, Daphne let the maid take her half-eaten porridge away in favor of a small platter of fruits and cheese. Her stomach grumbled at the substitution, but she had no choice. She had to get what energy she could from what she had. Dancing took more than her mother ever imagined, and Daphne couldn't even explain why she needed the extra sustenance.

"I know," her mother said, with a big smile. "Penelope's mother will be at the arts discussion Marilyn Fowler's holding. I'll arrange for you to call on her tomorrow if you'd like. The two of you must have so much to talk about. It'll be good for you to spend time with someone your own age."

Daphne stared at her mother, horrified. How had a simple smile led to this? "Oh Mother, I couldn't," she whispered, her mind filled with an endless stream of things taking her away from her only love.

"Oh posh, my dear. No need to be shy. You're just as good as any of them for all I let your father keep you a bit sheltered. I should have done away with that dancing years ago, but he thought it made you so happy." She shook her head at Daphne. "And now look where you are. I tell you it will be fun. You'll see quick enough there's no need to mope in your room." Leaning across, her mother patted Daphne's hand firmly. "You have a lot going for you if you'd only take a moment to look around."

Knowing that firm voice meant her mother's mind was made up, Daphne smothered an unhappy sigh. "In the afternoon then," she offered.

Mother smiled approvingly. "Of course. In the afternoon. We want you at your best." She looked at the dress Daphne wore and shook her head. "A pity we don't have time to get you into something more appealing, but that will come. No need to style you as anything more than the young girl you still are."

Daphne pushed back from the table, acutely aware of the way her gown stretched against her chest and revealed a full inch of ankle. She'd pulled it from the cupboard after practice without even looking, hunger gnawing at her stomach so much she almost went to breakfast in the wrinkled, sweat-stained dress she'd danced in. Only the knowledge that her secret would be out drove her back to her room to change. She hadn't taken the time to choose one that didn't show how her body had matured.

"I'm done," she said as she stood up. "I'll be in my room." Though she knew she fled, sometimes retreat was the better part of valor. She didn't think her mother would concoct any more grand plans with her absent.

Her mother nodded, "Probably wise. Stuffing yourself before being measured would be foolish. I'll send for you when I'm ready to leave."

Daphne barely paused at the door to acknowledge her mother's words. She'd forgotten about the gowns. Rest and quiet had been denied to her.

TUGGING THE SIDES OF HER new dress, Daphne struggled to recapture the joy of her morning practice. A yawn split her face as she fidgeted with the colorful ribbons lacing the front of the bodice, all dressed up for an outing when she needed a quiet rest with her books.

"Oh stop playing with them," her mother said, irritation coloring her voice. "It's the latest style, Hellenic, and you heard the seamstress. She couldn't have creamed of getting you a new dress in one day if not for the lacing that allowed her to readjust the size without extensive stitching.

Daphne dropped her hands to her lap, twining the fingers to keep them still. "I didn't need a new dress," she murmured, trying to keep the petulance from her tone.

Mother laughed. "You say that now, dearest, but just wait until you're in a room with all your rivals and they have the most beautiful gowns. Then you'll be happy for this." Her mother tapped Daphne's knee where the thick layers of pleated cloth lay heavy against her. "Just remember, no matter how much you might like them, each and every one is after the same man that you desire. Watch carefully. Learn both how to act and how to make yourself stand out."

She glanced toward the mantle and her husband's portrait. "How else do you think I could have snared your father? He might think the marriage arranged, but I didn't dance attendance on his crippled aunt for nothing."

Daphne stared at her mother, seeing a side she'd never really known before.

Lady Scarborough laughed. "Don't look so shocked, my dear. It's not as simple as you might think. You could leave the decision up to your father and end up second or third wife to one of his cronies. Far better to take a hand in it yourself no matter what it takes. Listen well today and you'll see that I'm right." She shook her head. "We really should not have sheltered you so much. Made all this too much of a surprise. You have a lot of catching up to do if you want your coming out to be a success. I'm so glad you've finally decided to put yourself out. Penelope may not be the cream, but she's far from the chaff. You do well to learn from that young lady. Why, I'd guess she has her husband already picked out for all she's not officially available."

A cough drew their attention to the parlor doorway and relief flooded Daphne as the conversation came to a sudden halt.

Daphne leapt up, bending down to press a kiss against her mother's dry cheek before striding to where Willem waited to escort her to the carriage.

"Now Daphne, no need to seem so eager. Don't let the girl know how dependent you are. You'd think all that time spent with that dance tutor wasted." A small gasp escaped her mother's lips as Lady Scarborough pressed fingers against her mouth as if to call back the words.

"I'll remember," Daphne said softly, her mind racing back to her practice in the morning where she achieved a step Monsieur Henre had shown her the visit before his dismissal. Remembering her triumph brought heat to her cheeks and grace back to her motions as she followed Willem to the carriage. No matter what she had to suffer, she'd have the morning to look forward to.

Another yawn stretched her mouth as the hard exercise took its toll especially after Lady Scarborough dragged her about the previous afternoon. She'd have the morning to look forward to only if she could stay awake through the night.

Chapter Five

The rhythmic sound of wheels against cobblestone lulled Daphne into a light doze. She noticed when the carriage stopped, but thought little of it until Willem called down.

"My lady, we're here. Want me to walk you to the door?"

She glanced up to the small window framing Willem's face and grimaced. "I'll be fine. Just call back for me in two hours. I'm not sure I'll last that long." With a small gasp, she felt heat rush into her face. "I didn't mean that…well, I did about the time." Shaking her head, Daphne gave up. She'd become much too comfortable with Willem during their morning sessions but that was no call to be rude to Penelope even where the other girl couldn't hear her.

He climbed down and opened the door for her, bowing as she stepped out of the carriage. "It'll be fine, my lady. You'll see," he whispered, giving her a small measure of encouragement.

Daphne glanced his way with a shaky smile before straightening her spine and marching up the steps, determined to survive this encounter.

The large, carved door swung inward as she approached and an intimidating butler held out his hand for her card. Daphne smiled as she fumbled in her reticule for the cards her mother had offered as identification since Daphne was too young to have her own made.

The butler stared down at the card then raised one eyebrow. "Lady Scarborough?" Doubt colored his tone.

Daphne raised her chin and looked him in the eye. "Her daughter, Lady Daphne. I'm expected."

The harsh demeanor cracked for a moment into an approving smile. "Lady Daphne. Of course." He stepped back to let her through. "They've gathered in the front salon. Just follow me."

They? Who else could she expect to see at this gathering? She walked the seven feet down the hallway, her shoulders tensing with each step.

He opened the door and a burst of laughter came from the room beyond.

"The Lady Daphne Scarborough," he announced, waving her forward.

Daphne crossed the opening to find a large group of both men and women, each staring up at her. A half smile tugged at her lip as she realized how right her mother had been about the need to dress. She took the fresh material of her new gown in her hands, hoped she had no carriage lines pressed into her face, and curtsied as best as she could.

"Oh do come and sit down," an older version of Penelope declared, pointing to an unoccupied corner of the sofa.

Grateful as attention turned back to Penelope's sister, Daphne slipped into the seat, trying to mimic the posture of the other ladies present. She managed to hide another yawn as she turned to admire a landscape hanging from the wall next to the sofa but when she turned back, no one was paying any attention to her anyway. She opened her mouth to comment on the painting when one of the young men spoke.

"Oh you can't seriously be mourning his loss, can you?" the man said, his voice strident. "Do you really miss him looking down that long nose of his at you?"

Penelope's sister laughed and touched the man's sleeve with her fan. "Now, Filbert. It's not very gentlemanly for you to speak ill of the man. Jealousy is such a weak emotion."

The young man frowned, carefully rearranging the lace extruding from his coat sleeves. "While I can't deny he's a handsome chap," he said in a tight voice, "for a leader in the ton to seek a bluestocking is beyond the pale. He fails to appreciate the finer things well-bred ladies such as are represented here can offer. He seeks instead the kind of discourse better reserved for gentlemen's talks over cigars and brandy."

Several of the ladies gave him approving looks, but Daphne felt her interest piqued. Who was this remarkable man?

"You can't fault his support of the arts though, Filbert. He's kept more than one personal eye on the most entrancing of stars," another young man broke in, this one seated on a stool near Daphne.

"Bernard, you watch your tongue," a young lady next to Penelope's sister said, the laughter in her voice undermining her scold. "We don't talk about such things in mixed company."

He flushed, gaze dropping to the floor for a moment before he recovered. "I only meant he patronizes many different art forms, music, theater, even dance."

The lady who had chastised him shook her head before turning away. "Even if some of us go masked to see the same performances," she added as though he had not spoken.

"Not that his preferences matter any longer. Rumor has it his mother chose the poor man a bride. I doubt she'll share any of the characteristics he might value, but maybe she won't shame the Pendleton name either."

The others nodded at the pronouncement from Penelope's sister and turned to talk about other members of the ton. Daphne sank back against the seat, her interest fading at the sound of his name. If ever she could have found a man she would have been willing to tie her life to, one who appreciated knowledge and enjoyed the arts seemed to have a chance. And yet, the name told a different story. He was her sister's choice, or at least the one their parents had found for her.

"Daphne, I was so surprised when your mother said you'd like to come," Penelope burst out, having emerged from whichever corner her sister had tucked her in. "Which is not to say you aren't welcome because you are. Just a surprise. Here, move over a bit and we'll chat."

Pushing closer to the woman on her left, Daphne made room for Penelope, a slender, nervous young girl who never seemed able to slow down at all.

"So, have you all your gowns picked out? My mother's dresser came up with a glorious plan to color my white dresses while not offending any of the grand ladies. I'll have patterned underskirts with just enough color to show through." Penelope clasped her hands together in her lap. "It's so marvelous. I can't wait for my first ball. It seems forever until the spring comes again. I just don't know why my parents couldn't have done my coming out this year. It's been a full season since my sister's and she's dangling several offers. She only has to choose. It's not like I'd interfere or anything."

Daphne tried her best to nod at the right places as Penelope's fierce whisper drowned out what the older people were saying. A headache began in the bridge of her nose. She struggled not to reach up and pinch it.

"Are you all right?" Penelope asked, breaking up a constant stream of information about the planning for her coming out. "You look a bit peaked."

Managing a wan smile, Daphne shook her head. "I'm fine. I just had a late night and an early morning."

"Oh you poor dear." Penelope patted Daphne's arm in a clear imitation of someone older. "I can't imagine what would drag you out of bed with the sun lower than the sky's height. Wait a moment and I'll be right back."

The other girl bounced up and raced across the room in quick steps until she reached the pull cord. Deep in the house, Daphne heard a gong sounding.

Penelope's sister glanced over at the movement. "Oh, be a dear and get tea for the lot of us. Run along and ask cook for some sandwiches. We're all famished. It's been hours since breakfast."

Daphne smiled, recognizing the origin of Penelope's imitation as her sister sent her off on an errand. Grace had always been her friend and confidant. Clearly, Penelope did not share the same closeness with her sister.

"And you are again?" the young man who had spoken of the arts before said, raising a monocle to stare at her.

She stared back, startled by the sudden attention.

"Oh, yes. The Scarborough girl. Younger, I presume? You look nothing like your sister."

Daphne blushed under the sharp gaze, knowing full well she lacked her sister's elegant looks. Her rounded cheeks and wide smile took away all chance of being considered a beauty, but she didn't need a stranger pointing it out to her.

"I'm surprised you've ever met her," Daphne shot, her tone as sharp as his look. "I can't imagine my father allowing her to associate with those who'd speak so about the arts."

He jerked back, the monocle falling to the end of its chain as he stared at her for a long moment, suffering the reminder of his earlier indelicacy. Then he laughed, a sharp bark of sound. "And unlike her, you have bite. Well, well, it'll be an interesting season once you're allowed out of those whites."

Daphne twisted one of the colored ribbons between her fingers, finding both his comment and his regard uncomfortable.

The young man smiled, softening his expression until he seemed almost approachable. "No need to undo the careful curls in that ribbon. I won't bite back. I like a woman with a little spice to her sweetness."

Dropping her hand away, Daphne looked to the others, only to find them focused on different conversations. Penelope hadn't returned from her errand, leaving Daphne to fend for herself.

"You're so young," the man said, suddenly seeming other than those gathered around Penelope's sister. "You don't really understand men at all, do you?"

He paused, but she said nothing, unsure what she could say.

"Never mind. Let's choose a safe conversation, shall we? You can practice your wiles and I can get a break from dissecting the latest gossip. Did I detect an interest in Lord Pendleton?"

Daphne blushed, shaking her head in silence.

"Now that's a pity. He's managed to capture the heart of one not even offered on the marriage mart and he's already claimed." The man raised his monocle again and looked her over most intently. "What could have piqued your interest, I wonder. It couldn't be the bluestockings. After all, as young as you are, I wonder if you can even read, much less so much that you worry about things well beyond your ken."

"I read what I please," Daphne muttered, suddenly tired of being examined as if a bug under a lens, especially when he seemed to take her for a child.

He smiled. "And what does please one such as you?"

Daphne's thoughts flew to her dancer's book, now tucked safely under her pillow, but she suppressed the memory. "Plato and Homer," she said instead, her tone defiant. Her father had let them read whatever they wanted to from his personal library, though none had captured her attention as thoroughly as the dancer's life.

A crow of laughter shook her out of her musing. The man stood up, pulling her with him. "Behold, I have Pendleton's bluestocking. A self-professed reader of Plato, she's pleasing enough to the eye and has a cutting tongue to keep him on his toes."

Daphne pulled away, heat suffusing her face. She wished herself anywhere but here, among those who thought such nasty games a sign of sophistication.

"Oh, Bernard," Penelope's sister said reprovingly. "Leave my sister's little friend alone. She probably read the names off books on her father's desk. You are so gullible at times. Besides, he has his own debutante already and probably gets more from the deal than any bluestocking could offer."

Bernard laughed again. "It's all just in fun, you know. No harm intended. She'll have to develop a thicker skin if she's planning to hang about here."

Daphne watched as he strode across the room toward another knot of people, grateful to see him leave. She couldn't imagine Lord Pendleton being such a brute. Maybe if she had to marry, he'd be able to find someone of like mind. She couldn't imagine being thrust in among ones like these for the rest of her life. At the very least, she'd want a husband she could talk to.

Shaking her head at how quickly she'd been turned from her true path by all this talk of coming out, Daphne pushed to her feet. She didn't want a husband, and she did not want to stay here any longer.

At just that moment, Penelope reentered the room, leading a seemingly endless stream of servants bearing tea and small sandwiches for them to share. She stopped suddenly when she saw Daphne on her feet, almost bringing the whole parade to a crashing halt.

Penelope cut across the room, giving no thought to the chaos she'd caused, and approached Daphne. "You're not leaving so soon?" she asked, her worried gaze scanning the two ladies who had shared the sofa with Daphne. "Can't you stay at least for tea now that it's here?"

Daphne opened her mouth to deny the request, but something in the other girl's eyes made her change her mind. If she'd felt out of sorts in this company, who's to say how Penelope had been treated.

Another flood of details from Penelope, ranging from the list of acceptable balls for first introductions to the possibility of small, private gatherings before, soon undermined her good intentions. When the butler came to announce the arrival of her carriage, Daphne felt a wave of gratitude toward Willem for the rescue. She said her goodbyes as quickly as she could and escaped before any additional arrangements could be made.

"Sorry I'm so late, my lady," Willem said as he bowed her into the carriage. "Your mother would not hear of me returning so soon and so sent me on numerous errands I had to complete before coming for you."

Daphne looked up at the sky, surprised to find that dark had fallen, though in summer the sun sank quite late. "I guess she saw no bother in me staying out so long," Daphne murmured to herself, letting her shoulders slump as reaction to the crowded room and deliberate teasing swept over her. "And why should she? This is what all girls my age want to be doing."

The bitterness in her tone surprised even Daphne. How could girls stomach such gatherings where the sole purpose seemed to be to tear people apart, both those poor victims present and those who did not grace the proceedings? At least her sister's betrothed did not seem the type to participate.

Daphne's head slumped against the seat cushion, and she fell asleep, her mind drawing pictures of an exceedingly handsome man, arm curled around her back as they spoke of the arts and philosophy.

Chapter Six

ady Pendleton reached out and tapped Jasper on the arm before pouring more tea into his tepid drink. "She's beautiful, darling. Clearly one of the cream. And her lineage is wonderful. You'll love her."

Jasper curved his mouth into a sardonic smile. "Will I, Mother? Will I love her?"

Undisturbed by her son's attitude, his mother smiled back. "Just drink your tea and try some of these ginger sandwiches. They're becoming the rage. A little jolt to prepare you for the long evening."

He took a cautious bite into the delicacy and choked, only just managing to avoid spewing the contents of his mouth out on their Persian carpet as the ginger burned his tongue. He took a quick gulp of tea, forgetting she'd just replaced the cooled liquid. Gasping, Jasper tried to regain control to the sound of his mother's laughter.

"Surely it's not as bad as all that," she said as soon as he stopped choking. "Cook came up with the idea when I was so drowsy the other day."

Jasper put his now mangled sandwich back onto the plate, shaking the crumbs from his fingers. "And how many of your guests have you tested this new rage out on?" he asked, swallowing hard and blinking to clear the liquid from his eyes.

"So far only you. What do you think?"

Glancing from her untouched sandwich to the suppressed laughter in her face, Jasper frowned. "If you need to ask, you need a pair of those spectacles I heard about to wear at events."

Lady Pendleton shrank back, her tiny hand pressed to the front of her dress. "Never," she declared. "I'll stumble blind through the room before that day comes."

This time laughter came from Jasper's lips. "I can just see you bumbling through the debutantes, squinting at their faces in the hopes of finding one with the right countenance."

She gave him a repressing look. "I won't have to go seeking among the debutantes. I already found you your bride. She's quiet, polite, and a rare find. You'll suit each other very nicely, I think."

"Mother, you make her sound about as interesting as a loaf of bread. It too as a form of beauty, is quiet, never says a wrong word, and suits me rightly after a long night. Only I would never consider sitting across the table from a slice of bread every morning.

His mother leaned forward and gave him a hard stare at odds with her fairy-like appearance. "As if that matters. Don't try to kid me on this. I know full well you plan to install her in one of the outlying mansions and only see her to do your duty. You'd better get used to those ginger sandwiches. I'll be ruling this roost for a long while the way your plans are going."

Jasper frowned. "You know you'll be welcome wherever I install my wife," he said. "You don't have to worry that I'll let her cast you out."

Lady Pendleton shook her head. "I don't worry about that. You'd be hard pressed to lever me out of here." She reached out a hand to grip his arm lightly. "It's you I'm worried about. A wife is so much more than an inconvenience to tuck away in a corner. What will you do if she doesn't fall in with your plans? She could make a mockery of you."

Surprise filled him as Jasper caught a look of true concern. His mother never made any bones about her lack of affection for his father. They barely managed to treat each other civilly back when his father was still alive. He'd never expected her to bring emotion into the discussion.

"Having second thoughts, Mother? You want me to go out and woo some of these pale beauties to see if any can spark my hardened heart?"

His mockery brought a frown to her features. "Just because your father and I never found affection doesn't mean such a thing doesn't exist. But you have to give it a chance to grow."

Jasper pushed to his feet, glowering down at his mother. "I doubt any of those girls has enough in her feather head to interest me. They're all cut from the same cloth, interested only in clothes, titles, and money. I should be grateful I have the last to offer them, but I can't find it in my heart to actually like any of the little schemers. As long as she goes her way and I go mine, I'll be happy. She tries to touch my name or that of my children, and she'll find the Tower a pleasant dwelling compared to what she'll get from me."

Not giving his mother an opportunity to add to the dark cloud hanging over his head, Jasper slammed out of the parlor, scaring the downstairs maid on his way to the stables. He only hoped a long ride would cut through this bad mood and let him put the idea of his mindless wife-to-be from his thoughts.

Daphne accepted a towel from Willem and turned away before dabbing at the sweat marking her brow and dripping down the front of her body. She'd practiced hard, bringing together the most difficult steps she knew, and every single one came fluidly.

When she looked at Willem, he had a grin pasted over his face. "You did right well, my lady," he said, taking the soiled towel from her. "Better than ever before."

She accepted the praise with a nod, knowing he spoke truly even though he had no way to judge. "I think good enough to do something about it," she declared. "I'm ready to find Monsieur Henre and offer my services." She swept into a deep curtsy, imagining the applause rising to the high beams of the ceiling and filling the theater in her mind.

"You can't be serious," Willem gasped out, any attempt at a respectful tone lost in his distress. "Master will never allow it."

Daphne put a gentle hand on his cheek and smiled at the man. "That's why my father is never to know." She spun away, her mind filled with plans she'd held to her heart ever since reading that book. "With your help, he'll think I'm off visiting friends." She turned back to Willem, pleading with her eyes.

He took a step back until he pressed against the wood paneling. "Lady Daphne, he won't believe that. You never go visiting. You haven't since Lord Scarborough brought you and your sister up from the country estate."

Daphne frowned, recognizing the flaw in her plan even though she didn't want to. She wanted to be able to slip away and see her teacher. How could things be so difficult?

The sharp sound of her dance slipper hitting the hardwood floor shocked Daphne. She jerked her gaze to Willem, embarrassed by the childish gesture. "I have to do this. I have to come up with something." Tears gathered in her eyes as she stared at him, scrambling for anything her father would believe.

"Och, don't cry now." Willem put out the towel before pulling it back with a shake of his head. "Do you have to go and try to find this man? Isn't it enough what you do here? Maybe if you spoke to Lord Scarborough he'd let you perform for his guests."

Daphne slapped her clenched fists against her sides and glared at him. "You don't understand. You don't understand anything. You think I practice so hard to be a party treat?" She stomped over to where she'd left her overdress, having given up on dancing in the heavy cloth in favor of her shift. Suddenly, she felt naked in front of Willem as she never had before.

Clutching the overdress to her chest, she glared at the coachman. "Was that what all this was? You offered to play for me so you could watch me prance around pretending to be someone?"

Willem twisted the towel between his hands. "No, my lady. You are very good. It's not your skill, but your father I worry about."

Daphne stepped close and shoved Willem in the chest. "I wouldn't have to worry about my father if you'd only help me," she charged. "He'd never question where you brought me. I could get a hire coach back and he'd never know."

Willem shook his head slowly back and forth. "You think your father a fool," he said. "He'll question me, and when I can't give an address, he'll suspect something right off."

She could feel the truth in his words as her chest tightened in fear. "You're right," she said, shoulders slumping. "I can't risk your job and my father's displeasure without a better story. I only wanted to prove I really am as good as Monsieur Henre always said." The last Daphne whispered, tears clouding her vision once more.

"How about that girl, my lady. The one your mother wanted you to meet with?"

Daphne looked up, trying not to hope. "What?" she asked, her tone faint. "What did you say?"

Willem smiled, as if finally finding some connection with her plan. "I think you called her Penelope?"

"Penelope?" Daphne echoed the name without comprehension, but then memory sparked of the scatter-brained girl mixed in with a crowd much too sophisticated for either of them. "Penelope." This time, the name had a level of consideration. "My mother suggested I visit her. No one said a word when I stayed out so late." Daphne nodded. "She'd calm any worries my father might have, thinking I'm only preparing for my coming out. That's perfect."

Overcome with enthusiasm, Daphne pulled Willem into a tight hug.

Willem jerked back, his features painted red. "Glad to be of service, Lady Daphne," he muttered, turning away from her.

Daphne shook her head before reaching out a hand to brush his shoulder. "I am sorry, Willem. I didn't mean to embarrass you. I was a little carried away. Your idea is perfect."

He cleared his throat and spoke in a gruff voice, making him sound much older than Daphne though he had less than five years on her. "I still think this plan isn't wise, my lady. Your mother will be crushed and what will your father do?"

Smiling, she dismissed his worries. "I can handle my parents. It's just easier this way. No one will be hurt."

"And what about when your name comes back to them? You don't see hurt coming from a father hearing his daughter's shown her underdress to everyone? Those dance halls are places nice ladies don't frequent even to watch the dancing."

Daphne laughed, tapping his chest. "You're starting to sound as old as a grandfather, Willem. No one would mistake you for a young man with those tones. Monsieur Henre doesn't direct in one of those places. You'll see. His dance hall is frequented by all of the ton, men and women."

Willem frowned. "And that's better? Everyone knows what kind of woman exposes herself on the stage."

She wanted to dismiss his concerns, but she couldn't help thinking her mother and father would not appreciate becoming the butt of the gossip for whatever reason. "I'll need a disguise," she said, without thinking. Only after the words left her mouth did she hear the truth in them.

"A disguise?" Willem echoed. At first, his frown stayed as fierce as ever, then the boy who'd helped her through so many scrapes before found his way through the demeanor of the man grown. "Like a masked ball," he said, excitement filling his voice. "No one would recognize you with your face covered. They'd never think to see you there."

Daphne grinned, covering her lower face and peering at her reflection. "It would have to be something simple, something I could wear with any costume and that wouldn't interfere with my dancing."

Willem laughed. "You dance with your eyes closed half the time. Anything not stretching out from your head would work."

She cupped her hands around her eyes, a frown of concentration puckering her forehead. "A simple mask. Black and just to cloak the eyes. Anything more and it would hint at my class. Don't we have some from the last ball? The ones my mother provided for unprepared guests?"

With a slow nod, Willem agreed. "I'll have to be careful, but I think I can get you one by the end of the day."

"Perfect," she said again. "We can go to visit 'Penelope' tonight then. Monsieur Henre should be there."

"And if he's not?" Willem asked, concern taking the place of his earlier excitement.

Daphne shook her head. "Don't worry. If he's not, I'll come right back and you can take me to Penelope's for real. It's little enough to suffer for my art." She thought of the worn leather cover enclosing another dancer's challenges. She had little to give up in comparison. And once she made a name for herself, maybe her parents would delight in knowing their daughter's prowess.

JASPER SLOWED HIS HORSE TO a walk, knowing he'd hear about his unrestrained canter through the gardens, but he'd needed the release. The gelding panted in rhythm with each step, not exhausted, but easily tired by the effort.

"Don't worry, old boy. I'll cool you down with a long walk before putting you back into the stables," he promised the horse, still feeling the twist of energy in his gut. "We'll just wander down and see the few folks up early to shop."

The horse tossed his head, as if contesting the pleasure of that path, making Jasper laugh out loud.

"You have so little faith in those of my class, you old mule, you." He tightened his knees and pressed on one side, steering his mount into the sparse traffic. Though he couldn't protest the horse's opinion, he did have a book to pick up at the bookshop. He'd requested the philosophy text when it came up in discussion with some of his old Oxford comrades. It wouldn't stand for them to be more aware of the world than he, but they'd played a pretty game on him a time or two so he'd read the text on his own before claiming a permanent copy.

Few of the elegant stores had opened their doors, knowing full well mid-morning was not yet time for their clientele. Jasper enjoyed the relative quiet and only had to acknowledge a few friends or acquaintances, none of which were female.

"Heard you've been snatched up in the marriage mart, my boy," an older friend of his father's called up to him.

Jasper smiled, hiding his own thoughts behind a social mask. "It had to happen sometime," he told the man who had not been to their house since his father passed.

"True enough. You need strong boys to carry on your family name. Only hope you have better luck than your father."

Giving the man a fierce stare, Jasper kneed the horse past him, wanting no reminder of the wedded bliss his parents had suffered for nigh on thirty years, though like as not the comment referred to the loss of his brothers. The man had often enough praised the late Lord Pendleton's perseverance. Unlike many of his generation, Jasper's father survived to a ripe old age, ducking the hunting and riding accidents that claimed many of his peers. And yet, to live so long beside the harridan Jasper's mother had become around his father would have been enough to test any man's will to live.

Jasper swung down from his mount, his movements no less smooth for his bad mood. After tying the reins to the mounting post, he strode up to the bookshop, taking a firm hold on the door handle and jerking it open. The loud jangle from a bell secured above the door made him flinch as it announced his presence. Still, the musky scent of books crowded upon themselves in the close-packed space calmed him as little could. As a child, he'd spent many a favored hour in his father's study, listening to the gentlemen's discourse or pouring over the books filling the shelves.

"Be right with you. Just a moment." The shopkeeper's voice came from among the stacks, muffled by the press of books.

Jasper scanned the books on the counter, then leaned over the divider to see what the shopkeeper offered to those just passing by. He lifted a book on land rotation, skimming the first few pages and then flipping to the middle to study the methods more intently.

"Ah, Lord Pendleton. Come for that philosophy text I'd guess."

He nodded to the shopkeeper, smiling a greeting. They'd come to know each other well in his Oxford days, and the acquaintance only deepened with Jasper coming into a modest fortune not too long after.

"I think I'll take this one as well," Jasper said, hefting the agriculture manual. "If its offerings are sound, you may have to request another copy."

The shopkeeper took the book from his hand and looked at it almost despairingly. "And I suppose you claimed this from the window? I'm having the hardest time keeping that display, though with so few copies, I don't see why I expect any different."

Jasper laughed. "Oh? Another long-limbed boy come snatching up your inventory?" he asked, bringing to mind an old joke between them.

"No," the shopkeeper said, without looking up. "A girl. Mere chit of a thing, but with a very good name. Wanted a novel."

"Figures. No female would want something of substance."

The shopkeeper stopped scribbling in the ledger and glanced up. "Oh, there you are mistaken. This book was no simple tale of love and woe. She's yet to return it, but I had second thoughts about letting a Scarborough take it home. It read more like a biography than fiction, even claimed to be one. And it certainly did not skimp on the harsh parts."

Jasper had been about to dismiss the contention when he heard a name he'd never expected. Scarborough. "A biography of whom?" he asked, intrigued at this sign that his affianced might have more to her than that he'd seen on the dance floors.

"Some dancer, my lord. The story ends well, but the path to that ending is very dark. Not what I'd expected to interest a young lady, let me tell you."

Jasper smiled then shook his head at this grasping for straws. "I'm sure she skipped to the happy parts. She must not have known what she'd chosen."

The shopkeeper laughed. "You may well be right. She seemed so fascinated and wouldn't accept my cautions, but when she actually sat down to read it, well, it could very well have been different. She may just be too embarrassed to return it."

Picking up the brown-wrapped package containing his two books, Jasper signed the promissory note with a flourish, having left his mother's presence with little coin. "A man can spend a lifetime trying to understand the feminine mind only to discover it contains solely two thoughts: titles and money. I'll be happy to stay with my philosophy texts."

"As you say, my lord." The shopkeeper gave a short bow.

Jasper returned the salute and headed back to his horse, unable to wipe the thoughts from his mind as easily as his tongue had dismissed them. Imagine the daughter of an earl reading something more taxing than a fanciful romance? He shook his head. "Fanciful is the right word for my thoughts," he muttered, swinging into the saddle. "I know just how to handle my wife-to-be. It's the best for both of us."

Chapter Seven

hat's a beautiful gown," Lady Scarborough said, gently rotating Daphne to get the full effect. "It should do nicely for your visit. It's so nice of you to spend time with Penelope. Her mother worries she'll be overshadowed by her sister. And I can't help but think the crowd her sister hangs with will only be bad for that girl."

Daphne ducked her head to hide her expression, sure the guilt showed plainly. She, too, had felt a tinge of pity for the other girl, though not enough to suffer another moment in that lion's den. "I think I look fine, Mother," she said, ignoring the rest. "But I don't want to be late."

Her mother laughed with a practiced twinkle in her eye. "It's fashionable to be a little late, dear. I can't tell you how glad I am to see your doldrums fading. It's not right for a young girl like you to spend her time moping. You'll have fun with Penelope, and when you both come out, it will be fabulous." Making a grand sweep of her arm, Lady Scarborough conjured images of a ball, bringing her hand up to simulate a fan masking her face.

Again, Daphne felt heat gather in her cheeks, as if her mother could see the mask hidden in the coach along with a plain change of clothes. At least her mask wouldn't be noticed when sneaking in. She'd remembered a comment from the last visit to Penelope's home that reassured her.

"Now, dearest, don't let it worry you. We'll start small and get you used to such august company before your first ball. After all, we don't want you to give the impression of a shrinking violet. No man wants a ninny for a wife."

Daphne stared at her mother in confusion before she realized her mother thought her discomfort due to the idea of a ball. "Thank you," she murmured. "I'm sure I'll do fine with your help, but I really should be going." She tugged free of her mother's hands and stepped toward the corridor.

"True enough. You have a good time. And mind your manners. The others may act like louts but there's no cause for you to be one. But don't insult them either. The ton has a long memory and you never know who might come to one of those gatherings. It's not like Penelope's mother doesn't run in the right circles."

Daphne smothered a laugh as her mother subtly condemned Penelope's sister's friends using basically the same tactics the sister had. "I'll do fine," she repeated, moving out of her mother's view.

The carriage waiting for her at the bottom of the step proved a welcome sight until Daphne's gaze fell on the crest painted in rich colors on the door. She climbed in, her mind whirling at this last impediment to her plan. She couldn't hope to escape notice driving up to the dance hall in this.

Waiting until they'd moved beyond her street, Daphne kept struggling with the flaw, trying to come up with a way to get around it. She didn't waste her time on mulling though. There wouldn't be many chances to get this right. She struggled with her dress, barely managing to get it off in the tight space without help.

If only she could have a female confident, Daphne thought as she pulled the plainer dress over her head and tried to fasten it by herself. No sooner had she had the thought than the carriage jerked to one side, sending her sliding to the floor in a pile of discarded clothing.

"Watch your driving," Willem shouted.

Daphne climbed up onto the seat and peered out the window. A hackney, the cause of her tumble, pushed past them almost close enough to scrape her father's crest. No matter how much mother supported her choice of destination, she'd never hear the end of it if any damage came to the carriage.

She moved from the back bench until she knelt right behind Willem, calling up to him through the grill. "Willem. Find a park to pull aside in." The glimmering of an idea teased her mind.

"Are you sure, Lady Daphne? This is not the best of neighbor-hoods."

His voice came down into the carriage, and she nodded, forgetting at first that he couldn't see her. "Yes. Please stop," Daphne added.

She waited for him to find a park and rein in the horses before unlatching the door from inside and slipping out, the mask clutched in one hand.

"Lady Daphne! Where are you going?" Willem called, the scrape of his shoe against the carriage side warning her of his approach. He grabbed her arm in a disturbingly familiar touch.

Daphne tried to jerk away, but his hold was firm.

"You don't want to be wandering alone here, my lady. It's not safe for the likes of you."

She pulled again, glowering. "What would you have me do? Ride up to the door in my father's carriage? Word would get back to my mother as fast as a lightning bolt strikes the ground. How will my father react when he has to account for his time? Do you think my secret, or that of your aid, will hold for long? If I have to walk to the theater, it's little enough to pay for my craft."

He frowned, but his grip did not loosen. "I can't let you go like this. I'd better suffer the consequences of discovery than if harm came to you in my care."

Daphne took a deep breath before she lashed out, giving her a moment to rethink her angry words. "How else can I go then?" she asked, keeping her tone mild with an effort.

With a jerk, he pulled her back to the carriage. "Wait inside while I think a bit. You won't get what you want if some man takes a liking to you."

She shuddered at the thought, not resisting as he tucked her back onto the bench. Her plan had seemed so simple back in the mirrored ballroom.

Willem leaned against the door, looking at her through the carriage window.

"You could walk me there, Willem. In the dark, your livery looks much like any other suit."

He laughed. "Thanks for that thought, Lady Daphne, but you're wrong. Your father's name might not be blazoned on my livery in the dark, but no one would mistake me for a regular gent any more than you could have gone in that fancy dress your mother gave you."

She twisted the curtain cord between her fingers, unwilling to give up so close to her goal. Her foot came out and pushed the hated white fabric now crumpled on the floor. She'd have enough of a time explaining how she sullied her dress. Her mother would be no happier to hear of the hackney and would ask what they'd been doing in areas frequented by them.

The glimmer of thought that had teased her before now came clear. "A hire coach. Willem, can't you find me one? You could wait here and I'll come back when I've spoken to Monsieur Henre."

Willem frowned, the lines in his face cut deep by the reflection of the lantern. "And how will you find one on the way back?" he asked, though she could tell he worked hard to restrain an outright rejection.

"Monsieur Henre can call me one," she said quickly, reaching out to tap his arm. "Don't worry. No one will recognize me. I've hardly been out in society at all and this dress is not reminiscent of a fine lady." She plucked at the worn fabric, chosen for its invisibility. "No one will notice me."

"That's where you're wrong, my lady." He gave her a long look. "But I see nothing will change your mind. Just make it quick. This really isn't a safe place for your father's carriage either."

Before she could say another word, he pulled away and walked down the street, seeking a hackney. She'd never felt so alone as when the lantern flickered in a slight breeze, sending the tree shadows stretching into her carriage. The silence became menacing, every little sound portending something dangerous.

A tap on the door sent her back against the far corner, a squeak bursting from her lips as the door swung open.

"It's just me, my lady." He stared at her in the flickering light. "Do you want to change your mind and go home?"

Daphne couldn't tell what he saw in her face, but she made an effort to school her features as she let her feet drop down to the floor and straightened her skirt. "Did you get the carriage?" she asked, her tone higher than normal but steady.

He grimaced, but lowered his chin in a nod. "Can you give it another thought, Lady Daphne? Is this really what you be wanting?"

She met his eyes, hers holding determination tinged with defiance. "I'd be untrue to my heart if I didn't go. I'd hate myself forever forward if I let simple fear keep me from my dreams." She put a hand on his shoulder, imploring him to understand. "I have to do this."

Willem nodded again, offering her a hand down from the carriage. "If you're sure, you're sure. Just take care with yourself. This isn't the area for nice ladies like you."

Daphne slipped her mask into place and leaned close to whisper in Willem's ear. "I'm not a nice lady anymore. I'm a dancer."

She pushed away, twirling in a circle, her feet slipping on the cobblestones but not enough to make her fall. Her heart pounded against her ribs as if it would burst free and fly up into the sky, so much excitement filled Daphne.

"Lady Daphne, the hackney is this way," Willem called, his smile visible even in the fading light.

Daphne laughed, her joyous sound bouncing in between the trees as she skipped over to join him.

Willem handed her into the coach, making her repeat back the address of this park three times before he was satisfied. After the door closed, she heard him give the coachman directions to Monsieur Henre's theater using the address from the hated dismissal notice. At least she'd never given in to the desire to rip it into tiny shreds.

THE HACKNEY CAME TO A stop and the driver called down to her. Daphne waited for a heartbeat, then laughing at herself, opened the coach door. She kicked the step until it fell down and she could climb onto the dirty street.

"Out of the way, miss. I have another customer to collect."

Daphne stared up at the driver, startled, before she stepped back and let the carriage roll away, leaving her in the middle of the road.

Another carriage approached, this one with a crest carved into its door. The gilt paint passed so close to her, she wondered if it now decorated her cheek.

"Stupid git. Move to the side."

Dazed by the close contact, Daphne stumbled over to the well-lit theater entrance, joining the masses just collecting there. She ducked her head when she saw one of the women from Penelope's house before remembering the mask hiding her features.

Sliding through the crowd until she stood at the edge, Daphne slipped free and walked down the alleyway on the theater's side. She sought a different kind of entrance than one given only to those holding a ticket.

Though she could hear the sounds of the crowd behind her, the dark alley seemed a world away from them. Daphne shivered as wind rustled against something ahead of her, her mind painting pictures that made her want to turn and run.

Some distance away, a door opened, sending a cheery glow into the alleyway.

"I won't have it," a woman's angry voice rang out. "If she can't keep her paws off my costumes, you'll have to find yourself another dancer."

Daphne stared as the woman stomped out, no sign of a dancer's grace in her tense form. She tried to find some pity for the woman who had clearly been pushed too far, but her nerves thrummed with expectation. The urge to jump up and down calling, "Me, me," swept over her as she absorbed the chance providence had shown her.

She didn't care what position the angry woman held. She wanted it.

Rushing forward on the balls of her feet, Daphne let her excitement have free rein as it drew her closer to her heart's desire. Not even the quiet thud when the door swung shut could dampen her enthusiasm, though she slowed, no longer able to see her way.

Her feet crushed some refuse and she tripped over a large object in the path, but she barely noticed the impediments. Her gaze stayed locked on the faint hint of light revealing the doorframe. When she reached it, Daphne hesitated. She'd always imagined the scene spent talking to Monsieur Henre, never once considering how she'd get to him.

Raising her hand to knock, instead, she rested her knuckles against the hard wood surface. What would she say to the person who answered? How could she convince them to let her past? Would she be ushered back to the front, her request unmade?

Her chin firmed as she washed away the doubts. She reached for the knob, choosing not to take the chance that the person who answered would send her away. The dancer in the book had done horrible things to get that first moment to present her desires. Ignoring etiquette seemed a minor sacrifice in comparison.

The knob turned in her hand, its smooth movement reassuring even though she'd half expected the door to be locked.

The door swung open, hinges groaning, a deep sound she hadn't heard from so far away.

"You came back did you?" The woman who spoke leaned out from one of the rooms, a smirk twisting her face. "Miss Fancy come to beg her way back into the troupe? You never expected the master would let you go, now did you?"

The words stopped as the woman actually looked at the one who had opened the door.

Daphne stared back, scared and embarrassed at her audacity. The courage she'd felt in the dark alleyway deserted her and her throat felt dry, all words to plead her case having escaped.

"Who are you?" the woman asked after an awkward pause as she stepped free of what must have been a dressing room. "You can't just come in here, you know."

Fully revealed, the dancer's clothes seemed indecent, even more than the racy styles Daphne had heard tell some of the ladies now wore. She doubted damp underclothes caused the woman's dress to hug her curves so closely and the material seemed quite insubstantial.

Daphne reached out and fingered a bit of the skirt, barely registering the question. "Do all dancers have to dress like this?" she asked, her words soft and hesitant.

The woman threw her head back and laughed, but the sound seemed more bitter than full of good humor. "I was more right than not when I thought you were her." She jerked her head toward the door, indicating the angry dancer. "Only the line dancers wear this." She jerked her skirt free from Daphne's hand and spun on her heel. Calling back over her shoulder, she said, "You should get out of here before the master finds you. He's not in the best mood and would love someone to take his temper out on."

Daphne watched the other woman leave, fighting the instinct to turn and run. She'd never seen Monsieur Henre in a rage and could not imagine it. Had she gotten confused somehow? Did someone else lead this troupe?

She half-turned back toward the door, torn between her need to demand a place in the world of dancers and the realization her whole plan hinged on Monsieur Henre. Without him, who would accept a dancer off the street? She flinched away from the thought of what the dancer in her book had done, actions only hinted at to protect delicate minds like hers.

Chapter Eight

S he'll learn quick enough just how hard it is to find work."

The voice issued from an open door further down the corridor. A small cry of delight slipped from Daphne's mouth. Even with anger hardening his tones, she'd recognize that voice anywhere. She skipped toward the sound, forgetting her purpose in the recovery of a friend. Without thinking, she stepped through the door, her arms thrown wide.

"Whatever you think you can earn with that body, go do it elsewhere. I've no interest in your wares."

Monsieur Henre didn't even look up from the desk, only glancing at the mirror in front of him to see her reflection.

Daphne dropped her arms, stunned at this side of him. He didn't resemble her dance instructor at all. Even the faint hint of accent had vanished from his harsh voice. She looked past him to the practice mirror, seeing not an elegant young noble, but a scruffy woman, her features covered in a simple black mask, her hair pulling free of a once-neat bun and a worn dress hanging limp from her shoulders. Oddly, the sight made her smile.

"It's me, Monsieur Henre. Your favorite student," Daphne said, stepping further into the room and crossing to stand next to him.

Her teacher frowned at the continued intrusion, raising his fingers to pinch the bridge of his nose. He fumbled as they met the spectacles he'd never worn in her presence, and he jerked them off his face in an almost vicious movement. After lowering them to the table in a controlled motion that made his hand tremble, he turned to face her.

Daphne grinned, expecting his mood to change when he finally accepted it really was her.

"I have nothing for you. This is not some whore house where you can twirl once and collapse across some gentleman's lap. Dance is an art form well beyond the likes of you." His voice grew louder with every word and Daphne cringed, suddenly fearing him.

Monsieur Henre pushed his chair back, the legs scraping against the wood floor with a harsh sound. She trembled when his hand tightened around her upper arm, the fingers pressing hard enough to bruise. "Get out of here. Take your wares to Covent Garden. My dancers earn their keep on the stage, not in dark rooms with red bed sheets."

He jerked her toward the door as if to escort her outside. Daphne cried out at the rough handling, stumbling forward before her determination reasserted itself.

"No," she said, pulling against his hold. "It's not what you think." Reaching up with her free hand, she pushed the mask up to reveal her features. "Don't you recognize me?"

He turned to yell at her again, but stopped, a stunned expression taking the place of his anger. "Lady Daphne?" The words came out tentative and his accent crept into his tones.

She tugged against the grip he'd obviously forgotten and smiled. "Yes, it's me," she repeated, relaxing as the teacher she knew returned, "But best you call me mistress when I'm here in case any overhear."

His eyebrows drew together and a frown pulled at his mouth. "You can't be here. You'll be ruined as will I. Put that mask on and get back home."

Once again he touched her, but this time just to press a hand against her back, forcing her out of his office.

Daphne turned to face him and stretched her arms out until she blocked the door, confident he'd do nothing to harm her now that he'd recognized who she was. "I'm not going anywhere. I came here to dance."

Monsieur Henre shook his head, stepping back until he sat on the edge of his desk. "We already talked of this, mistress. It's not possible. Even were I willing to take the chance, your father would storm my establishment and drag you home in disgrace. I have enough troubles of my own without inviting more." He waved at the table, his shoulders slumping. "You have no idea how much all this takes. First I lose the extra income because of your ridiculous dreams and now I've lost my lead dancer. I don't have time for your childish games."

Daphne tensed in indignation. How could he treat her this way? Even as the question stormed through her mind, she realized she'd have to accept this familiarity and worse if she convinced him. Letting her arms fall gracefully against her skirt, she wiped the belligerent expression from her face. "I could take her place," she murmured.

With a bitter laugh, Monsieur Henre dropped into his chair. "Haven't you listened to a word I've said? Even if you could carry off a professional dance—"

"But I can. You said so yourself." Daphne crossed the room quickly and leaned against the desk, her hand on her teacher's shoulder. "You need me."

He shoved back, shrugging off her touch. "I need you as much as I need some randy noble taking a liking to one of my dancers. You are trouble. More trouble than I can afford."

Desperation swept over her and Daphne snapped her mask back into place, refusing to give in. "You didn't know me. If you, who has seen me dance, who knows me better even than my family, didn't recognize me, who else will?"

He stared at her masked face for a long, thoughtful moment before shaking his head. "No, it still wouldn't work. This would be the first place they'd come looking when you slipped away. You made your intentions clear enough, and Lord Scarborough is not a stupid man."

Daphne smiled, feeling her plans finally coming together. "They think I've given it up," she said, brushing a loose strand of hair out of her face. "They think I'm focused on my coming out like any other young girl my age."

"Young noble girl, you mean," her teacher said. "And so you should be. This is not natural. Not the way things are."

"You'd turn me away?" she asked, strain making her voice higher than it usually was. "You need me, and I want nothing more than to dance. You can't really mean to make me go. Not after all I've done."

Her teacher looked worried. "What have you done?" he asked, his voice sharp.

She blushed, knowing the answer wouldn't speak well of her. "Does it matter? Can't you just accept that I will do whatever necessary to get this chance?"

"Oh mistress." He took one of her hands between his. "I know how the desire to dance can burn in you—I feel it in myself—but you have a different life to live. A much better life than this one."

Jerking her hand free, she glowered at him. "As a governess?" she asked, throwing his suggestion back in his face. "Is that the better life you see for me? At the beck and call of someone else's children, wilting away because I cannot dance?"

He shook his head, a rueful expression crossing his face. "Do you truly think it will come to that? Some handsome noble will snatch you up and make you his own. You'll have fancy dresses, parties with the best of the ton, and you'll forget these childish dreams."

Anger whipped through Daphne. She forgot herself as she slammed her fists against Monsieur Henre's chest. "You think so little of me, of my desire? I already have gone to a party with the best of the ton. That's where my mother thinks I am right now. I hated it. All I wanted was to be dancing, not exchanging false pleasantries knowing they'll laugh the moment my back is turned. I am not like them."

She stopped, breathing heavy in her agitation. With an angry swipe of a hand, she pushed the hair back out of her face and glared at her teacher.

Again, he gave her that thoughtful look she'd grown used to as he considered whether she'd mastered a step. "Perhaps I have been hasty. Perhaps you are truly driven to dance."

Something about his tone kept Daphne from relaxing. She had not won the argument just yet.

He shook his head, turning away. "Not that it matters. Your father would never allow it."

Daphne walked around the desk so she could look him in the face. "My father need never know. They think I'm bonding with some other young woman who will come out next year. Their paths cross so rarely, I needn't worry about discovery. Don't you see? This is my only chance." Forgetting about dignity, she pleaded with him. "You can't send me away. You need a dancer now and how are you to find one? Just let me try. Just let me dance while you seek a replacement. I swear you won't regret it."

He looked from her clasped hands to her face and sighed. "True enough I have no dancer. You're already here, and I certainly didn't recognize you in that mask or those clothes." He shoved back from the desk again, but this time a smile spread across his face. "Just how much harm can it do?"

He spoke the last quietly, as if to himself, and Daphne held her breath, hoping against hope he'd give in.

"Come. I'll take you to Cynthia. She knew Joan's wardrobe better even than Joan did." His smile turned down into a grimace as he added in a mutter, "That was part of the problem."

Daphne let the air go in a long sigh. She'd won. Unable to restrain herself, she flung her arms around her teacher, giving him a tight hug. "Thank you, Monsieur Henre. Thank you," she cried.

He slowly pulled her hands aside and frowned down at her. "I meant what I said earlier. This troupe doesn't go for that sort of behavior, mistress, and now you're no different than any of them. You'll have to practice mostly on your own because of your father, but when you're here, you will be one of the troupe."

She backed up, his admonishment failing to dent her delight. "Of course. One of the troupe. You tell me what to practice and I will. Father hasn't taken away the back ballroom so I've been practicing there."

A quiet bell rang through the corridor outside. Monsieur Henre tensed, then released his breath on a sigh. "I hope you have, mistress, because there's no time to run you through your paces now. The dancers have started their routine and you'll be on soon enough. I count my blessings that I taught you this dance though you'd never have the opportunity to use it."

Fear raced through Daphne as it all became real. She gave her teacher a shaky smile. "I know the movements by heart. I won't fail you."

He raised her chin and smiled. "I never thought you would. Now follow me. I'll show you the costumes myself. We have no choice."

SOOT RISING FROM THE OIL lamps used to light the stage tickled Daphne's nose and made her want to sneeze. She could hear the rustle of people but could not see them from where she stood behind a side curtain. Her mind drifted to when her father had brought her to the opera. She'd been entranced by the actors down on the stage so far below their box, and even then the longing to be there herself had infected her.

"From distant lands comes our newest star, never before seen on this shore."

"More like from Lancaster," a voice called, breaking through Monsieur Henre's introduction.

Her teacher kept speaking, ignoring the interruption, but Daphne no longer heard his words. She swallowed, the wonder replaced with nervousness. Her hands crept up to make sure she'd attached her mask securely. What if she stumbled? What if she crashed into something? She didn't know the stage. She'd never tried to dance with the mask on.

Panic fed on itself until she could only hear the hard pounding of her heart. She couldn't do this. She had to get out of here.

A hand closed over her shoulder as she turned, ready to escape. "It's always hard the first time. You just need to get out there and make your mistakes. No one is ever perfect, especially not on their debut, but until you get it over with, you'll be stuck in this moment."

Daphne turned to look at her teacher, her lips trembling though she tried to smile.

His stern expression dropped away, and a soft smile took its place. "Go. Your audience awaits you. Just remember how long you've wanted this. Nothing can take this from you now except your fear."

She stared at him for a heartbeat then firmed her chin, nodding sharply. As if in tune with her mood, the audience's restless sounds stilled. The musicians started again, a familiar melody soothing her nerves. She closed her eyes, letting the notes wash over her and invade her body until it thrummed with the need to express the music through dance.

"Go on," Monsieur Henre said, suppressed laughter in his voice.

Daphne didn't look at him again as she moved away from the sheltering curtain, taking swift, graceful steps toward the center of the stage.

As though in the distance, she heard some calls from the open seating at the base of the stage, but this time none of them bit into her. Instead, the violin pulled a spin from her and then the flute sent her into a dip until she continued through the routine she'd practiced so many times that her body required little reminder.

The audience vanished, the oil lamps became the warmth of a bright summer day, and the music transformed into wind and waves. Daphne couldn't tell whether her eyes were open or closed. She only felt the exhilaration pounding through her as the shortened skirt swirled around her legs and the springy wood floor gave her steps more lift than she'd ever experienced. She never wanted it to end.

The music slowed then stopped, only a single note of the flute remaining as Daphne collapsed onto the floor, unsure how much time had passed. Sweat dripped from her forehead, sliding between her lips. She licked the fluid, tasting her effort in its salty bitterness.

Had she succeeded? Or failed?

In the silence that followed the flute, she remembered every stumble, every time she missed a move or didn't raise her arms high enough. A single cough cut through the quiet and seemed to provide her answer.

When the sound first started, Daphne thought the audience was stampeding away, trying to escape her amateur efforts. Then, she realized the thunder held nothing of chaos. Daphne raised her head to stare into the darkness beyond the stage lights, and the noise intensified.

A smile pulled at her cheeks and tears slipped down to dampen her mask. They were applauding. They loved her.

The curtains came down from each side to close her off, but the thunder continued without faltering. She let the noise wash over her, let it wash away her doubts and replace them with a single certainty. This was her place. This was where she belonged.

"They always did like a novelty. Don't let it go to your head."

The sharp voice pulled Daphne back to reality. She turned to see the woman she'd met in the corridor. Her gaze drifted further and three rows of four dancers each now stood on the stage, ignoring her.

"You'll be trampled if you stay there," the same woman said, the edge in her voice making it seem as if she hoped Daphne would wait.

With none of the grace she'd shown before, Daphne scrambled to her feet, her knees shaking with exhaustion. She stumbled off the stage just in time as she heard the rumble of chain as the curtains pulled up out of sight.

"You did well, my pupil," Monsieur Henre greeted her, putting a robe around her shoulders before she even realized how the cold seeped into her bones.

Daphne managed a tired smile, happy to follow him back to the changing room, unsure she'd be able to find it on her own.

"I'll call you a hackney," he said as he closed the door. "You were wonderful."

She barely heard the click of the door latch. Her teacher's words meant more to her than all the applause in the world. She spun around in a circle with her arms hugging herself, stumbled and almost fell.

Collapsing into the chair, Daphne laughed breathlessly. She'd done it. Against all odds and with providence shining on her, she'd become a professional dancer.

Daphne didn't know how long she'd sat slumped in the chair, contemplating her success with a bleary exhausted elation, but she jerked upright when a heavy hand slammed against the door.

Without waiting for a response, an unfamiliar male voice called, "Hackney's here. Won't be waiting long."

"Just a moment," she called, her voice muffled as she dragged the costume over her head. She glanced around the room, looking for her dress. When she found it, she laughed again. The dress lay in an untidy pile, right where she'd dropped it. She would never have thought to look there. At home, one of the maids would always pick up after her, almost faster than she could drop things.

Shaking her head, she pulled the dress on and tugged the laces as tight as she could, using her wrap to cover her clumsy work. She'd just have to change again anyway.

"I'm ready," she cried, bursting through the door at a run.

"As if we care," the other dancer said, shoving past Daphne into the dressing room.

The rest of the dancers followed her, one shrugging. "Don't mind her. Cynthia's always like that," the woman whispered, before pulling the door closed on all of them.

Daphne's mouth pulled into a half smile. At least they weren't all nasty, she thought as she went to find her carriage and make her way back to Willem.

Chapter Nine

$\mathcal{D}$aphne massaged her arches before slipping her feet into normal shoes, unable to keep the smile from her face even though her cheeks ached from it.

"They love you. You should hear some of what they're saying. Half the young lords are begging to meet you while the ladies color when they mention your grace."

In the dark carriage, Daphne blushed as she heard the echo of Monsieur Henre's praise. It made the long nights and early mornings worth it.

She smothered a yawn, her body protesting the week of hard work in the morning paired with long performances at night. Even her mother had commented that Daphne looked a bit worn the other day. Daphne tensed at the memory, but once again her mother's focus on coming out remained dominant. She'd gotten off with a warning not to fall ill.

Daphne leaned against the carriage wall as she tried to do her laces, her eyes slipping closed even though she struggled to stay awake.

"My lady, we're here," Willem called down, his voice jerking her back to consciousness.

Her fingers were tangled in the laces, and Daphne pulled hard enough to pinch as she tried to reach up and check her hair. She froze when a sharp sound echoed in her ears. One finger stung as if cut. A lace had snapped under her rough treatment.

Still trying to wipe the sleep from her mind, she pulled the cloak around her, grateful most of the household would be out on visits of their own. If her luck held, no one would know about the snapped string until morning. She could always claim she'd broken it while getting undressed since she'd told the maid not to wait up for her.

Willem opened the door and put his hand under her elbow without waiting for her to ask, supporting her first down the carriage step and then up to the house. As much as she knew she should pull away, Daphne couldn't find the energy, barely managing to force one foot in front of the other.

If anyone saw her now, they'd never imagine she could be the masked dancer all the ton seemed to be talking about. Even Grace had mentioned the phenomenon, though Mother hushed her quickly.

Daphne's lips curled in a smile as she remembered her mother's ringing tones, "No one of our standing has any business being in a place such as that. I'll not hear it spoken of at my table."

If only her mother knew.

"Ah, there you are, dear."

Daphne froze, her hand on the clasp of her cloak, as her mother's voice echoed not from the past but from the front parlor.

"Well, Daphne? Don't just stand there," Lady Scarborough said. "Give up your cloak, and come and chat with me. You've been so busy with your new friends, I've hardly had a moment to speak with you."

The butler took her cloak before Daphne could protest, sweeping away her protection. Luckily, her mother had already turned back into the parlor.

Glancing at her side, Daphne checked to see if her torn lace showed. Some of her tension drained when she could not see it, only to return when she considered what possibly could have made her mother cut her evening entertainment short just for this discussion.

Her steps tentative, Daphne moved into the parlor, slipping into a chair and curling her legs under her.

"I do hope you sit like a young lady when you're at your friend's house," her mother said with a sharp tone. "You are much too old for such posture."

Daphne straightened abruptly, a blush staining her cheeks. She knew better than to sit so, but had been too worried to pay attention.

Her mother's sharply indrawn breath brought Daphne's attention to the loose string, now dangling from her side. She gathered it up, trying to hide it from sight even though she knew it was too late.

Tsking under her breath, Lady Scarborough shook her head. "And see what your childish posture has done?" she asked. "Though that more than anything makes what I have to tell you essential."

Daphne had relaxed just slightly when her mother credited the sitting position for the torn lace, but at the added words, she sat ever so much straighter, feeling tension bind her shoulders. She wanted to roll her shoulders and release the muscles as she'd been trained, but knew the dancer's move would only enrage her mother.

Lady Scarborough smiled. "Now don't look like a fox facing the pack of hounds. You should be delighted with my offer. I'm planning to take you on a shopping expedition on the morrow."

Daphne pasted a smile on her face but inwardly she cried out in protest. "In the morning, Mother?" she asked, forcing her voice into a semblance of joy.

"As soon as we're done with breakfast."

Before Daphne could relax at the partial reprieve, her mother shook one finger toward her daughter. "And no coming in after the rolls have cooled. I expect you to be up and ready by ten and no later."

Daphne smiled again, smothering a groan. Her mother rarely started breakfast before eleven and didn't show any signs of surprise when Daphne came in at noon for the meal. She'd lose clear half of her practice time. A yawn stretched her face, breaking through her agitation with the reminder of her exhausted state. She'd lose her afternoon nap as well, the way her mother liked to consider all dress styles. No doubt Lady Scarborough expected her to beg off going to Penelope's house tomorrow, but she could not disappoint Monsieur Henre.

That thought brought forth her first honest smile. Disappointment might have been the worry when he'd been her teacher, but now he employed her services and could just as easily send her on her way, dreams crushed. He had no care for her mother's desires, only that the theater beyond the stage remained packed.

Daphne couldn't help but be surprised at how her image of her dance instructor had changed now that she saw him as a businessman. He'd gone from beloved teacher to harsh taskmaster, leaving as little taste of his former self as she kept the look of a lady when she stepped onto his stage. She'd do anything to keep her place, and if that meant dancing when she could barely keep her eyes open, so be it.

She yawned again, finding the effort to raise her hand too much.

"You haven't heard a word I've said, have you?" her mother asked with an indulgent expression. "All these late nights begin to wear on a girl, even one as young as you. You don't want to peak too soon, my dear."

"Yes, Mother," Daphne managed, grateful she'd been forgiven for her inelegance without another lecture. Her eyes drooped shut and she tensed her neck to keep upright.

Lady Scarborough tapped her on the knee. "I can't tell you how happy it makes me to see you spending time with girls your own age and preparing for the same wondrous event. I know you've never liked our shopping expeditions," she added, showing a surprising amount of perception, "but you can't keep wearing the same old rags. Your father has enough to deal with without worrying about rumors started by your lack of fashion sense. They'll think we're in the poor house. And don't for one moment believe word wouldn't race around faster than you could blink. Penelope's a sweet girl and her mother's a dear, but her sister is all that's gone wrong with the young of our set."

Jerking her head up after a nod that threatened to turn into deep sleep, Daphne blinked at her mother as if echoing the statement.

"Don't you worry. Just stay by Penelope and keep clear of those others. I'm sure the good from all this greatly outweighs any chance that my daughter would be influenced by those uncouth gossipmongers. It means so much to see the light back in your eyes."

Daphne forced herself not to flinch as her mother came to stand by her chair, putting a soft hand under her chin. Guilt cut through any protest she might have made. She'd never considered the costs of her deception, the hopes she'd raised. "I won't," she stammered. "I won't be influenced by them, I promise." Not that she could be, having only gone the once. At least she could keep one promise. "And I'll enjoy shopping with you, Mother," she added, swearing to herself that she'd enjoy it even if the effort killed her. She couldn't give up the dance, but at least she could do this one little thing for her mother.

Lady Scarborough glanced at the mantle clock just as it started its short pattern of chimes. "Tsk. Would you look at the time? If you're to come down in the morning without looking haggard, you'd best be up in your bed." A smile softened her sharp tones. "Do go on now. We'll have time enough to talk tomorrow."

Grateful to be excused, Daphne rose and pressed a kiss to her mother's cheek. "Until the morning then," she said, turning toward the door.

"Sleep well," Lady Scarborough called after Daphne.

The gentle words followed her up to her room where she fell onto her bed, lacking the energy to do more than loosen her stays. Just before dropping off, she thought how much easier it must have been for the dancer in her book. Having a loving family could only be a burden when she had to deceive them. Daphne wished more than anything for the chance to show her parents, to show Grace, how well she danced and how much it meant to her.

A tear slipped down her cheek. Her family must never know. If ever they found out, they'd be crushed, their reputation destroyed. The guilt she felt now would be nothing compared to how she'd feel should her actions become known.

Wet lashes pressed against her face as Daphne slipped into exhausted slumber filled with dreams of dancing her heart out only to lift her mask and stare directly into her mother's horrified expression.

"I didn't mean to," she muttered, thrashing against the binding sheets. "I only wanted to dance."

WHEN DAPHNE WOKE TO THE sunlight glaring across her face, she dragged herself up to start her morning routine. Only after she put on her practice dress, did she remember most of today would be lost.

She rushed through her morning wash, determined to get in stretches and some basic routines before she had to dress for the outing. Willem never came to join her, probably having heard about her mother's plans. The sound of her panting breath and patter of her shoes against the floor provided unhappy accompaniment and did little to mask the boom of the longcase clock in the main hallway.

Tension raced through her when the clock sounded nine, but she refused to stop. Then she stumbled when the quarter struck.

"Enough," Daphne growled, throwing her arms into the air in a final pose. Her mother could send someone to check on her at any moment and discover her practice.

Gathering up her dress, she tugged it over her head and pulled the lacing tight enough for propriety if not elegance. The bustle as she slipped past the servant corridor warned her to take care. With the mistress of the house awake and about, everyone was even more determined to be seen at work, increasing the chances of her crossing paths and making the journey up to her room a tense adventure.

"Ah, there you are," her mother said as Daphne slipped into her seat at the table, this time properly attired as a young lady of her station. "I almost sent the upstairs maid after you. We have a lot to accomplish today."

"Yes, Mother," Daphne answered, buttering a steaming roll. She let the rest of the conversation pass over her head, focusing on fueling her body enough so she could manage this trip without embarrassing herself. Depending on how long they stayed, she'd have little chance for a nap before it was time to dance.

"Daphne? Daphne? Are you done yet? I swear, child, I don't think you've heard a word I've said." Lady Scarborough clucked with her tongue. "You need some sunlight to wake you up, my dear."

With a nod to the footman, she signaled for warm cloths to wash their fingers and wipe the crumbs from their mouths.

Daphne dabbed at her face, hurriedly pushing back her chair as her mother swept away from the table. Somehow, she imagined she'd be trailing after for most of the day.

Willem gave her a wink as he handed the two of them into her father's carriage, the coat of arms polished until it gleamed in the morning light. Daphne reminded herself that this outing was half for the show. If she could love twirling her skirts for an audience each night, surely she could keep a good face while being displayed for her mother's friends.

The trip to a row of small, tasteful shops took no time at all. Daphne smiled as they passed the bookshop, remembering her last visit and how her life had changed. She had yet to return the book, unwilling to be parted.

Lady Scarborough laid a hand on Daphne's knee and squeezed gently. "See, you can enjoy this if you try. Just imagine all the beautiful dresses and how your friend Penelope will gape. After all, the impressions you make now will determine how you start next season."

Daphne nodded, feeling the pinch of tension at her temples. How could her deception hold? And what would her family do when it came to light? Her stomach churned in time with the clop of horse hooves against the street. No matter what, she'd have to give up her love. This time was an idyll and couldn't last. She would be discovered and hadn't the strength to abandon her family like the unnamed dancer in her book.

Despair made her shoulders curl and her mouth pulled down at the sides, wiping out her attempt to keep a cheerful appearance.

"Daphne! Sit up straight," her mother commanded, rubbing chilly fingers against Daphne's cheeks. "No frowns, not now, not ever. They'll mar the beauty of your face faster than you can say 'release the hounds.'"

Struggling to obey, Daphne noticed the line between her mother's eyebrows. She didn't know whether to laugh or feel guilt at how she'd made her mother violate such an important rule. Pushing away the hands, she dragged a smile from the bottom of her heart and straightened her back.

"There. Much better." Lady Scarborough settled back on the seat across from Daphne, smoothing her own forehead with quick swipes of her fingers. "Nothing is so bad that a smile can't solve, I've found."

Daphne raised her lips a little higher on her cheeks before turning to look out the window again, this time with her back pressed against the seat. A few moments later, the coach pulled to a stop in front of her mother's dressmaker.

Lady Scarborough flowed out of the coach and into the small shop like a waterfall, unstoppable and overwhelming. The dressmaker dropped the hem of the skirt she'd been working on and rushed toward Daphne's mother, her face wreathed in smiles.

"Oh, Madame. So good to see you here. Come for another ball gown?"

Ignoring the whispered conversation as her mother leaned close and told the dressmaker exactly what they were looking for, Daphne wandered around the room, looking at the dresses hanging from special hooks. The styles seemed overblown to her and all required at least one other set of hands to put them on.

"You have good bone structure," the dressmaker said, appearing before her. "But you need more meat on your bones. Such a waif-look and people will think your parents starve you."

Lady Scarborough laughed, the sound more annoyed than anything. "She eats. She eats more than her sister. I can't quite understand why my little girl looks the way she does."

Daphne hid a smile as the two women exchanged an exasperated glance. Practice and performances had replaced what little cushioning she'd had with taut muscle, emphasizing her natural tendency toward being lean.

"Tsk, tsk. Well, we'll do what we can. If she carries herself with poise, maybe others won't notice how her cheeks seem sunken."

Turning away from the renewed discussion, Daphne saw the girl standing on a raised block, still waiting for her dress to be hemmed. A flicker of light made the girl look like Penelope.

Daphne stepped closer, her heart pounding as she waited for the greeting.

The girl offered a shy smile then looked away, but not before Daphne noticed her hair secured in a simple bun and the lack of rouge on her cheek. Of course. The dressmaker would never have abandoned a girl of Penelope's standing even to greet Lady Scarborough.

"How long do you think you'll have to wait?" she asked the girl with a smile.

The girl giggled, then forcibly restored a serious expression. "I don't mind the wait," she said, her tone firm.

Daphne shook her head. "I'd be impatient to move and my legs would grow tired."

Dimples marked both of the girl's rounded cheeks as her smile widened. "That's why I have this job. So ladies like you don't get impatient." A blush added color where before the girl's face had been pale as the girl realized her impertinence. "Your pardon," she whispered, making an awkward curtsy.

"You have it," Daphne whispered back, knowing full well she couldn't claim no offense. The girl wouldn't believe her and would spend the rest of the time waiting for the dressmaker to fire her. Little did this girl know she spoke to someone who also worked at a profession, if not for the same reason.

Daphne moved away, realizing she had no right to engage a shop girl in conversation. Her mother would be sure to offer a lecture in proper etiquette when they returned to the carriage.

"Come over here, Daphne. Bernadette needs to take your measurements." Lady Scarborough waved Daphne over, showing no sign she'd noticed the inappropriate conversation.

They moved into the back room where Daphne stripped to her underdress, again sparking tuts from the dressmaker at her muscled limbs. Daphne suffered the treatment without comment, shifting when she had to and holding still otherwise. She felt a moment of sympathy with the girl in the main room, having become little more than a dressmaker's dummy.

"That's all I need. It will take some time, but I think I can manage the first we discussed by midweek if the situation is as desperate as you said."

Pulled back out of her thoughts, Daphne asked, "What's so desperate?" before thinking.

"Your clothing situation, my dear. Every day over at Penelope's and a wardrobe falling to pieces. What could be more desperate?"

Daphne looked at the dressmaker, expecting humor at her mother's melodrama, but Bernadette's expression only mirrored her mother's concern. She shrugged. "You know best, Mother."

Lady Scarborough smiled at Daphne. "Of course I do, dear. Now let's go take a stroll down to the hatmaker. Bernadette says they have just the thing to go with your new dress."

The dressmaker cooed over the hats she'd seen, recommending ribbons over feathers while helping Daphne back into her dress. "Never feathers. They're only suited for an older, mature woman. A girl needs something to twirl in her fingers when a young man smiles in her direction."

Again, Lady Scarborough took the lead, approving of Bernadette's advice or shaking it off with a gentle laugh. Daphne trembled inside, imagining her life after coming out as a brightly colored nightmare filled with dressmakers, hatmakers, and who knew what else when all she truly wanted was to dance.

Chapter Ten

Daphne drew in a deep breath as they stepped through the door, relieved with the oppressive atmosphere behind her. She glanced around for their carriage and waved to Willem when she saw him waiting in an out-of-the-way spot.

Lady Scarborough placed a hand on Daphne's arm and pulled it down. "Have you forgotten already? We're going to the hatmaker next. Surely you don't need a carriage to take you such a short distance." She tucked her arm through Daphne's and tugged until they started walking. "I don't know how you stay so slender when you don't get the least bit of exercise. I imagine you sit and talk with your friends all day and all you do at home is sleep."

Daphne avoided an answer, laughing inwardly at the picture her mother presented. It could not be farther from the truth—a truth her mother must never know.

The bitter scent of thick glue announced their arrival even before Lady Scarborough pushed open the door. If the dressmaker's shop had felt like understated elegance, this one dazzled Daphne with its brilliant mix of colors and objects. Hats with feathers hung from dark walnut hat racks while bonnets decorated cloth-covered wire shapes.

She took a step toward the bonnets, their colorful yet simple forms appealing to her.

"Oh no, Daphne. You need something special for your new dress. You've outgrown bonnets for all but carriage rides." Her mother took Daphne's hand and pulled her toward the back, thankfully passing up the more garish, feathered structures near the entrance.

"Ribbons. We need ribbons," Lady Scarborough muttered under her breath as she scanned a row of hats. "Your dresses will be white of course, suiting someone of your age, but with emerald green highlights. Look for ribbons in that color, dear."

Daphne scanned the area they stood in, trying to distinguish one hat from another in explosion of fashion. She gasped, startled, when her gaze found another young woman in the shop. She'd thought they had the curious place to themselves.

"What's that?" her mother asked, turning toward the other woman. "Did you find something?"

Lady Scarborough also froze at the sight, but recovered almost instantly. "Meredith Smythson? Little Merry, is that really you?"

Daphne cringed at her mother's tone and recognized a similar reluctance as the other woman nodded.

"What brings you here?" Lady Scarborough asked, seemingly unaware of the tension. "Why, to get a hat, I suppose." She answered her own question with a laugh.

Meredith smiled slightly and turned to stare toward a small door, presumably where the proprietor had gone.

Lady Scarborough remained oblivious to the other woman's disinterest as she moved closer, one hand pulling Daphne along. A quick jerk put Daphne out in front just as they reached the other woman. Daphne looked up to share a commiserating look, only to be met by disdain.

"You must know my daughter. She's Penelope's friend, and from what I've heard, you've spent a good bit of time at that house yourself."

A fever flush heated Daphne's face as her worst fears came true. She stared at the other woman, hoping horror didn't show on her face. She'd thought to have much longer before her world came crashing down.

Meredith stared at Daphne, her expression unchanged. After a long moment in which Daphne felt examined and found wanting, the other woman laughed. "She's just a girl. Not even out yet. Why would I waste my attention on someone like that?"

Daphne gaped, aware of her mother's swiftly drawn in breath, but unable to react to such a complete dismissal.

"Enrique," Meredith called to the closed door. "I'll come back some other time when you are less busy."

Ignoring both of them, she pushed past and headed for the door.

"But Mistress Smythson?" the shopkeeper called, racing out of the door. "Your hat—"

He stopped as soon as he saw them, bowing low over the beribboned crown he held in his hand. "Lady Scarborough. How delighted I am to see you here," he said, the other woman forgotten.

Daphne glanced toward the door in time to see Meredith stiffen at the sound of her mother's title. When the other woman continued on her way, her step had little of the earlier arrogance.

With a smile, Daphne turned back to listen to her mother describe the dress. Little Merry had obviously not seen Lady Scarborough recently enough to recognize her, or to know whom she had married. Whatever their current circumstances, a countess was not one to annoy. The thought gave Daphne pause as she realized she ran the same risk, but her heart wouldn't let her give up her dreams. Whatever the consequences, when they eventually came, she'd face them knowing she'd had her moment on the stage. Far better than never having had one.

DAPHNE TOOK THE HATBOX FROM her mother, worried its stiff cardboard would fail to protect the bonnet inside.

"The nerve of that chit," Lady Scarborough said, continuing the low-voiced rant she'd begun as soon as they left the hat shop.

The shopkeeper, perhaps recognizing something had happened in his shop, went out of his way to help them, even offering a bonnet for Daphne to wear while he made a chapeau, as he called the hats, for her specially. Only his care had kept her mother silent that long.

Willem drew up beside them, leaping down to help first Lady Scarborough then Daphne into the carriage. He didn't offer her a wink this time, moving quickly and efficiently.

"If she thinks this is the last of it," Daphne's mother said, as if nothing had happened to disrupt her tirade, "she's got another think coming. No up and comer like that girl should dare dismiss my daughter, much less dismiss me."

"She didn't recognize either of us," Daphne said, attempting to soothe her mother.

"And more fault to her. In my day, we knew all of those we'd hope to impress by description if we hadn't been lucky enough to be introduced. And she should be ever more careful than the rest, being what she is."

Lady Scarborough stared at Daphne as if she should understand this cryptic pronouncement, but Daphne only shook her head, bewildered.

Her mother's lips compressed in disappointment, then she shook her head. "I don't know why I should be surprised. Thank goodness we finally cut your ties to that dance instructor. You need to be educated on the real world more than gaining worthless skills and reading books."

Daphne held back her anger at this dismissal of her dream, knowing better than to refocus her mother's upset. As if understanding whatever foolishness this Meredith had done would make her a better person.

Lady Scarborough leaned forward, whispering in a confiding tone. "Her mother married beneath her, Daphne. It was a scandalous affair. A lieutenant in the Navy, youngest son of a mere knight. We'd been friends as girls and I tried to keep relations, to give her someone to talk to when her lieutenant sailed off to sea. It became so difficult. Your father never said a word, but I knew people talked. When you were born, with both Grace and you to take care of, I just decided the effort was too much."

"You stopped seeing a friend because she didn't match your station?" The question slipped out before Daphne could censor it, seeing her mother in a different light.

Lady Scarborough laughed. "It was never that simple. I should have broken off the relationship much earlier, but you get half your stubbornness from me. Thank goodness Grace never gave me a moment of trouble."

Daphne stayed quiet, ignoring the tease as she waited for more of an answer. She'd always known her mother was acutely aware of social rules, but to go so far?

With a sigh, her mother settled back against the cushion and stared out the window for a long while until Daphne thought she'd never get an answer.

"It was a long time ago," Lady Scarborough started. "Helen always did like men in uniform. Her parents should have been more careful, but they never imagined she'd treat them so poorly. While they arranged a good match with a decent suitor, she slipped out with the lieutenant one night and raced up to Scotland. It caused an uproar, I can tell you. Her parents disowned her, leaving poor Helen to live on a lieutenant's salary. Sure enough he never did make captain after the disgrace."

Daphne shuddered, her motion masked as their carriage went over a hole in the road. Would her parents disown her? She could live on the salary Monsieur Henre held for her—she knew she could as her needs were small—but to never see her family again would be unbearable.

Lady Scarborough continued talking about how Helen's sister had taken pity on Meredith and practically adopted the girl, even supporting her coming out. Daphne barely listened, chilled to the bone by her mother's belief her friend had deserved the treatment. Where was the generosity of spirit she'd always believed Lady Scarborough sheltered? And how would her mother react to Daphne's deceit?

Numbly, Daphne stared out the window, unable to give up her dream, but only now really understanding what she risked in pursuing it. As much as she abhorred the artificial life her mother and sister seemed to thrive on, she'd feel its loss bitterly.

"Come on, dear. We're home," Lady Scarborough said, tapping Daphne's arm. "You look all done in. Why don't you slip up for a nap before the evening's entertainment? It'll do you a world of good."

Daphne summoned a smile for her mother and stumbled up to her room, suddenly feeling the exhaustion her mother had seen. She slipped out of her gown and crawled into bed in her shift, hugging her pillow to her chest.

Sleep provided no protection from her thoughts as the worries pursued her, throwing up images of her mother with frown lines cutting into her face. "We disowned her, of course," the phantom said, shaking its head with disapproval.

Chasing after the image, Daphne never managed to catch up as it flitted from group to group, each of which turned their back on Daphne, rejecting her presence. She'd never cared about other opinions before, but her dreams revealed she'd also never considered how she'd feel with her whole world turned against her. Even the image of Grace shook its head back and forth before slipping away.

DAPHNE JERKED AWAKE, HER HAND aching where it had hit the headboard. She stared around the dim room, unable to remember what day it was. Her gaze fell on the hatbox and memory returned along with frantic energy.

"Twilight," she muttered. "How late did I sleep?"

She didn't wait for an answer from the silent room, just pulled her dress over her head and struggled with the laces. The bundle holding her mask and plainer dress lay next to her bed ready for her to snatch. She'd packed it in the morning in case she was rushed, but never imagined this.

Daphne leaned out her window, releasing her breath in a sigh of relief as she saw the carriage already waiting for her. How long had he been down there? she wondered. Shaking her head, she picked up the bag and raced down the staircase with a complete lack of decorous pace. Her hair, loosened during her nap, fell forward to veil her eyes.

"You are not planning to go out like that, I hope?" her mother's shocked voice came from the hallway below.

Daphne brushed her hair back and stared at her mother in horror. Grace, standing next to Lady Scarborough, hid a smile behind her fingers.

Pushing the bag behind her, Daphne scrambled for an answer, another lie to add to her list of falsehoods. "Actually, I was looking for a maid to help me with my hair."

Grace winked at her, obviously seeing through the excuse though she probably assumed Daphne just forgot what she looked like in her rush.

The front door opened, and Willem stepped inside, his eyes widening when he caught sight of her. He shook his head slightly and turned to her mother. "Lady Scarborough, the carriage is ready."

"But—" Daphne silenced herself with an effort, trying to figure out what to do. How would she get to the theater without Willem?

"Hurry to your room and change into something without enough wrinkles to masquerade as bed sheets. I'll send one of the girls up to help with your hair."

Daphne stared at her mother, her befuddled mind unable to accept the directions.

Lady Scarborough glanced toward the longcase clock in the hallway. "We're going to be delayed as it is and you're making us later, Daphne. There is fashionably late and inconsiderate. I'm willing to drop you off as it's on our way, but not if you take much longer."

Meeting her mother's pointed look, Daphne gave up on any plans she could have hatched given enough time to think them through. She turned around and ran up the stairs, ignoring her mother's exclamation.

"How am I going to make this work?" she demanded of the air as she stripped off her dress and grabbed another from the wardrobe.

"Make what work, my lady?" the maid asked, coming up behind Daphne without warning.

Daphne jumped and dropped the dress into a crumpled pile on the floor.

The maid's lips pulled to one side as she stepped between Daphne and the wardrobe. "That's not a good style for this late in the year anyway," she said. "You go sit down, and I'll choose something that suits you."

Following the instructions, Daphne remembered why she'd discouraged the maids from helping her. Even though the girl couldn't be much older than Daphne herself, she treated Daphne like a child.

Fighting the urge to sulk, Daphne pulled out the ribbon holding the hair back from her face as she crossed to her dressing table. Steady strokes from the brush calmed her enough to realize she'd have to hire her own hackney on Penelope's street.

"Here you go, miss. You'll look right fine in this one."

Daphne stood and let the maid tug the dress over her, realizing too late that it had back laces. "I don't like this one," she said, her words panted against the sharp pulls.

"No time, miss," the maid said in a matter-of-fact voice. "Lady Scarborough didn't seem in the best of moods. I wouldn't delay longer than I had to. There. Now hand me that brush, and I'll fix your hair."

Reluctantly, Daphne handed over the brush, recognizing the truth of the other girl's statement.

A few quick strokes and her hair took an elegant form that would be completely out of place where she truly went and probably even at Penelope's house.

"Good enough," she said, standing up. "Tell Mother I'll be right down."

"But miss…" the maid protested, a colorful ribbon in her hand.

Daphne smiled what she hoped was a gentle smile and took the ribbon from the girl's lax hand, waving toward the door. She waited a moment longer before the maid took her hint and left.

She almost dropped the ribbon on the dressing table, but at the last minute, Daphne tucked it into her bag. She'd have to redo her hair into a simpler style if her plan would work. A quick glance in her dresser, and Daphne pulled out a plain shawl that her mother would be sure to question, but which might cover her dress enough to support her story. Another drawer offered up a small selection of coin to pay for her adventure.

Finally prepared, she rushed back to the staircase, slowing only when she would become visible to those waiting below.

Lady Scarborough bestowed a pained look on her youngest daughter. "Quite late, Daphne, but at least your sense of decorum has been restored along with your attire. Come along. There's no time to waste."

Daphne relaxed when her shawl drew no more than a head shake.

Willem gave her a regretful look as he ushered her into the carriage before her sister and mother. Daphne only had time to give him a faint smile before tucking into the far corner.

"I know you like your independence, but you cannot be so inconsiderate. Willem and the carriage are not at your beck and call. When your father has the family coach, this is for all of us. Next time, have one of the maids wake you so you have enough time to prepare."

"Yes, Mother," Daphne said, lowering her gaze to the bag twisted between her hands. "I'm sorry that I didn't think of your needs as well."

"Mother, you must know it was just a mistake. After you took her about all morning, I should have thought to wake Daphne myself," Grace offered, her soft voice soothing some of Daphne's tension.

Lady Scarborough tsked under her breath before heaving a sigh. "I know you don't mean to harm others, but you really seem to live in your own world. I'd thought after such a trying morning, you'd give up your evening entertainment and so deliberately let you sleep in. It's just with your sister's nuptials approaching, it's very important she doesn't seem to take on airs. We may be of good blood, but I don't have to tell you just how tenuous our position really is after that ship sank not two days out of port. We can't afford to offend Lady Pendleton, not now, and she's expected to attend, though her son is less likely to do so from what I understand. If we're unfashionably late, how will that appear to your future mother-in-law?"

"Why would she care?" Grace muttered, sounding nothing like her name in an uncharacteristic moment.

Lady Scarborough stared at her older daughter, drawing in a breath to give a flaming lecture, but something in her earlier words teased Daphne's mind.

In an effort to rescue Grace as her sister had done for her, Daphne said, "You could always tell Willem to drop me after you."

Her words provoked an angry glare from her mother that softened as Lady Scarborough considered the idea. Though she hadn't known what she was going to say before she said it, Daphne now held her breath in hope of a much better answer to her dilemma. If only her mother agreed, they could continue on in their normal pattern, though she'd be even later. She closed her eyes, trying to block out the thought of just how Monsieur Henre would react.

Lady Scarborough made an irritated sound and Daphne turned to look, praying her mother had decided to agree. Hope vanished with a shake of her mother's head.

"No, I can't let you keep the carriage and there's no sense in Willem going back and forth when we'll pass by on our way." Lady Scarborough settled back into her seat as if declaring the conversation over.

Daphne clenched her hands around her bag, struggling to come up with some other solution.

"It won't take that long to drop her off anyway, if we don't stay to see her to the door," Grace offered, straightening her skirt next to Daphne.

For a moment, Daphne thought her sister knew and her heart almost stopped from fear. Grace avoided her gaze, and a blush showed on her sister's cheeks when the carriage lamp swung near. That color more than anything let Daphne relax. Her sister only offered assistance because of the other trip. She couldn't know what Daphne did instead of visiting with Penelope. If she knew, even she would have tried to dissuade Daphne.

Daphne accepted the gift, adding her voice to her sister's. "She's right, Mother. I can easily run up the steps on my own. I don't need Willem's escort and you will save a little time at least. It's not like I can get lost on Penelope's doorstep."

Lady Scarborough waved a hand in front of her face as if to cool her agitation. "There's no point in it, Daphne. How much is the difference in a few minutes when we're sure to be unfashionably late? No need to strain yourself now that the harm is already done."

Daphne didn't need to pretend the guilt she felt as she glanced from her mother to her sister. What if this did harm her sister's chances? Grace deserved the best of everything. She'd always been the perfect daughter, unlike Daphne. "I truly am sorry," Daphne said, her voice filled with remorse. "If I'd known, I would have asked a maid to wake me."

Her mother reached out and patted her on the knee. "Now don't let it strain you, dear. What's done is done and there's nothing any of us can do about it."

Feeling the guilt tighten around her heart, Daphne laid one more mark against herself as she said, "It really would make me feel better if you didn't waste the time to wait on me. I know it's not much, but maybe, just maybe, it'll make a difference. There is a fine line between fashionable and unfashionable as you are wont to say."

Lady Scarborough shook her head, but the smile she wore gave Daphne renewed hope. "At least you listen some of the time. Well then, if it means that much, I suppose we can just this once. I wouldn't want guilt to make your evening painful." She laughed a short bark of humor. "After all we've paid for this, you better have the best time ever."

A broad smile curved her lips at hearing her mother's words. "Oh, it will be, Mother. I promise. The best time ever," she echoed, knowing her statement to be pure truth. If nothing else, this close call reminded her just what she sacrificed for her dream and how tenuous her hold on that dream might be. She'd enjoy every moment, because it very well might be her last.

Chapter Eleven

The carriage jerked to a halt and Willem rapped sharply on the roof, startling Daphne from an exhausted doze.

Grace nudged her with a foot. "Wake up now. We're here. You're sure to be the life of the party. Just try not to snore."

Daphne looked up to glare at her sister and met Lady Scarborough's concerned gaze instead.

"Are you sure you're up to a visit? It would be quite out of his way, but Willem could run you home after dropping us if you've misjudged your stamina."

Smothering a yawn behind her hand, Daphne said, "I'm fine. No need to put Willem out."

As if called by her mention, the carriage door swung open and Willem lowered the step for her.

"Enjoy yourself," Grace said, laughing as Daphne pushed past her to get out.

"Yourselves as well," Daphne muttered, focused more on slipping past her mother without revealing what she carried in the bag. Grace gave the large bundle an odd look, but said nothing, releasing Daphne to step out of the carriage.

Willem took her arm, moving away and pulling her after.

"I'll walk myself up," Daphne said, loud enough for her voice to carry back to her mother.

"What are you going to do?" Willem whispered, leaning his head close to hers.

Daphne smiled, trying for confidence even as her knees quaked. "I'll catch a hackney to take me down there. It'll work." She held back the thought that it would have to. Willem had enough worries without adding to them. "I'll get another hire coach back as well, so you needn't worry."

Willem resisted her effort to pull free, staring at her. "It's not the bother I'm worried about. You shouldn't be on your own."

"There's no choice," she whispered back. "And I have to learn to fend for myself sometime. It's not like we're on the West End. The driver will think me a maid servant."

He laughed. "No one will mistake you for a maid, Lady Daphne, not even in the dark and if blind."

"A shop girl then. I'll pretend to be from one of the dress shops, wearing a cast off gown."

The sound of knuckles rapped against the carriage cut through the air. "What's keeping you, Willem? You could have escorted her up the stairs by now."

Willem tensed at Lady Scarborough's comment, turning back toward the carriage as if divided between his responsibilities.

"Go," Daphne urged. "I've done enough to upset my mother this night. Don't let yourself become the whipping boy."

He hesitated only a heartbeat longer before releasing her arm. "Take care now, my lady. Keep yourself safe."

She didn't have time to respond as he strode toward the carriage and leapt onto the seat with surprising athleticism. Daphne wondered for a moment what he'd be like as a dancer, then dismissed the thought, focusing instead on what to do next.

Once the carriage moved around the corner, Daphne set off in the opposite direction, her steps awkward. She fumbled with the pins holding her hair, finally getting it down around her shoulders and falling into her face. The ribbon solved that problem, securing her strands so they fell down the middle of her back.

Daphne tugged the shawl tight around her shoulders, attempting to hide the dress as best she could while thinking hard about the young woman in the dress shop. How had she carried herself? It took a while to school her features into the stoic boredom she'd seen on the shop girl's face, but it didn't need to be perfect, just good enough to fool a driver in poor light.

Her disguise in place, she looked around for a hackney, only then realizing she'd noticed none while she organized herself. A thrill of fear raced up her back. What would she do if no cart came? Could she arrive unexpected and unannounced at Penelope's home, her hair down like a maid's and her dress covered in a tatty shawl? And what would Monsieur Henre say?

Daphne curled her shoulders inward, despair negating her training in posture. Nothing had gone right today. She stamped her foot, temper getting the better of her. She'd planned everything so carefully and her mother just had to spoil it all. First taking away her teacher and now taking away this chance.

She turned sharply, marching back toward Penelope's home with a determined step. If she couldn't find a hackney here, she'd make Penelope's butler get her one and darn anyone who tried to get in her way.

Her temper sustained Daphne until she'd almost reached the stairs, but then her pace slowed. Could she really go up there and ask a servant to run after a carriage when she wasn't even expected?

The sound of reins slapped against a horse's broad back could not have been more welcome, though Daphne shrank against the stone pillar marking the step, hiding in its shadow in case the noise signaled the arrival of another guest.

The carriage didn't stop and Daphne could see no coat of arms on the door as it passed her. She grabbed her skirt in one hand and ran after it, waving her bag to attract the driver's attention.

He kept going, apparently unaware of her frantic signaling.

"Wait," Daphne shouted, ignoring all convention. What had she left to lose if anyone saw her like this?

She thought all was lost, but then the hire coach slowed and stopped, waiting for her to catch up, breathless and panting.

"Where to, miss?" the driver called down, apparently taken in by her disguise or behavior enough that he didn't come to help her inside.

Pushing down her annoyance, Daphne tried to mimic the dressmaker's attempt at a learned accent. "Take me to Drury Lane. Monsieur Henre's theater."

The man pushed back his hat and stared down at her with a smile she found uncomfortable.

"An actress are you?" he asked, still staring.

Daphne shook her head, mute with embarrassment. She reached up and opened the door, pulling herself into the carriage without even lowering the step.

He clucked to his horse, then leaned sideways to peer through the window as they started moving forward. "What are you then?" he asked, his tone impertinent by any standards.

She shuddered, suddenly feeling as vulnerable as Willem seemed to think she would be. "I'm a shop girl," she stammered. Her fingers tightened around the bag as if it provided some protection. It might not keep her safe, but the crinkle of cloth within gave her an idea. "I have to find his lordship," she murmured. "Lord Pendleton. He ordered something from my master and he needs it tonight."

The driver laughed, a bark of sound that held a world of contempt for her kind. "They got you running their errands even this late at night? A decent girl like you should be safe at home, not out here where any stranger could catch you."

She mumbled something in response, unsure even what she'd meant to say, grateful only that her reason struck a chord with him. The driver showed no more interest in her activities, keeping to a smart pace and delivering her as promised.

Daphne dug in her bag for the coin to pay him, surprised when he opened her door and lowered the step.

"I've a sister about your age," the driver said in a gruff voice when she raised questioning eyes to his face.

He ran a finger along his cap as thanks for her payment and waved goodbye as though they'd become friends on the trip, a bond formed in serving those of noble blood, one she deserved only because of the entertainment her dance provided.

Daphne tried for a smile, but facing the dark, empty entrance, she could hear her heart beat out the words "you're late, you're late," over and over until sweat broke out on her palms. Still clutching her bag, she scrambled toward the back entrance, only remembering to put her mask on when her hand touched the doorknob. She risked too much to be revealed now.

THE WARNING BELL RANG THROUGH the hall as soon as she closed the door behind her. Clutching her bag, Daphne ran to the costume area on feet driven by panic. The sounds of laughter reached her, and she spared a grateful thought for flexibility as she fought to undo the back ties, almost tearing her dress in the need to change rapidly.

Before she'd completed the transfer to her costume, other dancers swarmed into the room, filling it with their voices. She shrank toward the corner and concentrated on doing up the laces holding her costume close to her body.

"What have we here?"

Daphne tensed at the voice of the one dancer who seemed to resent her: Cynthia, the woman she'd met first of any of them.

"That was your bell, dear," the dancer prodded. "Guess you think you're so good the audience will wait on you. Think you're better than us 'cause you've got the starring role."

Daphne straightened her skirt and turned to face Cynthia. "I don't think that," she said, her voice soft. "I know I'm late."

Cynthia dropped into a curtsy, a mocking smile on her lips. "And see how she admits to her faults?" Her voice dropped to a fierce whisper, "Just wait until you hear from Henre. It'll be the crowning moment of your short-lived career."

Pushing past the other woman, Daphne struggled against a tension filling her gut with worry. What would Monsieur Henre say to her? She'd only done it for his protection, his and hers. She shuddered to think what her father would do to Henre if he ever found out.

Then she squared her shoulders, pushing back the concerns. No matter what happened after, she owed her audience a wonderful dance.

Though her heart was focused, Daphne knew she'd failed by the second twist. Her mouth threatened to open into a wide yawn and her feet seemed to collapse at every opportunity. She begged the Lord above to give her strength, but her day had taken its toll.

As she bent over her legs, freezing into position with the last notes of the musical piece, instead of the silence she'd earned before, this time Daphne could hear rustles as people adjusted their clothing or their seat. The deafening silence before applause never came. Instead, some made half-hearted efforts to bring their hands together while others jeered.

Tears welled up in her eyes, soaking the edges of her mask. She'd tried her best, she really had.

"Get off the stage."

"An imposter? Does he think he can pawn us off on someone with so little skill?"

Daphne desperately waited for the curtain to drop, needing that slight barrier between her and the dissatisfied audience. She feared they would throw hard or rotten fruit next as the other dancers had warned her they sometimes did.

She glanced up at the cloth that should have been her salvation, and it had snagged. One of the workers struggled to release it, but Daphne could tell rescue would not come in time.

Gathering her courage with both hands, she pushed to her feet and swept an apologetic curtsy to the crowd before moving quickly off stage, almost running.

There, she ran full tilt into a grinning Cynthia.

"You've done it now, mystery lady. Henre's giving me the center stage to try and rescue your mess."

Daphne stumbled as Cynthia shoved past her. She saw the other dancer look back with a grin before going into a swift tumbling routine that threatened to upend her skirt over her head. Daphne clenched her fists at the display, but the audience didn't mind the performance at all. She could hear laughter where just moments before the same people had mocked and condemned her.

Tears welled up in her eyes, clouding her vision though she kept her gaze fixed on the other dancer. She knew she'd failed to give the audience what it deserved, but she'd tried her best. Shoulders slumped, Daphne turned away, wondering if she really had what it took to dance professionally.

Behind her, she heard the thump of Cynthia's feet against the floorboards, feeling the vibrations through her thin-soled slippers. The music from the pit masked every mechanical part of dancing, from the harsh breath to the thud produced by even the most delicate movement. The audience had no idea just how hard they had to work to produce such beauty and grace.

Daphne straightened, regaining a measure of confidence as she realized she'd had no choice in what happened and she'd just have to accept that she'd failed this night. Tomorrow, she'd come ready.

A rough hand closed on her upper arm as she stepped down from the stage wing. She squeaked, more from surprise than pain, jerking against the hold.

"What? You think you can enact that disaster on my stage and have no consequences?"

She turned to meet Monsieur Henre's sharp glare.

"In my office now," he ground out, giving her no choice as he pulled her behind him.

Daphne bit her lip to stifle a cry when she stumbled over an uneven board, her slippers providing little protection. Her heart pounded against her ribs as fear returned. Would he take all this away from her? Would the audience remember only this failure?

Determination grew within Daphne. No matter what he said, no matter what he did, she'd get the chance to prove tonight an accident of circumstances and nothing more.

Monsieur Henre pushed through his door, leaving it open as he tossed her into a chair before moving around his desk to stare at her, his chin resting on steepled fingers.

Daphne looked back, keeping her spine straight enough to impress her mother had she been there. Not even his strongest glare would make her flinch, not with so much at stake.

He frowned, dropping his hands to the desktop where he clenched them, random papers protesting the movement with their crinkling. "So. You come in late, from partying no doubt, and disgrace yourself on my stage. All this and you have the audacity to attempt to stare me down?"

She tried to protest his interpretation, but he slammed his hand flat on the desk, silencing her.

"I should have known better than to take on one like you. I thought I saw the heart of a dancer, but really you are only a spoiled noblewoman who thinks to amuse herself at my expense. You're no dancer. Go." He pointed at the open door. "Get out of my sight. I have no need to be your dalliance."

His shoulders slumped and he looked not at her, but down at his folded hands. Until that last moment, anger had fomented in Daphne's breast, but suddenly sympathy replaced it.

She rose and moved forward, wrapping her hands around his. "You were not wrong," she whispered. "I do have the heart of a dancer. This,"—she waved toward the stage—"was all to protect that heart and protect you. I wasn't off at parties; I was keeping my mother happy in the belief I spend all my time preparing for my coming out. She practically demanded I spend the day shopping with her. If I hadn't, she would've questioned why I spend so much time at Penelope's. Neither of us can afford for my parents to start an investigation into my time."

Her words ran out, and Daphne stood there, waiting on a response, hope and despair fighting for ownership of her heart.

Finally, Monsieur Henre looked up, shaking his head back and forth. "Why should I trust you?" he asked. "And even if I do, allowing you to continue in this only endangers everything I've worked for. Why should I let you stay?"

The last question came out as if he begged her for an answer. Daphne could think of none but that which drove her to this dance hall in the first place. "Because I have to dance," she murmured.

He laughed, a sound full of bitterness. "Ah, therein lies my problem. I do feel the dance pounding through your veins, feel it and see it on all other nights reaching out to capture the audience, leaving them rapt with attention to your every move. They feel your soul as they watch you. I've heard them talk. I'm too much of a dance instructor to let such skill, such heart, go to waste locked up on a country estate and rolled out only in the orchestrated dances allowed the nobility."

She sank back into her chair, relief filling her as his face twisted into a half-smile.

"You were always my best student and desperation has added something to your skill that I cannot quite describe. I'm a fool to take the risks you offer me, and I'd be a bigger fool to throw them away." He pushed up from his desk, once again her instructor as the bitter manager vanished beneath renewed faith. "Go," he said again. "Go get washed up. You've still got one more performance to manage tonight and you'd better dig deeper to find the strength." He paused, one hand upraised. "Unless you'd like me to give away the set. I won't make my performance hall into nothing more than a street fair if I can help it, but I may have no other choice. Only say the word and I'll tell Cynthia to perform once again. Let the audience laugh at her antics tonight. Tomorrow, you'd better provide me some *art*."

Daphne leapt to her feet, his faith giving her a rush of energy. "No, not tomorrow. I'll give them back the real dance, the art you so want them to see. I swear I can do this."

Monsieur Henre smiled then his expression hardened as he glanced behind her. "You do that. Go change your costume and ready yourself. There isn't much time before you're due on." He put his hand on her shoulder, drawing her gaze to his. "I know you can do this. Don't disappoint me."

Unsure how to respond to his intensity, Daphne dropped into a curtsy, a smile curving her lips. "I won't. I promise I won't," she said before turning away.

Her eyes met a fierce stare full of more hatred than she'd ever seen before. Cynthia stood in the doorway, listening to their conversation. Fear twisted Daphne's gut as she reviewed their words for any hint that their secret was out, but relaxed when she realized they'd named no names or even spoke of anything more than generalities. She could be the youngest daughter of some recent-made knight for all the other dancer knew, not an earl's daughter with much to lose.

Daphne brushed past her, trying to recapture the confidence she'd felt only moments before. She had to prove herself all over again, and this time she wouldn't fail her teacher or herself.

"He's got his eye on you now, girl."

The nasty words made Daphne stumble a bit. She hadn't realized Cynthia followed her to the now empty dressing room.

"One more error, and no amount of sweet talk will buy back his loyalty. I don't know what hold you have over the man, but he wouldn't have made it this far without being able to handle what problems come his way."

Daphne stared at the other woman for a long moment before reaching for her laces. "What's between Monsieur Henre and myself is none of your concern, Cynthia," she said, keeping her voice even with effort.

The other dancer smiled, an expression that failed to reach her eyes. "Just don't make another mistake is all I'm saying. A friendly reminder."

Turning away, Daphne closed her eyes and reached for strength to make it through this night. She didn't relax until she heard the door open then close, signaling Cynthia's exit. "If she's a friend, I'm as much of a clown as she made herself into," Daphne muttered to herself, unable to still the unease creeping up her spine.

For the first time since she'd snuck her way into this hall, Daphne couldn't wait for the night to be over. She wanted to curl up on her bed and cry out her exhaustion and tension, both from the near loss of her dream and from the other dancer's vicious behavior.

Instead, she straightened her shoulders, finished the costume change, and focused on her next dance. The bell echoed through the room, giving her enough warning to slip into the wings before the other dancers left the stage. There was no empty stage when her music started this time. She gave the audience what it wanted—her heart and soul.

Chapter Twelve

aphne collapsed into a sweating, clumsy lump, her legs shaking and her head aching.

Willem stopped mid-note and came up beside her. "Maybe you should stop for the morning, my lady. You're working yourself to death over this."

She raised her head to blink at him, her eyes squinting in pain as they found one of the lanterns. Daphne braced her head on one arm, too tired to rise. "You don't understand. Monsieur Henre still doesn't trust me. He checks every night that I've arrived on time and I can feel his stare as I perform. If I don't do something different, something spectacular, he'll decide I'm not worth the trouble. I'm sure of it."

Willem put his hands under her arms, a touch she should have resisted, but he'd helped her up often enough now that she barely noticed as he maneuvered her over to a chair to sit down. "Why would he give you up? I've heard tell you're something special on that stage. It's been all I could do to keep your secret and not blurt out that I know you."

That brought Daphne's head up as she stared at the man in horror. "You wouldn't." she said, her voice a harsh whisper.

He laughed, a casual, calm sound. "Of course not, Lady Daphne. I wouldn't betray you for anything. Certainly not to bring more attention on my shoulders. I've got enough vying for my time."

Willem looked at her intently for a long while, but Daphne couldn't tell what he sought from her. She shrugged, accepting his assurance. "I'm sorry. It's just that this seems so much more difficult now than it was. Two days ago, I had to deny my sister a moment of my company for fear I'd be gone too long. I hardly see her at all anymore and keeping secrets from her burns me."

"So tell her," Willem said, this time not looking at her. "It would do you good to share the secret with one of your own."

Daphne laughed, but her noise held little humor. "Grace isn't the girl she used to be, Willem. If I were lucky, she'd urge me to speak with Father, to confess. If not, she'd march me before the two of them and force a confession. Heaven forbid the slightest hint of scandal mar her chances with that baron."

For a heartbeat, she remembered the day at Penelope's house and how she felt a surge of interest as they described her sister's future husband. If she could find someone like that, would she give up dancing? Could she find happiness in tending hearth and home?

She shook off such unlikely and dangerous thoughts, vigorously rubbing her knee to loosen a knot.

"Let me." Willem put his warm hands over hers.

Daphne pulled back a bit, but then relaxed into his soothing touch. "It's not proper," she whispered.

He smiled up at her. "None of this is, my lady. And you can be sure I'd never do anything to hurt you. Never."

She looked down into his sincere gaze and recognized that which she'd never seen before. Stretching out a hand to touch his cheek, she frowned. "You love me." The words came from her as if driven by something other than her will. "You love me and that's why you risk so much."

This time she did pull away, scrambling up off the chair and backing to where she'd left her clothing. Suddenly, he'd become more than just an invisible servant and she felt naked under his regard.

As if hearing her thought, he turned away, his tense back facing her. "I never meant for you to know," he said in a low voice, "but it changes nothing. I am beneath your regard and always will be. It is enough to serve you."

Daphne jerked her overdress on, pulling it into place as quickly as she could manage. Finally dressed, she walked around to face him, her heart beating a little faster as she considered the implications.

When she came to a halt, he stared at the floor, waiting for her to speak.

Daphne twisted her hands together, not wanting to meet his gaze any more than he sought hers. "I can't let you do this," she muttered, staring at the frayed cloth of her slipper. "It's not right. There's no way."

He put a hand under her chin and raised it until she looked him in the eye. "Do you think I don't know this? Even if you felt the same, I know it wouldn't happen. You may deny your family for the dance, but you'd never love enough to deny them for me."

"Then why?" she burst out, tears collecting in her eyes from exhaustion and strain. "Why do you torture yourself?"

This time he offered up a genuine smile. "Because this way I get even a small piece of yourself for me. Don't worry, Lady Daphne. I'll find someone willing to share my life. I have no plans to spend it moping over you. But for now, let me have what I can take without an obligation. Let me help you in this."

Daphne pulled away from his touch, giving him a helpless shrug as she forced her tired mind to consider his words. A part of her felt disappointed that he could so easily dismiss her while the rest could only be relieved.

"If you're sure?" she said, her tone questioning his choice. She found it odd how she looked to a servant for direction, but she'd learned more about the other world since breaking free of her own, enough to know it was full of people not much different than herself and her family. "Without you, none of this would have been possible." Daphne swept the room with her arm, taking in the pipe he'd left abandoned by his chair, the mirrors where she studied her every movement and finally settling on the two of them. She sighed, her shoulders heaving with the motion. "I cannot refuse your help, not and still live out my dream no matter how much of a burden it is becoming. Only promise you'll tell me when it becomes too much."

She looked at him willingly for the first time since she'd heard his argument. Viewed through opened eyes, she could see why the girls must flock after him, but though he was a handsome man, he did not make her heart beat faster. Only the dance held that power, and for it, she'd make any sacrifice she had to. She just wished the sacrifice wasn't someone else's heart.

DAPHNE RETURNED TO HER ROOM only moments before the maid her mother had assigned to dress her knocked gently on the door. It took no dissembling for Daphne to look the part of someone who'd just woken up. She yawned as she called out, "Come in," grateful only that she'd already stripped off the dress she'd worn down to the ballroom.

The maid, a young woman hardly older than Daphne, clucked under her breath as she opened the windows. "The master's in a right mood this morning, Lady Daphne. You should take the time to look nice and make him happy. Even our Lady Scarborough is looking strained."

Daphne's heart rose into her throat. They'd found out. Somehow, even with all her caution, they'd discovered where she went each night.

Light crossed her bed, making Daphne blink, blinded. With the brilliance came a realization that she'd be summoned down to face her parents if ever they discovered her. Whatever had set Father on edge, it had little to do with her.

"Oh, my lady, you look so pale and there are dark shadows under your eyes. That won't do."

She let the maid putter around, dabbing at her face with powders and selecting a white dress trimmed in peacock blue.

"It will bring out your eyes, my lady. You'll see," the maid assured her.

Standing up when instructed, Daphne let the maid dress her like a life-sized doll. She felt the pinch of a real corset before she remembered to tell the maid to use her corded one.

"Now let out your breath and I'll get just a wee bit more."

Daphne pulled away. "That's enough. Just help me into my dress." Meeting the woman's gaze, she saw how the maid fought down her emotions. Did Willem feel the same way every time he saw her? Guilt made her let the maid finish dressing her hair without complaint, not that she wanted to rush down and meet her father's temper anyway.

By the time she headed for the main staircase, Daphne looked as fancily presented as her sister always seemed to be, but on Daphne, it felt awkward and fake. Still, she managed a half smile for the footman waiting at the bottom of the stairs.

Her smile froze into place when she saw Willem also in the corridor, heading out to ready the carriage from the sight of his livery.

He gave her a solemn nod before continuing on his way.

Daphne's hand clenched on the banister. She'd never planned to marry, but neither did she want to abandon the possibility of love. How could she ask Willem to do the same? After all he'd done for her, could she torment him like this?

"Daphne Louise? Just what do you think you're doing standing out there? You think we have nothing better to do than look you over?"

She jerked her hand off the railing and almost ran down the last steps, driven by her mother's unusually sharp tone. Stumbling to a halt before the entryway to the breakfast room, Daphne reached out to take her mother's hand. "Is anything wrong," she asked, her mind scrambling for what could have set both her parents on edge. Again, her fears rose, but she pushed them back.

"Just go sit," Lady Scarborough said, pulling her hand away.

Daphne took one slow step after another, grateful for the maid's efforts. At least her appearance wouldn't spark criticism, but somehow she knew it would not be a pleasant breakfast.

Her father stood at the mantel, staring into the fire with a frown cutting deep on his forehead. Grace had yet to come to the table.

He didn't turn as Daphne slipped into her place and accepted a piece of warm toast with her porridge. The longcase clock struck noon, much later than she'd expected, making Daphne's hand shake. She almost dropped her toast, but at the last moment she regained control, sparing herself a reprimand.

"Do you know what your sister's been up to?"

Daphne did drop the toast this time, startled by her father's harsh tone. She watched it fall to the table, scattering crumbs across the polished wood surface. A small chip rolled across to land right where Grace should have had her place.

Tense, she waited for the rebuke, but none came. Instead, her father marched up next to Daphne and thrust a paper into her face.

"Where has she gone?" he demanded, crumpling the paper in his hand. "This is no childhood prank. Your mother always said I was too lenient, but this is too much. Does she have no regard for the family's name? Does she want us disgraced?"

Daphne shook her head, bewildered. "Grace would never do such a thing, Father. I'm sure she'll come down soon enough. She's never done anything to besmirch the family name." She couldn't say the same, but her secrets had stayed that way. "What happened?"

Lord Scarborough paced to the head of the table and sank into his seat, holding his head between both hands. "What will we do now?" he asked his wife, ignoring Daphne. "How could she do this to us?"

Staring from one parent to the other, Daphne couldn't imagine Grace—proper, sweet, obliging Grace—doing anything to cause such distress.

Some of her feelings must have shown on her face because her mother stood up so quickly that the heavy wood chair scraped against the floor loud enough to make Daphne wince.

"You better not be hiding anything, Daphne Louise. No matter how innocent you might think this, we could be ruined. At the least, we'll be laughing stocks unable to show our faces in London again." Lady Scarborough marched toward her husband and grabbed the crumpled paper from his hand.

He didn't even look up.

Lady Scarborough rounded the table with such a determined look on her face that Daphne shrank back.

"This. This is what we're talking about."

Daphne tried to focus on the crinkled paper her mother waved before her, but could not see anything besides that it contained writing. Carefully, she took the letter from her mother's hand, shoved her bowl out of the way, and smoothed it out on the table.

"Read it," Lady Scarborough said, poking a rough finger against the paper. "Read what your sister has done to us."

Beloved Mother and Father,

It hurts me more that I can say to have disappointed you, but I cannot go on pretending any longer. I know you want me to marry the man you have chosen for me, but my heart has found another. If you ever had the opportunity to meet him, I feel sure you would love him as I do. I cannot face a life without him. Against his best wishes, we have decided to elope. I hope you can find it in your thoughts to forgive me. I love you both, and Daphne as well, but I must do this for my own heart.

Yours,
Grace

Daphne read the letter through twice before she could comprehend the words. "Who is it?" she asked in stunned disbelief.

Her father raised his head and slammed both fists against the table. "I don't know, but when I find out, I'll pound him into the mud." He took his linen napkin and twisted it in a violent gesture so unlike him that Daphne only stared.

"Anyone who would agree to such a plan is a scoundrel," Lady Scarborough said, rubbing her husband's back. "He deserves to be run through."

Lord Scarborough shrugged off her touch, staring at Daphne with a concentration that made his youngest daughter nervous. "I have only one daughter," he ground out. "One daughter who will complete the agreement with the Pendleton family."

Daphne wanted to break eye contact, to look away, to deny his words, but did none of them. Where had her sister gone? Would she ever see Grace again?

Her mother clapped, a gentle smile replacing the frown that had threatened to score Lady Scarborough's face. "I knew you'd think of a solution, my love. All is not lost."

"But what about Grace?" Daphne burst out, unable to accept the loss of her sister this way.

Lady Scarborough shook her head. "Daphne, my dear, it's not that simple. I'm sure she started as an innocent, but even if this rap-scallion swept her off her feet, any decent girl knows elopement is not respectable. She's no longer one of us. You must put her from your mind."

Daphne pushed back from the table, her appetite as congealed as the cold porridge on her plate. "I'll be in my room," she choked out, keeping to a walk by supreme effort as she left.

It wasn't until she reached half way up the stairs that she absorbed the rest of her father's pronouncement. Daphne sank to the step, her fist crammed in her mouth. "Oh no," she muttered, rocking back and forth in shock. "What will I do now?"

"My lady? Are you okay?"

Daphne raised stricken eyes to see Willem leaning over her. Was Grace's love one of the servants? she wondered as she looked at the only man ever to declare he loved her. Had Grace given up every-thing to follow her heart?

She shook her head mutely, caught up in the loss of dreams she hadn't really known she'd held. She'd always thought she'd marry sometime in the distant future and only to a man who filled her heart. Now, she'd be promised to someone she'd never met and who hadn't wanted her at all.

A tear slid down her cheek, but she brushed it away, not wanting to concern Willem any more. She pushed to her feet and turned to face the stair again. "I'm fine," she told him, struggling to keep her voice firm.

Willem put a hand under her arm, supporting her, and leaned in close. "They didn't find out, did they?" he whispered.

Daphne shook her head again, unwilling to explain what had tran-spired. Surely her father would pass out a story anyway, one that would preserve their name and her mother's standing. Suddenly, exhaustion overwhelmed her. She couldn't face another heartbeat holding together under the hawk-like eyes of the staff.

She shook off his hold and repeated to her new audience, "I'm going to my room."

Willem accepted the implied rebuke and stood tall, one step below her. "And will you be needing the carriage tonight?" he asked, his tone as formal as hers had been strong.

The thought of dancing, of performing under the stares of the audience all the while knowing her sister was out there somewhere, lost and abandoned by her family, seemed too much to bear. She closed her eyes, feeling this a crowning moment in her wish to become a professional dancer. With a sigh, she nodded again. "Yes. I'll need the carriage."

He gave her a long stare, as if wanting to ask for confirmation one more time, then turned and made his way back down the stairs without a word.

Relieved, Daphne finished the climb to her room and sat on her bed, staring at the other mattress that Grace had once used back when they shared what had been the schoolroom. "Why did you do this?" she murmured to her missing sister. "Couldn't you have asked them? Surely he isn't so low they would refuse to meet him?"

Memory of her sister's strange behavior that day they went shopping rose up. Had they been trysting on that day, right under Daphne's nose? If she'd only spared a moment for Grace, perhaps she'd know better, but she'd been too caught up in her own secrets.

The thought gave her pause as she considered who else had been there that day. Did Willem know anything about this?

She half rose, thinking to march back downstairs and quiz him, when a quiet knock sounded at her door. "Come," she said, sinking down on the realization all she'd gain would be Willem's dismissal. If her father had any suspicion, he'd toss the coachman out onto the street.

A maid entered with a tray, setting it up before Daphne. "Cook says you needed to eat, my lady," was all she said before slipping back out as quietly as she'd come.

"Wake me at six," Daphne called after her, wanting nothing more to go wrong on this horrible day.

Though she didn't feel like eating, Daphne knew she'd need her strength to dance, especially after what she'd learned. Each bite tasted like sawdust as she forced it down, "her last dance," echoing in Daphne's mind. She'd known her time would end, but never so quickly.

Determined, Daphne vowed to keep on with it as long as she could manage, storing up memories to hold her in the years to come. A yawn surprised her, making Daphne aware of just how much energy she'd used with the morning's revelations. Tears seeped from her eyes as she thought of her lost sister and she curled up in her blanket, hugging her pillow to her for comfort.

Though not intended, she soon drifted off to sleep, a sleep filled with memories not of dancing, but of the moment when she first heard a description of the man who would claim her. She'd thought then that they might suit, and at least in her dreams, they did.

A smile curved her lips when she curled into her husband's lap to read, sharing her thoughts as she once had with Grace. The dream turned darker at the thought of her sister, images gleaned from the dancer's diary mixing with her sister's elopement to show Grace shivering in icy rain with no home to call her own.

Chapter Thirteen

aphne woke to the sound of a knock at her door. She dragged herself out of bed, unsure whether the nap had helped or worsened her exhaustion. Her heart pounded faster than it should have. The restless sleep left a bad taste in her mouth.

She pointed to the dress she wanted to wear and freshened up at her water bowl.

"But my lady, this is so plain," the maid said, reminding Daphne why she usually dressed herself.

"I'm not feeling much like dressing up," Daphne muttered, toweling the cold water from her face and neck.

Pulling out the dress Daphne wanted, the maid tutted under her breath. "I don't suppose you do have much to celebrate what with Lady Grace done run off," she said.

Daphne froze, the toes of her front foot just touching the ground where she'd been walking back to the maid. "What do you know of it?" she asked as she continued forward.

The maid smiled shyly, glancing over her shoulder before returning to the task of pulling wrinkles from the dress Daphne selected. "The master is putting about that she's sick with something, but we know that's not true, don't we, my lady? Word is she's gone with a minister."

Daphne knew she should discourage this behavior. The maid had no business gossiping about her betters, but finding the energy seemed beyond Daphne. "You really shouldn't be talking about this," she said, her tone weak.

The maid rushed over and put a hand on Daphne's arm. "Oh, my lady, you know I won't be saying anything outside the family. We have to protect the family reputation no matter what might be going on."

Smiling faintly, Daphne accepted the reassurance even as she thought on how Willem struggled to keep her secrets from the rest of the staff. No matter what her father said, the real story would get out soon enough, a caution she'd do well to remember.

Her chest tightened as she recalled what else had come about because of her sister's elopement. She knew well enough that the Pendletons would have to be appeased and a new agreement made long before the ton started passing whispers of what truly happened to Grace.

"My lady, I can't very well put you into this dress with your arms so stiff."

Daphne forced herself to relax under the maid's soft chiding, her vow to make the most of what time she had left coming back to her. She had to make this sacrifice if her family was to keep its standing in society. If she balked, their financial ruin would be exposed on the heels of this scandal.

For a moment, she considered the possibility of retiring permanently to one of their smaller country estates. Even though it would still mean giving up dance, she'd be free of a husband, for who would want her, penniless and disgraced? But she realized it meant a lifetime with her mother moaning about what they'd lost. Could a husband, even one she did not love, be so much worse?

She considered what manner of men the dancer in her book met. It could be worse, much worse.

"Not so tight," Daphne said, pulled out of her thoughts by the maid jerking on her laces. She swallowed the last of her complaint, that she had to get out of the dress on her own, choosing to pull away instead. "That's enough. Can you go tell Willem I'll be down shortly?"

The maid gave her an odd look then shrugged, pausing only long enough to grab the breakfast tray before heading out of the room without a word.

As soon as the door shut behind the maid, Daphne pulled out her bag and checked that her mask hadn't fallen out. She tucked in another worn dress "borrowed" from the servant pile. Her mother would never accept that she wore such a ragged bit of clothing, but it made her blend into the crowd around the sides and back of the theater so she didn't stand out as she slipped to the stage door.

Checking her appearance in the mirror, she frowned at the fancy hairdo the maid had created. One more thing to redo in the carriage, but she'd manage whatever she had to. Tonight, she'd dance for everything she'd lost today.

Daphne grabbed the bag and headed downstairs, her look and posture having little in common with her breakfast elegance. However, the scene remained the same as she came down the last flight to find her mother in the drawing room doorway.

"Nothing changes for you, does it?" Lady Scarborough asked. "Whatever happens, you still go out to visit your friends."

Her mother's bitter tone surprised Daphne after the callous dismissal of Grace earlier. Daphne leaned over the banister to really look at her mother, noticing a redness in Lady Scarborough's eyes that she'd never seen before. In the time when Daphne had slept off some of her grief, her mother had apparently been crying, a luxury she'd never indulged in that Daphne knew of.

Hesitating, Daphne considered just not going. If she was late or didn't show, Monsieur Henre would declare her gone forever. Tension bit into the back of her neck, and she realized even if she'd have only one more night, she could not give up so quickly. But how could she explain the urgency to her mother? Lies bound Daphne in place, unable to comfort her mother or excuse her apparent quick recovery.

"Let her go."

They both turned to face Lord Scarborough as he came from his study. He sounded so tired, his earlier anger drained to nothing.

"Grace has gone to the country…ill." He gave each of them a long tight look before continuing. "There's no need for our little flower to cloister herself. Grace wouldn't have wanted that, and we must show a presence now more than ever. It's a good thing you started work on getting Daphne an audience earlier than the next spring. When Grace dies—"

Daphne stumbled down the last few steps to grab her father's sleeve. "Grace is dying?" she asked, begging him with her eyes to deny his words as images from her nightmares rose to cover her sight.

His expression hardened into the texture of granite as his anger returned. "She is dead to us already; her illness is fatal, or will be once you're safely married." He bit down on each word with barely controlled violence. Lord Scarborough took her wrists in a tight clasp and pulled her hands away from him. "You're not to tell anyone, do you understand? Not your best confidant or the members of the ton whose attention you court. No one is to know of your sister's *illness* until I've managed to make things right."

Daphne turned to her mother, hoping for what she couldn't tell, but Lady Scarborough stepped back into the drawing room, closing the doors behind her with a quiet click.

Her father took hold of her shoulders and shook Daphne hard enough to break through the numbness that surrounded her. "Do you understand?" he barked into her face. "Appearances mean everything."

She smothered a humorless smile. No one would know or care the source of her grief. With her face hidden behind a mask, she could pour her emotions out to the ton and their servants alike with none the wiser and no fault touching her family name. As long as no one found her out.

"I understand," she murmured, waiting only for his hands to release her before she spun away and moved toward the waiting carriage with an unladylike burst of speed.

THE CLIP-CLOP OF HORSE HOOVES and the gentle sway of the carriage slowly melted the ice that had built up around her heart. She hadn't understood until the moment her father had rewritten history just what it meant to be the only daughter. Suddenly, why her dutiful sister would break free in this way made a horrible amount of sense.

You never have to work for anything.

Father will let you get away with mischief because he knows you'll have little else as a second daughter.

If I marry well, at least I'll make sure you have a worthwhile dowry.

Her sister's words echoed from the past, biting deep into Daphne's heart. She had pursued her own dreams, chancing everything, selfishly unaware of the burden Grace bore. And now? she asked herself mockingly. Would she give it all up to protect the family? She hadn't so far.

A low moan issued from her mouth at the thought, her heart twisting in agony. Could she become what Grace had been? Or had Grace done anything more than pretend, just as Daphne pretended when she hid behind a mask?

Daphne raised her hand to tap on the wall behind Willem, unsure whether to tell him to turn around and let her dancing fall into the past. She'd lost the position of indulged second daughter. If she were caught now, the impact would be much greater and her family could lose everything.

"Are you all right?" Willem called down.

She let her hand fall back to her side, searching for what to tell him. Was she all right?

"Is he really a minister?" The question popped out without a conscious decision on her part, even though she'd determined earlier that questioning Willem would be unwise.

"I know only what you do, or even less," he said, clucking the horses to speed them up a bit.

Daphne slapped her hand against the wall where he leaned. "Stop this carriage. Stop this carriage now." Her demand sounded overly loud in the small space, but she felt the horses slow. When they stopped, the only sound came from the wind and occasional creaks of the carriage or harness as the horses shifted.

Willem jumped down from his seat and walked around to the door, leaning in the window so he could face her. "Didn't you speak of the risks if you should arrive late again? We haven't much time to spare."

Daphne shook her head, for once dismissing all concern about her dance. "I need to know she's all right," she said, her voice low and tense. "Don't lie to me. I know you helped her; I know because you took me shopping on that day and dropped her off without a word. You'd done it before, possibly many times, and surely many after."

She scooted up to the door and brushed trembling fingers against his cheek. "I can keep your secrets as you keep mine. I just have to know."

His obstinate look slowly faded under the pressure of her stare, and Willem sighed. "I can't tell you much. I never met the man myself, but Lady Grace spoke of him a time or two."

Daphne leaned forward eagerly. "What did she say then?" she prompted, unwilling to waste a moment. "Is he really a man of God?"

Willem nodded, a half smile pulling his lips up on one side as he gave in. "She met him doing her works with the children. At first, she'd just talk about the children, but then it became more Simon this and Simon that. It seemed so natural, my lady, I'm not even sure they realized when it began to change. She does love him, of that I'm sure. And he must love her back."

"It'll be little enough to sustain her," snapped Daphne, remembering again the struggle depicted in her book.

Willem pulled back from the window, a frown on his face. "Oh, it's that you be wanting," he said, his uncultured accent thicker than usual. "And here I thought you'd be different than the rest."

A blush stained her cheek at the disdain in his tone but she didn't withdraw the question. "It's not so much to ask. I need to know if my sister will be left to scrounge on the street or well cared for."

"Set your mind to rest, my lady. He's not what her father be offering, but he has the right color blood for the likes of her despite his works among the poor. He's noble he is, a fourth son she said. The one destined for priesthood. Wouldn't want her eloping with the likes of me, now would we?"

Daphne stretched out a hand in apology, but he pulled back before she could touch his arm.

He swept a deep bow and leapt back onto his seat, calling down through the wall, "We'd best get you on your way. Wouldn't want you late for your visit among the lower classes."

Daphne frowned, angered by his attitude. Still, she couldn't help the relief she felt in knowing her sister would not be sitting on a street corner, a beggar's cup in her hand. Was it wrong to want a little pleasure and security for her delicate sister, she who had never done anything but the best she could?

Willem might be unhappy with the truth, but he did not have enough to support a woman of her class and never would. Daphne could not imagine her sister managing on what a servant earned, and she'd never made any effort to give Willem that impression.

Daphne remembered her idle dreams of supporting herself with dance. How young she seemed back then, though very few weeks had passed since that time. She'd never be happy as a governess, but she'd waste away on the pittance offered a dancer.

Chapter Fourteen

Jasper pushed past Aubrey's butler, calling out for his friend in a tense voice. He needed to share the news with someone, someone he could trust.

"Dammit Aubrey, where are you?"

Aubrey stepped out of the library, a book dangling from his hand. "What is it now? No need to rouse the whole household." His laughter silenced abruptly as he saw Jasper's face. "Come into the library. You look in need of a strong drink."

Following his friend, Jasper sucked in a breath full of old wood and leather, something that never failed to calm him before.

It had little effect in this moment.

Jasper dropped into one of the high-backed leather chairs and stared glumly at his friend. "Is there something so unlikable about me then?" he asked, voicing the question that had stung him since his mother passed on the news.

Aubrey tried for a laugh but once again sobered. "Why would you even ask such a ridiculous question? You're the toast of the town, have your very own following, and behind every biting word hangs envy. Women swoon to see you, no matter how many years they've put behind them."

"Not all women," Jasper muttered, bracing his head between his palms.

"So that's what this noise is all about? One of your light-of-loves has taken off with the jewels you've showered on her." Aubrey rose and put a hand on Jasper's shoulder. "There'll be another soon enough. It's not like you weren't tiring of the latest anyway. You told me so yourself."

Jasper shrugged off the touch and also rose, pacing back and forth along the shelves. "If only it was something that simple," he bit out. "I'd be relieved to have my lover take herself off to the country permanently and save me the whining."

"There. You see. If a lover whines when put aside, it's surely not from a lack in yourself."

Jasper turned back to look at his friend. "And is that all I'm worth? The pleasures of the moment and all too fleeting regard bought with expensive baubles?"

Aubrey sank into the chair Jasper had vacated and stared at him. "You sound as if you regret that fact. You think there aren't girls across London who would die for the chance to be your bride? It's you who has earned the reputation for skill at dodging their grasp, not any effort on their part to turn you aside."

Placing his hands on the back of another chair, Jasper leaned heavily against it. "Tell that to the one who caught me," he said, unable to keep the bitterness from his tone. For all his parents soured him on the thought of marriage, he'd discovered a small part of him had hoped to prove them the exception.

"Blast it, Jasper. I'm not some kind of mind reader, you know. Out with it. I'm done guessing at what has you in a tangle."

Jasper stepped around the chair then sank into it, wishing he'd never raised the subject. What man wanted to admit, even to his closest friend, that he'd been duped?

"Whatever it is, it can't be half as bad as you're making out," Aubrey said in a coaxing tone.

That pulled a laugh out of Jasper, the sharp bark of sound surprising even him. "Oh," he said, "and what could be worse than having the only one ever offered the privilege of becoming my bride declining the gift?"

Aubrey stared at him for a long while, clearly dumbfounded. "She what?" he sputtered. "The bride your mother chose for you said no?"

Finally seeing some humor in his friend's face if not in the situation, Jasper managed a true smile. "She not only declined, she gave up everything to escape being bound to me for all time."

"Speak plainly, man. You make no sense with all your riddles."

Jasper inclined his head and responded, "She took herself off to elope with another man. That's the care she had for me and my charms." He wondered if she had been the one to read the book after all. Maybe she had more depth to her than he'd supposed and found his own character too shallow.

"Now wait," Aubrey said, "Are you truly saying your mother's handpicked bride has absconded?"

Jasper nodded.

"Why that's wonderful." Aubrey leapt to his feet, clapping his hands together. "Don't you see? Your mother chose so poorly that if word gets out you'll be a figure of pity. She has to let it go now. You're free—"

"Free to be mocked behind my back and pitied before my face? What kind of freedom is that? Do you really think all those adoring women, and don't forget their mothers, will not be staring at me to see what flaw they could have overlooked. I'll not be considered a leading bachelor, but rather a monster or idiot who just managed to deceive them all this time." His head dropped back into his hands as he stared fitfully at the carpet.

"Hmm," Aubrey said. "I can see your point. How far has word spread?"

Jasper frowned. "The earl's keeping it quiet for now so only my family and now you know the truth. He plans to spread a story about her falling ill and going into isolation. My mother was too sharp to fall for such a tale, and she's likely not to be the only one. He's offered up his youngest in her place so the agreement can still stand."

"There you go." Aubrey laughed. "You're free. If no one knows the true story, they'll think you a saint to take on the younger daughter."

"Sure," Jasper grumbled. "And how long before the truth gets out? Someone saw them together; you know they did. It's just a matter of time."

Aubrey crossed to Jasper's side and patted him gently on the shoulder. "Seems to me as though you were almost looking forward to this matrimony. If not, this wouldn't hit you so hard. It'll blow over."

Jasper almost looked up in protest, but found he couldn't gather the energy. The picture he painted would mean an end to everything he'd been without much to replace it. "Don't you see? My mother's acceptance of the younger daughter won't help at all. She's barely out of the nursery and hasn't been presented to the Prince Regent. I can add cradle robbing to my grand list of accomplishments, a desperate attempt by a desperate man who none in their right minds would choose." A groan passed his lips, and he laced his fingers over his bent head.

"See here, Pendleton, you can't let it get to you. She didn't know you from Adam. If anything, this escapade makes her look the fool, not you. Buck up. There'll be others still vying for the position as your bride if you reject the schoolgirl."

Jasper laughed, finally managing to pull his head up. "You forget my mother's already decided how to seal my future. I have no choice in the matter. I'll spend my life tied to the younger sister of a woman who refused me. Even if the mocking would have died down in time, how can it with the constant reminder of my future wife crawling at my side, her curls tucked into a country bonnet."

Aubrey's expression surprised another laugh out of Jasper.

"Is she really that young?" his friend asked, horrified.

Jasper waved the thought away with a sharp gesture. "Had she finished her schooling, she'd have been presented this year. Age has little to do with it. What will such a girl know about anything?"

Recovering from his shock, Aubrey crossed to the bar and poured two fingers of fine scotch into each of their glasses. "Some things require a stiff drink," he said, pressing one glass into Jasper's hand and keeping hold of the other. He took a long sip then lowered his drink with a thoughtful look on his face. "That may be the best thing of all," he said. "Just imagine what you could teach her. You could grow your very own perfect wife."

Tossing the full measure into his mouth, Jasper grimaced, not at the fine liquor but at Aubrey's suggestion. "I'm not some nursemaid to teach a child the ways of the world," he ground out. "I'd prefer someone with a bit of conversation and who knows her way around the bedroom rather than a parrot who copies everything I say. It'll be hard enough to lie with her, knowing she won't have a blessed idea what to do."

"Jasper, Jasper, Jasper," Aubrey said, shaking his head. "You're determined to see the harm in this without ever recognizing the good. No goodly wife has experience in the bed, and that means no annoying habits to tolerate." He took the glass from Jasper and placed it next to his own on the bar. "To put your suckling bride from your mind, you need a fine distraction. I've heard incredible things about a dancer down at Monsieur Henre's. Nothing like the others I made you see. Solid has never been spoken with her in the same sentence. More like brilliant and stunning. I've been meaning to check her out myself. Come with me. If she's half the artist everyone seems to think she is, it'll be sure to take your mind off this mess."

Shaking his head, Jasper headed to the bar to reclaim his glass. "I don't think some fancy performance is what I need. More like a few more slugs of that scotch then I'll head a little further west to find myself something pleasurable."

"I thought you wished to cool things with your latest. Melissa, was it not?"

Jasper twisted his lips into a sardonic smile. "With the current state of things, perhaps I should be grateful to her, but no, I've delivered her parting gift and hope only our paths won't cross until she finds a new lover. I was thinking along the lines of more strong drink and a round or two of cards."

Aubrey put a restraining hand on his arm. "I promise you, from what I've heard, this dancer is stimulating enough for all your senses. And I can't let you go down there alone. Not in your current state. You'd end up in a brawl or worse. You won't regret this, I swear. And if you do, I'll take you wherever you want to go afterward. Only say the word."

Shrugging off his friend's grasp, Jasper sighed. "If it will get you off my back, I'll give your dancer a look. But if she isn't all you've said, I'm gone and you'll be coming with me."

"It's a wonder you have any skills at all," Cynthia said as Daphne slipped into the costume area. "You can't even dress yourself and your hair is a mess."

Daphne didn't respond, just turned her face away as the other dancer passed, forcing herself not to tug on her skirt in an attempt to straighten it. With so much time lost getting Willem to talk, she'd barely managed to change before he handed her into a hire coach, his face blank of any emotion, a perfect servant.

She cursed under her breath as the brush tangled in the strap holding her mask on, wasting precious time.

The ribbon tightened against her face sharply as a hand pulled from behind.

Cynthia leaned over her shoulder and whispered, "I'll bet you wear this mask so the boys down at the pub don't recognize you. You couldn't handle the comments they might make about how you flaunt yourself. Or is it the master's rules you find too constricting." The dancer stepped away, framing Daphne with her hands like a grand painter. "Maybe that's why you wear the mask, hmm? Don't want the master to find out how you spend your time away from here. Always rushing in late with your hair and dress awry." She leaned close again, sniffing loudly. "Not a hint of sex about you, but a good wet rag can take care of that."

"You should know," Daphne muttered, unable to keep herself from responding, especially since, on the few times she'd managed to come early, she'd often found Cynthia in the alley wrapped around a man, rarely the same one.

"What did you say?" Cynthia's enraged tone echoed in the small room, calling attention to their altercation. The other dancers turned to stare as Daphne tried to focus on the brush, now hopelessly entangled with her hair.

"Don't you turn away. Don't think you can say such things when we all know you found your place by padding the master's bed. No other reason he'd choose someone off the street to take the lead."

Daphne leapt up, her chair falling back to strike the floor with a loud clatter. "I have not," she cried. "I would never."

The other dancers moved closer, as if drawn in against their will.

"Then why the mask?" Cynthia asked, her tone scornful. "Why do you hide your face not just from the audience, but from all of us? You think we're blind? All those special meetings, the allowances he makes for you. Even your quarrels sound more like equals than a dancer desperate to keep her position. If not your body, what did you sell to him…or do you hold something over the poor man."

Daphne's knees shook but she refused to back down as she scrambled for something she could say. The truth would cost her everything and they probably wouldn't even believe it.

"What is going on here?" Monsieur Henre's voice had never been more welcome as he burst into the room.

The dancers who had yet to finish changing into their costumes squealed and dove for more cover, but he didn't pay them any attention as he stalked across the room.

"You may not have heard over your yells, but the chime sounded," he said, his voice low and threatening. "You are due on the stage."

Daphne flinched under his pointed glare and ripped the brush out, taking with it a good bit of hair. She stepped behind one of the dividers and changed faster than she ever had before. She needed this dance more than anything, and no petty jealousy was going to take it from her.

"Cynthia. I'll see you in my office. Now."

The dancer let out a squeak then Daphne heard Monsieur Henre's heavy footsteps marching the other woman toward the door. It closed firmly, but without a slam.

A smile started to pull at her face, but Daphne shook away the emotion. She didn't have time for it. She needed to get ready and get out on the stage.

When the carriage pulled up outside a quiet building, Jasper turned to look at Aubrey, a question in his eyes.

"Don't worry," Aubrey said. "We've missed the opening, but we'll still be able to get in."

Without waiting for a reply, Aubrey pushed open the door on his own and swung down, moving forward to talk to his coachman.

Sighing, Jasper followed him. If Melissa hadn't become too clingy to continue with, he'd have gone to her for soothing instead of trailing after Aubrey. The last thing he needed was something educational.

"Come round for us in two hours," Aubrey told the coachman.

Jasper took quick steps to his side and grabbed Aubrey's arm. "Two hours? Are you mad? I doubt I'll last two minutes in there."

Aubrey laughed and shook off his hold. "Such faith in me. It's a wonder you ever let me choose where we'll go on any night. But don't worry. This place caters to all walks of life, and hackneys are plenty. If you really need to escape, we'll find a way. My driver knows well enough to wait for a short while then head back home if I don't appear."

Still grumbling, Jasper let his friend direct him to the heavy wood doors, closed against the night. He could feel an ache starting at his temples, and another stiff drink, or maybe several, would enact a better cure than a cultural event.

"I'm sorry, sir. You can't go in."

Jasper heard the tail end of the argument as he stepped inside.

Aubrey pulled out some money and waved it at the man. "How much for a box?" he demanded, his annoyance obvious.

"No one is allowed in once the performance starts. It's policy." The man matched arrogance with arrogance despite their difference in station. "Besides, there is not an open box in the house. If you'd come earlier, then maybe you could have found space on the floor, but I'm afraid it just isn't possible. You'll have to come back on another night."

"I don't want to come back another night." Aubrey visibly reined in his temper and grabbed Jasper's arm, pulling him up to the small desk. "My friend here has had a bit of a shock, and I want to cheer him up. Can't you do something for us?"

Jasper could see the trace of a smirk, quickly suppressed as the man adopted a sympathetic look instead. "I'm sorry, gentlemen. If I had a choice…" He shrugged. "But it is not my decision. You'll have to leave now. I need to see to our paying customers. Maybe you can find some cheer a little further to the west."

Aubrey gaped, staring after the man who had abandoned his desk and slipped through a door that closed soundly behind him.

"Give it up, Aubrey. He obviously didn't fall for your charm. This just proves we weren't meant to play voyeurs this night. Let's go somewhere where we can participate, preferably with a nice drink in hand." Jasper tugged on Aubrey's sleeve, pulling him toward the exit.

His friend resisted for a moment, still staring at the door that had swallowed his quarry. "We could sneak in," he muttered.

Jasper laughed aloud. "This isn't a brothel when we were still in short pants, my friend. If you want scandal, let the new gossip be all about how you were dragged kicking and screaming out of a cultural event. It'll make my own woeful tale pale in comparison."

With one last glance at the inner door, Aubrey shrugged. "I suppose you're right. I'd hoped…well, it doesn't really matter what I'd hoped now. I guess the waterfront it is. Do you think we can find a pub serving something more than the scrapings left when good ale has been sent to the better establishments?"

Clapping his friend on the shoulder and steering him toward the door, Jasper grinned. "We'll find you one if it means testing every establishment from here to the other end of the Thames."

"Aubrey? Aubrey St. Vincent?"

They both turned toward the sound as doors opened all along the inner wall, spilling out members of the ton in one area and those from the floor in another.

"It's one of Mother's friends," Aubrey whispered. "Maybe she'll share her box."

The gentleman they'd spoken to earlier appeared out of the small door again, this time leading servers with snacks and drinks. He passed them at the same time as the older couple who had called to Aubrey. The man gave them a disapproving stare, frowning when Aubrey took two champagne flutes and handed one to Jasper with a flourish.

The woman pinched Aubrey's cheek hard enough to leave a lingering red spot. "Now Aubrey, your mother will be so delighted to know you came to this. It's rare that young men come out to cultural events." She paused to fan herself, a flush coloring her cheekbones. "Though you're probably just here to see the masked dancer. She's a phenomenon that's for sure. A powerful dancer, wouldn't you say, Charles?"

Jasper turned to her husband, expecting him to grunt a reply as most men did at these types of events. Instead, the man gave him a wink.

"She's certainly got something to her. Why this is the only event with my wife that's ever stirred me, if you get my meaning."

His wife slapped Charles in the chest with her fan, frowning at him.

"Oh just go drink some wine, dear. Let the men have men talk," Charles said, waving her off. "Don't mind her. Women just don't want to understand a man's needs."

Aubrey shared a glance with Jasper, surprise mingled with distaste. They didn't want to hear that much about the randy old goat's needs either.

"I tell you that girl can dance. You'd think she didn't even know we watched from how much feeling she puts into the performance. It's like she bares her soul. Not that I'd have much trouble watching her in any case. She's a beauty. Nicely formed and graceful. A few years back I'd have sought her out myself, but now I leave such things to young bucks like the two of you."

Jasper smiled in response, the description almost making him regret their lack of an entrance, though he didn't know how reliable a judge this Charles could be.

Dorothea returned, sweeping through the crowd like a sailing ship on its maiden voyage, fully expecting their consideration. She stopped next to them, taking a deep sip from the glass in her hand, the flush on her cheeks having become permanent since she'd left them.

"A bit of a lush, my wife," Charles whispered confidingly.

"Am not a lush," Dorothea pronounced in an overly loud voice. "You don't think so, do you, dear?" she asked Aubrey, leaning in his direction.

He smiled an expression that almost resembled a grimace. "Of course not, my lady. It's just a bit hot in here."

She patted him on the chest, though Jasper guessed she'd been reaching for Aubrey's shoulder. "I always thought you were a nice boy," she said. "You and your friend will have to join us for the second half. I won't hear any objection."

Aubrey bowed his thanks but shook his head at the same time. "I'm afraid we came too late to gain entrance. That gentleman,"—he waved at the man—"said we could not enter."

"Oh pish. You'll be sitting in my box. I paid for it and I can put whomever I like there," she declared, directing a slightly clouded glare toward the gatekeeper.

Charles nodded. "It's true, you know," he said, taking his wife's arm. "Just follow me and we'll get you settled. We have lots of space and no one is going to mind if you slip in at intermission."

She claimed Aubrey's arm as well and grandly led the way, only stumbling once on the staircase. Jasper followed them, already bored but seeing no good method to extricate Aubrey from the older woman's clutches. He smothered a sigh and settled into one of the forward seats, leaning out over the balcony to see who else came to this cultural event.

He saw a surprising number of young men, younger even than he was, taking up booths and boxes without any sign of female frippery. The lights began to dim and Jasper settled in, his curiosity about this dancer growing.

Chapter Fifteen

asper propped his chin on top of crossed arms, staring blindly down at the moving figures on the stage below. Music, no different than what he'd heard in concerts since he'd been old enough to leave the nursery, swelled up from the orchestra. He could see how the dancers' movements in some way paralleled its sounds, but none of it affected him. He yawned, wishing for a mug of even bad ale and an easy way out of this torment.

Behind him, Aubrey's new closest friend whispered non-stop, creating an undercurrent of noise as she conversed at Aubrey, who occasionally grunted a response. Jasper felt his lip curl up into a smile. At least his dear friend had received a proper comeuppance for dragging him here.

Another yawn stretched his cheeks and Jasper amended the thought. No torture would be enough to repay Aubrey for this insult. This offered no distraction at all from the chaos his life had become.

The hall went black. Jasper tried to raise his eyelids only to discover they were already open as a pale, purple glow started in the center of the room. The music changed from the multi-voiced orchestra to a single flute, the sharp, clear notes haunting.

"This is the dancer," their hostess hissed from the back, her overly loud voice attracting the irritation of those in nearby boxes.

Jasper tensed at the confirmation even though he'd already guessed. His nerves seemed to come awake as he stared at the glow, expecting it to explode into action.

Instead, a deeper-voiced instrument joined the flute, creating a mournful counterpoint. The lit area remained the same, no angel dropping from above nor demon rising from below.

Without being aware that he'd moved, Jasper found himself pressed against the side of the balcony straining for his first glimpse of this mysterious woman who drew even jaded young men into her web.

The dancer, when she entered the stage, looked lost against its expanse and much younger than he'd expected. Her unbound hair fell around her shoulders in a cascade of locks that moved with her until they seemed alive. She walked to the brighter spot, each step a study in grace and passion. He could almost feel her sorrow, see it in the slight hitch of her breath, the inward curve of her shoulders.

Jasper forgot to breathe until his lungs begged for air, wanting nothing more than to comfort this woman, living her pain as if his own. Her movements changed, dragging him with her through sorrow into acceptance, into joy and through frantic desperation until he could feel the pounding of her heart next to his, the sweat slicking her flesh. He wanted her more than he'd wanted anything in his life, even knowing his desire held little rationality. He felt closer to her, that he knew her better, than any woman before, though he'd never seen her face.

The music grew louder and stronger, instruments having joined to swell the sound as he'd lost all awareness, trapped in the net of her beauty. She moved faster and faster, in a race with the music, a race against time, against fear, against whatever held her bound, whatever drove her to the sorrow.

Jasper found his own heart beating faster, his fingers clenched on the railing, fitfully tensing and relaxing in time with a deep bass drum. He couldn't turn away, didn't want to miss a moment of this vision.

He could feel her moving with him, their touch primal. He didn't know if his eyes were open or closed as he felt her pressed against his throbbing groin, his hand curled around her hip, her nipples hard stones against his chest, the connection visceral.

The lights came up before Jasper could make a fool of himself. He jolted back to reality, aware of a pain he had no way to relieve, a pain deeper than simple lust.

"Guess you didn't choose to leave after all, eh Jasper?" Aubrey clapped a hand on Jasper's shoulder, surprising him.

Keeping his body facing out over the balcony, Jasper found a smile, hoping the flush heating his face didn't show in the dim lighting. "I didn't feel right abandoning you to the tender mercies of…culture," he said in an attempt at a languid voice.

Aubrey leaned in close and whispered, "I'd trust your words if the heat from your face didn't warm the room." Pulling back, he added, "So what do you think of the dancer?"

"She's really something, eh, boys," Charles said as his wife ushered him out. "We've got some function or another to go to now. Take your time and come down when you're ready."

Jasper watched the two leave, not interested in moving away from the place where he'd experienced a revelation. He'd found the one woman for him and he didn't even know her name.

"Come on, my friend. She's not coming back on stage tonight and we have some pubs to explore, remember?" Aubrey nudged Jasper hard enough to rock him in his seat.

Rising, Jasper discretely adjusted his clothing to a more comfortable fit before heading for the staircase. Somehow, the search for a perfect mug of ale held little interest for him now.

THE CROWD FILLING THE STREET made a marked contrast to the barren space they'd arrived in. Aubrey craned his neck, trying to find his carriage, but Jasper only leaned against the wall, reliving the moment of oneness with the dancer. He grimaced, wishing he knew something to call her besides a generic title. Though arrogance itself, he knew if she only could meet him, she'd feel the same.

He glanced around at the other patrons, startled to see a familiar lust on practically every male face, regardless of age. Narrowing his eyes, he denied what he saw. His feelings were more than simple desire. He wanted this woman for more than a short tryst.

Jasper shied away from any deeper meaning, knowing he didn't have it in him to love, and even if he did, it wouldn't be some dancer who showed off her attributes for all to see. No, he had just the perfect offer for this one. A nice house on the edge of London, fine clothes, some jewelry. Surely she'd find his suggestion more appealing than working here no matter how much attention the audience paid.

"I think I see him. Over there," Aubrey shouted, pitching his voice to be heard above the crowd.

Jasper shook his head, trying to focus, but he couldn't shake the sudden determination that took hold of him. "You go on ahead. I have to do something."

Aubrey's exclamation echoing in his ears, Jasper shoved through the crowd back to the doors, pushing them open and slipping through. The entryway stood empty, the former occupants all out on the street, except for the gentleman who had first barred their way.

Jasper schooled his features into the calm arrogance that had served him well since becoming a man. With a purposeful stride, he crossed the space to where the gentleman strung chains through the door handles.

"Excuse me, my good man," Jasper said, mentally declaring the earlier confrontation gone. "I wish to speak with the dancer. The masked one."

"Doesn't everyone," the man said without turning. "The answer is no."

"How much will it take?"

"Look, mister, Monsieur Henre runs a clean house. His dancers are dancers. Nothing less. Nothing more."

Jasper saw recognition cloud the man's expression as he turned around, and rushed to make amends. "No, I meant what do I owe you for my friend's and my own entrance tonight." Jasper pretended that meaning all along as he pulled out some money. "We had no intention of skipping the fee, only a bit of a scheduling issue."

The man frowned and his face tensed in suspicion. "The box was paid for," he said. "Is that all?"

With a sigh, Jasper went to put the money away. "I really would like to meet her though. Is there a fee for an audience? I just want to tell her how much I loved her performance."

"You and every male with eyes. I know what you're offering and the answer is no." He moved away, heading for the same entrance he'd escaped through before.

Jasper strode after him, jamming his foot in the door before it could close. "I must talk to her," he said, annoyed to hear the desperation in his tone. "What do I have to do?"

The man pressed against Jasper's foot with the door hard enough to hurt. "Nothing. There's nothing you can do to meet her. She's not available and never will be."

Slamming his hand against the door, Jasper frowned. "Then Monsieur Henre. I want to talk to him."

"Oh, Monsieur Henre," the man said, a twisted smile crossing his face. "Of course." He opened the door wider and Jasper brought his foot back to take a proper step forward.

The door slammed shut, barely missing his fingers.

"Not." Jasper heard through the closed door. "Go away with the rest."

Jasper slammed a fist into the door then pulled back to curl his fingers against his chest, sucking in a breath as the pain reached him. "I'll find her somehow," he muttered, turning away. He'd retreat now, but he had not given up.

By the time he went back outside, most of the crowd had left. He glanced around and saw Aubrey's carriage still waiting patiently despite his delay. With a laugh, he crossed the distance between them. "It's good to know I can count on my friends at least," he said, tugging on the door.

"Oh, I wasn't waiting for you out of kindness." Aubrey laughed. "I had to know if you managed the impossible feat and actually met her."

Jasper sat down and stared out the window as the driver clucked to his horses. "I will," he whispered under his breath.

As they pulled past the building, he caught sight of a woman leaving from a side door and walking toward them. His chest tightened in anticipation even as his hand slammed into the wall behind the driver. "Stop!" he shouted, already reaching for the door handle. Then he froze, his fingers clenched around the metal bar.

Slumping back onto the bench, he released his breath on a sigh. "It wasn't her," he said, waving at Aubrey to tell the driver to continue on. His disappointment melted away though when he realized he knew the secret. He knew where the dancers stayed when not on stage. Someone back there would help him. They had to. Maybe not tonight, but soon. He could be patient for a short while.

"You were marvelous," Monsieur Henre told Daphne, pulling her away from the other dancers who were preparing to leave. "I've never seen such emotion from you."

Daphne managed a faint smile, exhaustion dragging at her limbs now that the energy had drained.

"The crowds were entranced. They've completely forgotten your earlier failure. The comments I heard tonight…just wonderful."

The front room man brushed between the two of them, his perpetually sour expression unchanged by Monsieur Henre's delight. "So wonderful I had to fight off another man. Nobility thinks they have the right to all of us."

Daphne reached for the wall, suddenly feeling faint as she wondered if her father had found and recognized her. Would he be waiting for her when she got home? Or even when she stepped out of the performers' door? She raised a trembling hand to her forehead, her fingers scraping against the edge of her mask.

"A man?" Monsieur Henre asked, his tone sharp.

"Yes, a young man probably out to choose his next lover. They see our women as playthings and too many a young girl's head is turned by it." He looked at Daphne as he spoke, but she only smiled, relieved to hear the intruder could not be her father.

"You handled him?"

"Of course. Don't I always?"

Their conversation continued, but she couldn't find the energy to follow it. Instead, she leaned back against the wall and closed her eyes, trying not to feel the fist of pain that had taken up residence in her chest and which clenched whenever she thought of her sister.

"Are you all right?"

Daphne started at the touch on her shoulder, looking up into Monsieur Henre's face. At that moment, the other dancers flocked out of the changing room, and she groaned, knowing they'd see only what Cynthia had implied and not the truth.

Monsieur Henre frowned at her, shaking his head. "Come to my office. We need to talk."

She could hear the women laughing and gossiping behind her as she reluctantly followed her teacher and now master.

He waited beside the door and closed it firmly as soon as she entered the room. "What is wrong, Daphne? It's more than just improving, isn't it?"

Daphne moved to the visitor's chair and slumped into it. What could she tell him? She'd promised her father not to speak the truth to anyone and knew he wouldn't consider her former dance instructor an exception to that promise.

Monsieur Henre leaned against the front of the desk and tilted her face up with one finger under her chin. "Such powerful emotion leads to quick rises and even quicker falls. Don't let it eat you up from the inside."

She slumped, pulling away from his finger to bury her face in her hands. Fighting back tears, she struggled with the need to lie and finally gave in to protect her family name. "It's my sister, Grace," she managed. "She's sick. Father sent her to the country."

He pushed up from the desk with a laugh, circling around to take his own seat. "You had me worried there. It'll pass. Illness comes and goes, never worse than when our loved ones suffer."

Daphne shook her head, staring at him through tear-filled eyes. "She's not coming back—ever."

Leaning forward to capture one of her hands between his, Monsieur Henre smiled. "I know it seems harsh, but the country air will help her heal, and she'll return to you in no time."

A frown pulled at her face, bringing back images of her mother's warning and then the sight of Lady Scarborough with blood-shot eyes. "Then why does Father want me to marry her affianced?" she burst out, unable to contain the knowledge.

He sat back, his expression mirroring hers. "But you said…never mind. When do I lose you?"

Daphne could almost see the calculations already whirling about in his head. Her mentor had vanished under her master. "The other family must agree to the change. I pray they won't. I haven't even had my coming out."

"I thought you didn't care about such things," Monsieur Henre said, his tone harsh. "I thought you only wanted to dance."

She managed a strangled laugh. "I don't." Her words came out flat and bitter. "But why would one of the most eligible bachelors want to saddle himself with a schoolroom miss? And yet, if he turns me aside, what will we do?" Her voice rose much higher before she regained control, the devastation of her hopes and dreams spread out before her.

"Well, then your sister must recover. When she returns, he'll transfer his affections back, and it will all be as if none of this even happened. You'll be able to dance unimpeded until old age makes you tremble."

She took the pat on her hand as the dismissal he'd intended, furtively wiping her eyes before opening the door. If she hadn't seen the calculation, maybe his reassurances would have meant something. As it was, she knew her time of dancing had almost ended. She would dance hard with her heart out for all to see. If nothing else, she'd have the brilliant rise to remember before she vanished from the public's mind.

Chapter Sixteen

Three days passed without word.

Daphne kept on dancing as if each night would be her last, but she'd started to hope just a little. Why indeed would a ton leader want to tie himself to an unpolished girl? After all, there must be many girls already out who had a title for sale.

She skipped down the stairs, for once looking forward to an outing with her mother if it would break the cloud hanging over them. Since talking to Willem, Daphne knew in her heart that Grace was well cared for no matter where she was.

A frown broke through her determined good mood at the thought of Willem. He still played for her during practice, but he kept his distance, acting the servant more than he ever had. She only realized how much she'd counted on his impertinent words and winks now that he'd become a proper coachman.

Just this morning, she'd wanted to startle him out of his proper form, to force a reaction. She'd tried so hard, but he kept up his stoic look even when she braced her leg across his knee, pretending to use him as a chair against which she could stretch. He'd tolerated the touch without a word, bringing the pipe up to his lips the moment she moved away.

"Remember your face," Lady Scarborough said as she passed Daphne on the stair. "I know it's hard, dear, but don't let what you cannot change ruin your life."

For a heartbeat, desolation stared out of her mother's eyes, but then Lady Scarborough blinked and slipped her arm through Daphne's.

"Time we were down to breakfast. I have in mind the perfect bonnet for you to wear to meet your betrothed."

Daphne moved down the stair, pulled by her mother's arm. "Don't you think we'd have heard by now?" she asked, unable to keep silent. Her heart pounded as she waited for the words to free her from this trap.

"Nonsense, my dear. It has all been a bit of a shock, but never you worry. Your father will work everything out. He always does. He fixed your sister's situation didn't he?"

They stepped onto the landing and Daphne slipped free, clenching a fist against her skirt as she fought the need to lash back. Disinheriting her sister then lying about why had nothing to do with fixing in Daphne's mind.

"Wait, Daphne," her mother said, putting a hand out to delay her. "I know you're worried. We're all worried, but there's no reason to suppose he'd reject you. You're beautiful and accomplished. Had we not held you back for Grace, you'd have had your pick of suitors." She tugged on Daphne's hair, pulling a strand free. "Given the chance, he'll love you as much as we do."

Daphne mumbled something in response and continued toward the dining room with a determined stride. She didn't *want* him to love her. She didn't want him to agree to take the younger daughter as easily as he had offered for Grace. Her older sister might have been willing to accept this fate, but she wasn't ready to be married off to the highest bidder. Daphne knew her place, her responsibilities to her family. She only wanted some time to live before falling in line.

She stomped into the room with none of her usual elegance and threw herself into the chair without even acknowledging the footman who pulled it out for her. Any bit of enjoyment she'd felt when looking forward to the day had vanished.

After liberally adding salt to her porridge, she stared at it without raising her spoon. Her mother's words had taken away the hope that time passing meant a rejection and killed what little joy she'd gathered around her.

Lady Scarborough sent a reproving glance her way, but said nothing except to call for a fresh scone.

Daphne felt her stomach curdle and could barely face the thought of food much less the reality. She pushed her bowl away, taking a deep gulp of water instead.

"You have to eat, Daphne. It's hard to be graceful on an empty stomach."

She didn't look up when her mother spoke, but the offending porridge vanished and a scone already spread with jam appeared in its place. Daphne raised the bread to her lips and took a tiny nibble, more to appease than out of hunger. Her body, however, wanted sustenance after the hard dance practice in the morning, harder than it should have been as she'd tried to spark a reaction from Willem.

Soon, she found herself brushing the crumbs from her fingers and waving for another.

"That's my girl," her father said, sweeping into the room with a smile on his face. "You never were one to let circumstances keep you down. Don't you worry. I have here the answer to all our troubles."

Daphne eyed the thick sheet of paper in his hands with horror, remembering the last missive he'd brought to the table. She cringed, knowing whatever it might contain, she'd like it no more than the letter that had stolen her sister forever from her life.

"Well don't hold us in suspense, dear."

Smothering a protest at her mother's words, Daphne crumbled her scone into tiny fragments, her gaze on the table. She had too good an idea of what the paper held to wish his information any speed.

Her father crossed the room to stand next to Lady Scarborough. "When I saw it came from Lady Pendleton, I brought the missive straight in. We can all read it together."

Daphne glanced up quick enough to catch the worried look her mother gave him. She tensed, thinking maybe, just maybe, this letter held her freedom not the loss of same.

The thick paper rustled as he opened the missive.

She couldn't help watching him, his lips moving as he scanned each word. She reached for a drink of water and almost sent the glass tumbling across the table.

A footman leapt forward with a cloth to clean up what drops had splashed at the same time as her mother lashed out, "Do be careful, Daphne."

Knowing her mother shared her tension if for different reasons provided little comfort and suddenly she too wanted the contents known. "What does it say, Father?" Though she'd meant to keep her peace, the indulgent smile from her mother almost made up for it.

Lord Scarborough cleared his throat then read the letter in a loud, clear tone. When he reached the end, he winked at Daphne and bestowed a smile on her mother.

The words echoed in Daphne's mind, unwilling to settle down so she could comprehend them. The Pendletons had agreed. She'd been sold off with little thought to her own wishes and no care to her sister's feelings.

Daphne managed a tight smile, holding back her tears with all her might. How could Lord Pendleton have done something so callous? Had he no care for the woman to share his table?

"Oh dear, just look at poor Daphne. She's overwrought. She's been under such strain these past days that I can't imagine what relief she must feel."

Daphne struggled to suppress her churning stomach, her mother's words only increasing the violent swirl surrounding the scones she'd eaten. Pushing away from her place, she managed a quick, "I need to go lie down," and rushed from the table.

"Don't worry, dear. We can go out shopping some other day," Lady Scarborough called after her.

Throwing herself down on her bed, Daphne reached under her pillow and pulled out the dancer's story that she still had not returned. A tear fell down to mark the cover, and she wiped it away, opening to one of her favorite passages, a description of the dancer's first night on the stage.

"I'm done," she whispered to the page. "It's all over now. I'm to be the wife of some uncaring brute, never to set foot on the stage again."

The dancer in the book seemed to mock her, asking if Daphne had ever had the heart for the dance if something as simple as a betrothal could make her give up. She stared down at the book for a moment longer before pushing up off the bed. Scrubbing a hand across her face, Daphne crossed to her mirror.

"I won't give up," she told her image. "Not for this. I'll manage somehow. It's not like he'll want to spend much time with me anyway. He wants my pedigree, not my person. Our wedding is soon enough for us to meet."

Her determined glare looked back at her. Daphne did nothing to prevent the smile pulling at the corner of her mouth. If she'd managed around her parents for this long, why not around her betrothed. They probably had little in common anyway. He'd go his way and she hers.

"SHE SENT THE LETTER," JASPER told Aubrey, finally breaking his silence on the issue as the curtain fell. "It's done. My future happiness is in the hands of a girl just out of the schoolroom."

Aubrey tapped him on the shoulder. "Don't look so glum. It's not like you'd planned to give your future wife much say, anyhow. Why should the sister be any different?"

Jasper continued to stare at the curtain, wishing the masked dancer would return for one more encore and distract him. "A mature woman would know the score," he muttered. "This chit probably looks at the world with stars in her eyes. I'll go from being respected to condemned for my treatment of an innocent, naive girl."

Aubrey laughed. "What makes you think she's an innocent? Pure, she better be, but with her sister?"

"Hsst," Jasper said. "Her sister fell ill, terminally ill, remember."

"Sure enough. Don't worry. I'm just saying she may not be the horror you expect."

With a frown, Jasper pushed to his feet and waved Aubrey out of the box. "I can tell enough that she won't be the masked dancer, and that's the only female who has caught my interest at the moment."

Aubrey strode down the stairs and Jasper followed, feeling the disapproving stare from the man who kept the audience orderly.

When they stepped outside, the absence of other people showed just how much time he'd wasted fantasizing about the dancer.

"If you want her so much, why don't you try for her?"

His friend's laughing comment made Jasper aware he'd spoken aloud. "I did," he muttered, remembering his humiliation when the same man whose eyes still bore holes in their backs had blocked his every path.

"Not like you to give up so easily," Aubrey said, waving to call his driver over. "Used to be you'd scale walls and bribe brothers to get at whatever fluff caught your eye. You, my friend, are getting old. Maybe settling down is just what you need. Are you worried she's going to wear you out, this new wife? Want one with more years under her belt so she has a mite bit less energy?"

Anger rose up in him and Jasper almost lashed out at his friend, just barely managing to control his temper. "I'll show you just how old I've grown. Don't wait for me because I'll be a while. As you said before, it's easy enough to find a hire cart in these ways."

"Are you sure?" All humor had vanished from Aubrey's face. "I didn't mean to challenge you, and I don't know about the neighborhood this late. Once the hall closes, there's no cause for hackneys to be here."

Jasper summoned up a smile, finding the effort less tiresome than expected. The thought of catching his graceful lady had restored his good humor and a sharp excitement now raced through his veins. "I'm a big boy, Aubrey. I can take care of myself. You just worry about how you will be begging my forgiveness when I show up with my dancer on my arm."

Aubrey laughed again. "Just make sure it's a masquerade or I'll have to question her identity. I only know her with her features covered." He put up his hands to cover his eyes in a mockery of her mask.

"There's ways enough to know her without needing so much as a glimpse at her face, but you'll not know them if I have anything to say about it. Go on now. I see no need for you to wait for me like a nursemaid. I outgrew my keepers long ago."

Jasper stood still, waiting until Aubrey swung up into his carriage before crossing to the building's far side. No need to reveal his secrets to anyone. He knew this one was a prize he'd hate to lose even to his best friend.

The alleyway emphasized the late hour, its sheltering darkness almost complete when he stepped around the corner. The building blocked what little light still spilled from the hall. Jasper paused to get his bearings and let his eyes adjust before heading toward the door he'd only glimpsed once.

The door swung open, a rectangle of brightness almost blinding him. He pressed close to the wall, watching first one then two other women step through. For a heartbeat, he thought she might be one of them, but as they turned away, heading the opposite direction, he found nothing to match his knowledge of her step.

Jasper grimaced, wondering what he'd have done if they'd passed him on their way to the street. How would they react to a man lurking in the shadows?

Dispelling the image of the watch dragging him away, Jasper strode toward the door now that its location was known. He didn't give a moment's thought to how he would get inside until his hand closed around the doorknob, feeling the resistance of a lock.

Jasper frowned as he raised his hand to knock. His purpose, while not entirely respectable, would certainly offer her a better life than this. Whoever answered his knock should be grateful of his interest.

The door swung open again before he could put fist to wood. He flattened his palm to stop it from slamming into his face.

"What?" a deep, feminine voice exclaimed in reaction to his resistance.

Jasper stepped around the door with a smile, half expecting his dancer. He pushed aside his disappointment when he found a nicely proportioned but taller woman in the doorway. Sweeping into a short bow, he smiled at her. "Jasper Pendleton at your service," he announced himself, leaving off the lord because he wanted success not fawning.

She put out a hand for him to clasp or kiss, a throaty laugh caressing him. "Cynthia," she replied. "Always welcome the attention of a man as handsome as yourself."

He squeezed her fingers lightly, not missing the frown that came and went on her full lips. "Perhaps you could help me then, Cynthia." Jasper smiled but kept his expression neutral.

Reaching out to brush against his cheek, she smiled back, her expression full of lust. "How could I refuse to help you? Anything you want, governor." She leaned forward, her breasts lifted by her costume so they created sizeable curves.

"I want to step inside."

She stared at him, her eyes narrowed. "And why would you want that?" she finally said, her expression unattractive.

"I…want to speak with the mystery dancer." He barely swallowed back the word he'd almost spoken: desire.

His intentions must have shown on his face because she frowned. He could almost see the calculation in her face and wondered if he should have revealed his rank, or handed her some currency.

"So you want to see her, then?" the woman said, her smile not reaching her eyes. "You've got a proposition for her?"

Jasper hesitated, something about this woman making him alert.

"Well?"

Her prompting matched his thought that he had no choice. If he shoved past her, he'd only get dragged outside, but with an invitation? "Yes. A proposition I hope will be welcomed." He kept his words short, keeping his own counsel as best he could.

"Hmm."

Jasper reached for his purse, the universal solution. He didn't mean to buy the dancer, well not really, but it seemed he'd have to buy his way in.

She stared at the coins in his hand for a long moment before shaking her head. "No, I don't want your payment. Only be clear just what you want from her."

With that odd statement, the woman stepped away from the door, moving back inside.

Jasper stared after her, unsure what he should do.

"Well? Are you coming or not?" she called over her shoulder.

The words convinced him and Jasper stepped over the threshold, letting the door bang shut behind him. He stretched his legs to catch up with her, passing through silent corridors with several doors.

"Wait in here," she said, jerking a door open and pushing his shoulder until he moved inside. "I'll bring her to you."

Jasper turned the wick up on the only oil lamp in the room, the light revealing a small office complete with papers on the desk. He smiled, surprised to find a dance hall office not much different from where he did the work of directing his stewards to manage the various lands for which he now held title.

At first, he felt reluctant to pry beyond a quick glance, but as the minutes passed and his dancer did not arrive, Jasper couldn't restrain his curiosity. He wanted to see just how similar his life as a wealthy landowner was to the artistic pursuit of producing beautiful motions set to music.

The first paper covered a project for replacing part of the stage floor where apparently boards had started to weaken. Jasper imagined the disaster if the floor gave way under the heavy pounding of feet and winced. He pushed that paper aside to read the next, a bill for costumes covering both the fabric and seamstress work. It cost almost as much as Lady Pendleton's gowns.

Page after page listed the costs until Jasper wondered how the doors stayed open. Using the financial acumen that had turned his family's modest fortune into a sizable one, Jasper estimated the number of customers and the price. He frowned, shaking his head at the cost to earnings. He'd sell any land with such a poor ratio.

Chapter Seventeen

The door swung open, jerking Jasper out of contemplation. He dropped the paper in his hand and tried for a smile, ready to persuade his dancer to agree by any means possible.

Instead, his gaze met that of an older gentleman in worn but quality clothing. Jasper noticed the thickening around the man's fingers, indicating a life of labor or at least one to build up calluses. The man's shoes also showed signs of wear. Clearly not another guest having slipped behind the curtain.

"What are you doing in my office?"

The low, calm voice confirmed Jasper's supposition and fears. A wash of guilt rushed over him for having pried into this man's business, an intrusion he'd never have accepted with such grace. Curiosity and boredom seemed to have little value as excuses.

Jasper twisted his mouth into a wry smile and stepped away from the desk to offer a respectful bow. Should he win over the manager, maybe he would find an ally in the effort to persuade his dancer. "I apologize for my rudeness, sir. I had but thought to pass the time while waiting."

The man moved past him to straighten the papers into tight piles, unlike the scattered layers Jasper had found. "And my papers seemed like novel reading to one like yourself, I suppose."

Meeting the man's unblinking stare took more of an effort than Jasper would have supposed. It was rare he found a man willing to stand against him, and never in the lower ranks. Then Jasper realized he had not introduced himself.

Stepping forward with his hand raised, Jasper offered a handshake. "I found them intriguing for sure, both like and unlike the papers I handle myself. Lord Pendleton at your service."

The man had seemed about to speak, but he stilled at the sound of Jasper's name, lips pursed as if in thought.

"It seems the theatrical life is hardly a source of good revenue," Jasper offered.

Reaching out to clasp Jasper's hand, the man smiled sourly. "Those of us who go into true theater do so for the love of it, my lord, not for the money."

Jasper smiled back, tensing his fingers once before releasing the man's hand. "So you hold yourself in the class with those who find patrons and give up on a normal workday?" he asked, trying to keep the contempt from his voice. It seemed wrong for a woman of such grace to be clutched in the hands of one unwilling to work for his living.

"I am Monsieur Henre," the man barked out as if the name should have significance. "I do not run a brothel from my theater. I make the money to keep it afloat by the hard work of my hands and using my skills. I teach your ladies one fraction of the grace I pass to my dancers and yet you see which is valued. My dancers would be more appreciated by your kind if they sought invitations or brought you back here where you have no business being."

Any deference his title might have earned had vanished from the man's voice as he lashed out.

Jasper's smile broadened. He nodded, accepting the rebuke. "So, Monsieur Henre. You keep the talent here skilled and pure while the theater rots about your ears." He waved toward the desk and Monsieur Henre's fingers clenched on the pile of papers. "It seems you are in need of a patron despite your best efforts."

The man's eyes narrowed as he stared back at Jasper, then his breath released on an exasperated sigh. "Is that why you burst in on my office, setting foot where none but the dancers should be? To offer yourself as my patron?"

Jasper froze, surprised and a little taken by the idea.

"I thought not," Monsieur Henre said. "You snuck back this way in the hopes of catching one of my girls in less than honorable circumstances. Despite all your talk of patrons, you don't understand true art. Your groin tightens instead of your heart when you watch the dancers, focused on their short skirts and revealed flesh rather than how their movements enhance the musical presentation, bringing it to life. Get out of my office. I have no use for you besides the entry fee you pay up front."

The man slammed his hands onto the table, leaning forward with a ferocious expression that would have made a lesser man tremble. "You have no business back here where I conduct my work. There are no tickets sold to get you here and nothing for you to buy. Get out of my theater before I bar you from the front as well."

Jasper stepped backward not out of fear, but out of respect and discomfort. Though he'd never have thought himself one of the dandies, hadn't he done just that? Hadn't he watched his dancer's body? Hadn't he lusted after her, wanting to capture her for his own? As much as he wanted to protest that he'd touched her soul and she his, how could he when they'd yet to speak?

A frown pinched Jasper's eyebrows together even as the bluster drained from Monsieur Henre and the older man sank into his chair as if the weight of the world rested on his shoulders.

"Just go. As you saw, I have much work to do. Many depend on my efforts to keep the theater open."

Moved by the man's exhaustion, Jasper stepped close again. "I have a bit of a reputation for supporting the arts," he said, keeping his voice soft. A bark of laughter escaped his mouth as he continued, "A bit of a bad one since I only choose endeavors where the artists actually labor rather than spending their time wooing young ladies. I could help."

Monsieur Henre glanced up, a look of hope gracing his features for a moment before a frown soured the expression. "And what will you ask for this offer? A tour of the theater? A free box?" He shook his head. "My dancers are not for sale, sir. Not for any amount."

Jasper struggled to keep the guilt from his face. Though he had not considered bartering for her favors, the thought would have come. Still, he couldn't give up this chance, this possibility. He soothed his conscience with the firm belief that his interest in the dancer extended beyond a wish to get under her skirts. She absorbed him, trapped him as Nimue trapped Merlin. He had to have her.

"Then your stage will rot and those precious dancers will fall, losing their limbs if not their virtue. I ask little enough in return for my heavy purse: a box, a tour, to meet those upon whom my coin rests." As further inducement, Jasper pulled out his coin purse, heavy with the plans to meet at White's later for cards. The coins jangled together, showing amount if not value.

The older man thrust both hands through his hair, conflicting emotions clear on his expression. His gaze fell to the papers on the desk and he groaned, a sound Jasper took as encouraging.

Monsieur Henre muttered, "All my life I struggle for every penny while you are happy to exchange more than I'll ever see on a whim." He glanced up, staring at Jasper as if to weigh his soul. "Yours is a devil's bargain. If I don't accept, I lose everything I've worked for. If I do, my dancers become little more than brothel workers, available to the highest bidder. And yet, if the theater is gone, where will they go? I know what reputation other dance halls maintain. I know what happens to those of talent and heart." He surged to his feet, slamming a clenched fist down on the wooden surface. "I swore to provide a place where they could be just what they wanted to and no more. Dance is beauty, art in motion, and needs nurturing to survive in this harsh world." He sank back down, bracing his face in his hands. "And yet it's come to this. I'll take your purse," he said without looking up. "I have no other choice."

Once again, guilt pulled at Jasper. He hadn't lied, but neither could he say his reasons were as lily white as this man kept his dancers. A grimace creased his face as he opened the mouth of his pouch and removed most of the coins. He'd have to skip cards tonight, but maybe he'd have something else to occupy his time.

Monsieur Henre stared at the money now decorating his desk, looking more like a man facing the gallows than one with salvation within his grasp. "When I was a younger man, more hopeful as I set out on the world, I promised I would never sell myself for any cause. Age weakens more than just the bones and life is rarely as simple."

Jasper mustered a smile, putting his hand over the older man's. "It's not blood money. No one will be surprised that I've taken another artistic enterprise under my wing. I ask only for an introduction."

Monsieur Henre's answering smile had a wry twist. "And when word gets round that what amounts to pocket change for your class buys my dancers? What will it matter whether you bed her or not?"

"Word won't spread unless you choose to spread it. I have no need to talk up my deeds."

"And you managed to make your way through a locked door, found my office, and chose to wait patiently in it all on your own?" Monsieur Henre raised a hand to stop Jasper's response. "No, I won't ask. There are plenty who find my rules too confining and I'm sure one of those aided you in. Probably thought I'd head on home after the last performance and that this was the safest place for an assignation. They don't understand what it takes to keep the soaring beams above their pretty heads." He swept a mocking bow. "I think you've missed your chance for this night at least, and paid a pretty penny for the privilege. She probably heard us talking and scampered away as fast as she could, hoping your good manners would protect her."

Jasper shrugged, unable to give the woman's name anyway. If she'd told him, he'd forgotten in his need to speak with the mystery dancer.

"Come," the older man said, rising to his feet with half the energy he'd shown earlier. "Now's the best time for that tour, if a bit dark. At least we won't be tripping over performers and the others who keep this hall running."

Jasper let Monsieur Henre usher him out of the office, hearing the underlying thought that this tour would provide no tantalizing glimpses that a younger hour might have.

DAPHNE DREW THE BRUSH THROUGH her hair one more time, staring at her face in the mirror. She looked pale, her features pinched as if she tottered on the edge of a collapse. At that thought, her eyebrows moved closer and her lips turned down, the expression reminding Daphne of her mother's warnings.

The frown deepened. What did she care about keeping pretty? She'd never have the opportunity to find someone to love. Even in dance, her features hid behind a mask. She could make as many lines on her face as she wished and no one would ever care.

Fingering the ribbon she used to secure her mask when on her face, Daphne wondered if anyone would ever truly know her. Willem would never really be a friend even if she somehow repaired the breach while whom else could she trust? Even her sister hadn't known, or shared her own secrets either.

Daphne froze as sounds of movement came from outside the dressing room. She'd been careless, believing herself alone. Grabbing for the mask, she knocked it off the table and it slid behind the room's only privacy screen, a leftover from the former lead dancer.

Panic welled up, but then Daphne relaxed. Monsieur Henre. It must be. She'd stayed late, hoping to tell him of the new development in her marriage situation. Everyone else had left long ago.

She stood, turning to face the door as she considered what she could tell him. Daphne refused to give up. No matter how unlikely, somehow she'd make it work. She wouldn't give up dancing for some title-seeking upstart who cared nothing about her.

The door opened without even a knock, Monsieur Henre's familiar form filling it.

Daphne opened her mouth, ready to tell him everything, when another, taller form appeared. With a squeak of surprise, she dove behind the privacy screen, scrambling on the floor for her mask.

"Hello?" Monsieur Henre called. "I thought everyone had left."

She stepped out as soon as she'd tied the ribbon, one hand pressed against her blouse as she tried to still her agitated breathing. "I'm here," Daphne's voice came out barely a whisper. "I wanted to speak with you."

Monsieur Henre paled, his expression holding as much strain as hers had in the mirror. "Ah. I didn't expect you or I wouldn't have burst in."

Daphne let his words fall into the silence, unsure what to say. Instead, she glanced at the man who had followed her teacher, curiosity pulling at her.

At first, he seemed no different than the other gentlemen she'd seen with good looks, stylish clothing and nice grooming. Then something pulled her attention back, whether the command he exuded or the delight on his face at the sight of her, she couldn't tell. Daphne couldn't take her gaze off him, wanting to understand the puzzle of his athletic form matched to lines she'd seen on her father's face formed by serious thought. Who was this man?

As if in answer to her question, Monsieur Henre coughed, drawing her attention back. He waved at the stranger. "This is Lord Pendleton. He's agreed to be our patron."

Daphne sucked in her breath on a gasp, all curiosity vanishing in the face of horror.

The mask must have hidden her reaction because her future husband swept a bow and took hold of her hand, picking it up from where it hung lax at her side. "A pleasure to make your acquaintance," he murmured, placing a kiss on the back of her hand as if they stood in some fancy ballroom rather than in the dingy dressing room of a dance theater. "May I have the honor of seeing your face?"

She directed a terrified stare at Monsieur Henre, begging for rescue. Her teacher couldn't have known or he'd never have risked this encounter.

Monsieur Henre clapped Lord Pendleton on the back, releasing a laugh that sounded forced to her ears. "Now what would be the mystery in that? She must stand silent and separate or half the draw will vanish and your investment with it. A one such as that needs to be worshipped from afar or else her flaws would show."

Daphne pulled her hand free, just stopping herself from angrily refuting her teacher's implication. Instead, she looked at her future husband to see his reaction, unable to stop her fascination even with so much at stake.

Memory of the description once given conflicted with what she'd imagined to find. Could he really be interested in the arts? And looking for a wife who had more to offer than fine fashion sense and a piercing giggle?

He turned to face her, startling Daphne with his intense regard. "A name then? Can I have your name?"

A strange heat started in Daphne's center and moved lower, bringing with it sensations she'd never felt before. A blush crept across her face, and she ducked her head to break the connection.

"She needs no name for you to enjoy her dance," Monsieur Henre said, stepping physically between them. "I think you've seen enough of the dressing area. Why don't we go admire the stage?"

The lord looked like he was going to argue, his body tense, but then he nodded, a short, jerky motion. Before either of them could react, he stepped around her teacher and captured Daphne's hand one more time, pressing his lips to the back. "Until we meet again," he whispered, claiming her gaze with his own for a long while.

Daphne released the breath she hadn't known she'd been holding as the door closed behind them. She sank to the floor, one hand pressed over her pounding heart. How could she hope to deceive someone like that? He didn't seem the type to be happy with a simple lie, not with his commanding air, nor could she imagine him letting her go her own way.

That last thought melted away the last of his influence, anger taking its place and sending her back to her feet. "How could he?" she demanded of the empty room. "How could he plan to marry me in the morning and that very night go chasing after dance hall perform-ers?"

She stamped her foot, unsure whether to be angry for the poor, sheltered maiden suffering a contracted marriage or insulted by his obvious assumption that a dancer was available for more than her performances.

"This is the man you want me to spend my life with?" Daphne charged her absent parents. "No wonder Grace left him. He probably flirted with all the young ladies present right in front of her." The memory of those smoldering eyes distracted her, calling up emotions she'd only considered in the abstract.

What would it be like to have such a man at her side? From what Penelope's sister had said, he appreciated a thinking woman. Daphne shivered at the thought of being appreciated by him and her lips curled into a smile.

She raised a hand to touch her mouth, and her fingers brushed against the mask. His reasons for being here returned to the forefront, and a frown wiped out her pleasant thoughts. Daphne turned to gather her things. She'd hoped to talk to Monsieur Henre, but she wouldn't take the chance of meeting that man again. She'd have to find a hackney on her own.

Chapter Eighteen

"If only I could peel off that mask, I'd die a happy man," Jasper told Aubrey as the coach headed back to the dance hall for the third time that week. He'd gone every night, unwilling to miss a moment with his dancer, knowing she must feel his presence from the comments others made of her increased intensity. She knew he watched, and she danced only for him.

Aubrey laughed, the sound sour. "You are obsessed, my man. You talk of nothing—and probably think of nothing—else. I never thought to see the day when your interest exceeded mine in something so refined, but I've just about exceeded my patience as well. We never do anything else anymore."

Jasper shoved his friend's shoulder. "And you didn't behave the same when that West End trollop caught your eye? At least what I have is pure. You were full of plans to undercut FitzWilliam."

Aubrey frowned, no sign of his normal good nature in the expression. "That's what worries me. What fool ever characterized a mistress with the word 'pure?' Certainly not you, before this. Just because you can't touch her doesn't make her better than any other woman down here. Don't pin too much on her or you'll fall hard when her cracks show."

Shaking his head, Jasper stared out the window rather than at his friend. "Her manager said much the same the other night," he muttered. "But I don't think so. She's everything she appears to be and more."

"I guess you did manage something the other night, you sly fox. How much did it take? Will you keep her on Regent Street? Or do you have another place in mind?"

Jasper gave a half smile as he named the amount he'd pressed on Monsieur Henre, waiting for an outburst worthy of his mother. "And I've made no offer."

"You're insane. What did you get for your coin? Did one of the other dancers offer up? Or did you pay so much for the fatherly advice of the manager. If I thought you'd be willing to part with such a stake, I'd have acted the father for you."

The heat of Aubrey's gaze was such Jasper turned to face his friend. "Only if you can put on a performance at the same time. The money went to keeping a theater over their heads, not to buying my dancer. She can't be bought."

Aubrey laughed, some of the tension draining from his face. "I should have expected it. You went in there looking for a tender hand to soothe away your hurts and ended up adopting another failing cause. If you weren't such an astute businessman and farmer, you'd be in the poorhouse and no family would be willing to tie their name to yours."

If anything, Aubrey's words only soured Jasper's mood. "It's not like any to-be-wife eloped or anything just to get away from me and my money, now is it?" he burst out, his tone bitter. "How long do I have to wait before the sister does the same?"

The coach stopped, a roar of sound from the crowd outside revealing they'd reached their destination. Jasper moved for the door only to stop when Aubrey put out a hand to block him.

"She's not her sister," Aubrey said, holding Jasper captive. "And her sister ran to someone from all accounts, not from you. Someone her family would never have accepted. It had nothing to do with you."

Jasper sank back onto the seat, reluctantly letting thoughts of his new fiancée wipe the dancer from his mind. "How can you say that? Did she tell you so herself? I know I'm considered a catch by the mothers, but their daughters seem quick enough to escape me."

Aubrey put a hand on Jasper's knee. "One daughter. Listen to yourself. You'd think elopements trailed after you since you gave up short pants from how you're going on. Why is this eating at you so?"

Jasper waved off Aubrey's question with a laugh, unwilling to share the gut feeling that love had no place in his family. His parents proved that often enough. Why should he be any different?

"You're right. I know you are. It's just that for the first time I'd actually let myself think about marriage. I don't know, maybe I considered for a moment that my mother knew me well enough to choose someone favorable."

Aubrey's bark of laughter echoed back in the small space loud enough to deafen Jasper. "You think your mother a good judge? Should I turn the coach for a visit to the doctor? She judges your worth by the letters before your surname and the coin jangling in your pockets. The first she finds lacking, the second lush. She found you a bride to fulfill her ambitions and not one to touch your heart. I doubt any who shared your intellectual pursuits would have scampered off to elope with some poor minister. Word has started to spread despite the earl's efforts. You're best free of that one."

Jasper shook his head, refuting his own misdirected feelings rather than anything Aubrey said. "I suppose I've just been listening to too many gossips. I never imagined the paragon of virtue my mother chose would throw me away as if I had as little value as watered-down, one-year-old scotch." Again, a sense of worthlessness washed over him, and Jasper wished he'd never started the conversation.

"You met Lady Grace a time or two, didn't you?" Aubrey asked, waiting for his nod before continuing. "So she seemed perfect? Like the one you wanted to spend your life with?"

Aubrey's question made Jasper pause. He forced his mind over those few meetings, an opera once, a ball he'd been forced to endure, a tea. He couldn't remember a single word the girl had said and could barely draw up a vision of her face, though he knew it had been beautiful. "No," he said slowly, "If we had anything in common, I certainly couldn't see it. She seemed a good looking, properly brought up female who would give me children. If she had anything more than that, I certainly didn't delve deep enough to discover it."

"And this is the paragon of virtue you are in the doldrums about? This is the woman who has undermined your practically historic self-confidence? Dash it all, man. Give me an hour and I'll bring you five like her or more. You can bet against me at White's, and I'll rake in your coin as each and every one agrees to be your devoted wife."

Jasper shook his head. "You forget. I already have a wife waiting. If you're right, she'll still be there when I go before the chaplain so I might as well enjoy my time now." He pushed up again, this time swinging the door open.

"As if you will give up keeping mistresses for a lily-white wife. I suspect you'll be having as much fun after as before, maybe more, without your mother pushing debutantes at you."

Laughing aloud at his friend's statement, Jasper stepped down from the coach, his attention focused on those waiting for the theater doors to open. The crowd seemed to be thinning and urgency set a fire in his veins. Soon, he'd see her again.

Aubrey swung out of the coach, dropping to the ground in a controlled leap rather than deigning to use the steps. "Or you could give her a chance before you plan your neglect," he added, straightening his coat. "You never know what you might find. If one sister is the consummate debutante, the other might even be your bluestocking. You have yet to meet her."

With a glance toward the rapidly clearing steps before the theater, Jasper nodded, ready to agree to anything if his friend would only hurry. He couldn't help remembering their first visit when he'd almost been denied an entrance. Though his patronage might have bought him a box, somehow he suspected the front man would still deny him if the curtain rose before they arrived. "I'll promise to meet with her soon if you only come now."

Aubrey resisted the hand placed on his arm and stared at Jasper. "Tomorrow. You'll meet with her before I return to this place. I'll take you there myself. Until you deal with this odd notion, you'll never know if you seek this dancer just to distract or because of true interest. For all I tease, I know this dance theater's reputation. Those dancers really are virtuous. As nuns in a nunnery, from some comments. You could hurt the girl when your interest moves on."

Exasperation filled Jasper as he met his friend's gaze, his obsession with the dancer momentarily forgotten. "Since when have you been the keeper of any woman's virtue? You barely manage to keep your youngest sister within the bounds of propriety. I'd not think you had the time to stand guard over performers."

"These performers are as much people as my sister, and deserve the same."

Jasper laughed out loud, slapping Aubrey on the shoulder. "Never thought to see the day, but you've been reading too much. Such thoughts won't gain you many friends among your fellows, but you've got the right of it. I promise should I pursue this dancer further, that more than just the temptation of flesh will drive me."

Starting across the street toward the theater, Aubrey murmured, "Perhaps you had more in common with your lost fiancée than you thought."

Jasper stopped for a moment, Aubrey's words finding a deep chord in his heart. A hackney driver who sought to drive past cursed him, but Jasper hardly noticed the offence. Could he really quiz her motives? If she'd fallen for a lowly man, it was not like she could have taken a lover. No wife of his would keep a man on the side.

His mouth quirked into a smile as he started walking again. A silly chance of fate made her a woman, not a man. For him to keep a mistress would raise no eyebrows, but she had to throw away her family to hold true to her heart.

By the time he caught up with Aubrey, his good mood had returned. Even the prospect of meeting the simpering fool he'd have to marry couldn't shake him. The lights lowered, declaring bare heartbeats kept him from the one who captivated him. Whatever marriage held for Jasper, here he'd found his heart.

DAPHNE PINNED HER HAIR FOR the second time, her hands tense as she tried to relax. She'd almost lost a battle with her mother tonight, almost had to do an informal coming out. The thought made her breathing accelerate again, and she clenched the side of her dressing table, trying to restore her balance.

If the argument had only risked her dance, she could have brushed it off, but no, that man's mother was going to be present. How could Daphne have faced the woman, knowing her son even now sought out a simple performer practically on the eve of their marriage? And what if Lord Pendleton himself arrived, finally wanting to meet the woman he trapped for a lifetime?

The slap of her brush against the polished walnut jerked her out of the bitter thoughts. Daphne stared at the dresser top, grateful only that her blow had struck wood and not the hand mirror she'd inherited from her grandmother.

A soft rap called her attention to the door.

"Yes?"

"Lady Daphne, you have a caller."

From the hallway below, the chimes of the longcase clock sounded the hour.

Daphne pushed to her feet in a panic. "I'll be right down," she said, grabbing her things. She needed to leave for the theater soon, but with both Father and Mother gone, she couldn't fob the visitor off on anyone. Besides, the caller was probably Penelope, the only girl Daphne had the remotest acquaintance with, so her parents' absence was probably for the best.

After pulling a cloak off the hook, Daphne raced down the steps, remembering only at the last moment to drop her satchel and cloak at the foot of the stairs. No matter what the urgency, her mother would never forgive her if she were so rude.

Pausing before the parlor door, Daphne pulled in a steadying breath. She pushed the handle, realizing only as the door swung open that she should have had the butler introduce her. With a slight shrug, she stepped into the room, unsure if she should stand on ceremony with one of her own status.

"Hello, Penelope," she called out, "I wasn't expecting to see you here." Daphne let the door swing closed behind her, leaving the servants to pass her greeting on to her mother, a greeting that left the impression they'd visited often.

A deep cough jerked her attention to her father's chair.

"I'm afraid you're mistaken. I am not Penelope."

Daphne could only stare at the man relaxing in apparent comfort in the parlor, the same man who'd acted the rogue not so many nights before. Steam rose from the cup of tea at his elbow. She thought he'd probably prefer something stiffer but ruthlessly pushed the idea of offering anything aside. She wanted him gone.

Calling on all the training her mother had drummed into her over the years, Daphne gave him a haughty glance. "I'm afraid the maid failed to tell me the identity of my caller." She stepped back toward the door. "It's unseemly to have a gentleman visit without a chaperone, and I'm sorry to say my parents are out for the evening.

Pulling the door open, she stood by it, indicating he should leave.

Lord Pendleton frowned and pushed to his feet, strolling toward her with an easy grace that struck her as almost menacing. The impression strengthened when he took the door from her hand and pushed it firmly closed.

"Any gentleman maybe, Lady Daphne, but not this one. Though you do not know me, I'm the man soon to be your husband. I thought we should learn a bit about each other."

He reached for her hand, but Daphne jerked it away, feeling the pressure of his frown as she crossed the room to settle in an uninviting, high-backed chair.

"I can't imagine my mother would approve, Lord Pendleton," she said, her tone cool.

"And I can't imagine she'd disagree. Unless she hopes to hide your flaws, that is. Is that why you've yet to come out?" He tossed himself casually back into his chair, tipping the cup in a salute before taking a sip.

Daphne fumed underneath but struggled to keep her demeanor bland. "There's no secret to my coming out. It's scheduled for the next season. It's your interest in one not even formally presented that is out of order." She almost gasped as the words slipped from her mouth, the cut biting.

Instead of anger, her comment provoked a laugh. The man leaned forward, bracing his arms on his knees as he studied her with sudden intensity.

Daphne tried harder to project disinterest, but his attention made her uncomfortable.

"And here my mother told me your parents seemed quite relieved to get her note. Are you saying you don't share their sentiment?" He stared pointedly at the dress she wore, a new one she'd chosen to appease her mother.

Daphne blushed at both the subtle accusation and the hint about their circumstances. Confused, she almost missed the mention of his mother. "So you didn't send the letter?" she asked before she could stop herself. She'd seen him as the master of his fate, but what if he was only a fellow sufferer?

"It went with my full knowledge," he said. "Does it matter so much whose hand penned it? Are you now going to languish in misery, your hopes dashed?"

Daphne straightened in the seat, tucking her feet under her skirts as all fellow feeling vanished with his mocking tone. Though he'd misunderstood her intention, she understood his image of her all too well. "Lord Pendleton, I'm not planning to languish over you or any other man," she bit out, each word colder than the previous.

He surged from his seat, towering over her before she could draw a breath. "You will not have any other man," he said, his voice every bit as icy as her own tone. "Whatever you may think, I'm not one to be taken advantage of. You may have a higher title, but you will honor me as your husband if I must lock you up to ensure it."

She stared at him, his eyes dark with passion and conviction. A chill ran up her spine. No, he wouldn't be easy to deceive.

Lord Pendleton grimaced and pushed away from her chair, shoving a hand through his carefully arranged locks. The movement disordered them into an almost boyish look she found appealing even as she pushed the thought away.

With his back to her, he muttered, "My apologies. I did not mean to speak so harshly."

A spark of hope started in her chest as she let her gaze roam over his tightly muscled back and legs, a spike of sheer feminine interest racing through her body. When he turned back to face her, his expression seemed more relaxed and much kinder.

Then, as if noticing her attention, he swept her body as well, pausing at places no gentleman would have dared to skim. He bowed, nothing like his stiffness earlier.

"Call me Jasper," Lord Pendleton said as he reached for her hand. "My given name seems more appropriate considering our lives will soon be joined. And I shall call you Daphne."

Instead of offering her hand as he clearly expected, Daphne gave a regal nod, agreeing though he had no right to claim her first name without permission. His gesture had brought back the night before, and she knew him to be a cad. Who was he to question her faithfulness when he went through the streets courting ladies of the night?

Into the silence, the mantle clock's chime sounded overly loud as it counted out the half hour, the quarter having passed unnoticed in the heat of their discussion. Fearful, Daphne darted a look at the clock face, confirming the time though she knew she'd heard correctly.

He followed her gaze, a frown cutting into his elegant features. "Do you have a more pressing engagement?" he asked, the mocking tone back in response to her rejection of his gesture.

"As a matter of fact, I do," she said, standing. "You'll have to be going now. Next time, maybe you could send a card ahead?" She felt one eyebrow rise in an expression she'd seen on her mother's face before but never managed to emulate successfully.

From the anger gathering in Lord Pendleton's features, she'd succeeded this time. His stride forceful, he walked to the door, jerking it open and waiting for her to pass outside first.

Daphne swept past him, calling for the butler to show him out. She had no intention of giving him the chance to see her leave.

He caught her arm, jerking her against his side. "Your behavior does not become you. If you cannot learn manners at your mother's side, be sure they will be taught at mine."

She stared at him, stunned for a moment, unable to believe his audacity. "Do you purport to be my mother, my father, or my husband? I doubt you have the substance to be them all," she said, her voice savage. "Look to your own manners before thinking to tutor mine."

He stared down at her, his expression going from angry to something she couldn't quite place. Then his eyes twinkled and his mouth quirked into a smile. "You're not much like your sister, are you?" he asked, shaking his head when she didn't—couldn't—respond. He ran one finger down her cheek, stopping just before the corner of her mouth. "I could melt that ice," he murmured.

This time, Daphne could find no words to answer him, though her chest heaved with tangled emotions. As if to support his statement, a fire started burning inside her with such strength she feared it would consume her.

"Lady Daphne. You called?"

The butler's haughty tones broke through the thread holding Daphne trapped, and for once, she felt grateful for his manner. Stepping away, she kept her eyes pointed over Lord Pendleton's shoulder, unwilling for him to see how shaken she felt.

"Yes, Thomas," she replied, her tone just as condescending. "Could you show Lord Pendleton to his carriage? I'm sure he has more important engagements to attend to." Against her better judgment, she glanced at the man who would claim her, her expression showing just how little importance she attached to his schedule. A flicker of annoyance tweaked her as she realized he probably went to visit his latest mistress, or even worse, came to see her dance.

Chapter Nineteen

$\mathcal{J}$asper watched her march away toward the back of the house, something about her angry strides absorbing his attention. A discrete cough from the butler had him shaking his head. She did have a fiery center, that one. If nothing else, he wouldn't have to worry about facing a shrinking violet across the table on mornings to come. It might even make the meal a bit more interesting.

He took his outer coat, letting the butler assist in settling the cloth around his shoulders. "She's got spirit," he muttered to himself, unable to keep the observation bottled inside any longer.

"Spirit and a good heart," the butler said, fixing him with a pointed stare. "It's not my place to say so, but she needs a gentle hand."

Jasper stepped away, wondering at the change in the butler's demeanor. "Sure enough. It's not your place," he said, unwilling to take advice from the enemy's camp.

He almost laughed aloud, but at the same time, couldn't quite escape it. She'd shown her opinion of him quite strongly, especially since they'd never met before. Even had he been inclined to fawn over her, she had already decided to fight him every step of the way.

With that thought lingering in a not completely unpleasant manner, he strode down the outside steps to where Aubrey waited in his carriage to take them off to the evening's entertainment.

"So? What did you think of your future bride?" Aubrey asked the moment the door closed them into the semblance of privacy.

"It's obvious enough why she's been kept to the schoolroom," he said without thinking. "Her sharp tongue and icy manner would turn aside the most eager suitors and probably send the sponsors into faints."

Aubrey laughed. "That passionate? Maybe you've met your match after all."

In short, succinct sentences, Jasper recounted his visit, sparing neither in his description. His own behavior had been as wrong-headed as hers, a fact that left a sour taste in his mouth, he who was known for his persuasive nature. "As you see, she's against the match and determined that all will know it. A shrew and nothing more. This is the woman you're so happy to see me paired with?"

Even as the words left his mouth, Jasper couldn't help his growing respect at how she stood up to him. Though his title was no match to hers, her family had to pick among those well-heeled enough to fix the family fortunes. He knew the agreement his mother had made up. He'd not just acquire a wife but pay a hefty bride price. Could his mother really think a title worth so much? And did this mere girl think her family welfare worth so little?

A different memory rose to wipe out the annoyance still lingering from his meeting with his bride. She'd been so quick to get rid of him but he couldn't argue her point. He did have a more important engagement, one that engaged his heart as well as his pocketbook.

His fickle mind flashed back to his bride standing against him and then replaced the figure with his masked dancer. How was it the two women who held claim to his future both found the strength to thwart even his best intentions? A smile crept across Jasper's face as he remembered how the dancer had stared, her expression masked but her body giving away her interest. Though it take time, he'd have her for his own soon enough.

Across from him, Aubrey grimaced. "Well I know that expression. I'm a man of my word. I'll take you to your fancy now that you've seen the face of your future wife. I'd had hopes, but sometimes it's just not to be."

The sound of wheels against pavement stilled Aubrey's hand as another carriage moved into place before them. Curious despite himself, Jasper leaned out the window to see the girl, his fiancée, rush down the steps as if chased by the hounds of Hell, a bag clutched in one hand.

"Now I wonder where she's off to in such a hurry," Aubrey mused, leaning forward as well. "She's got a nice form for all her tongue has edges."

Jasper laughed. "I think gagging is only in style for highwaymen, my friend, so her looks will do little to comfort." Though he joked with Aubrey, his gaze remained on the girl, her lithe form springing into the carriage ahead of them without even a look to the stairs. Intrigued, he wondered what had her in such a rush.

As if reading his thoughts, Aubrey commented, "We could follow her. Maybe you'll learn more than you thought possible about the girl and her family. Maybe you've sent her running scared after her sister."

Jasper shot him a sharp look and Aubrey had the grace to look ashamed, waving a hand as if to erase his last statement. "Still, it might prove more entertaining than just another performance."

Reaching past his friend to slap the wall separating them from the coachman, Jasper called, "To the theater," his voice unnaturally harsh. Taking a deep breath, he added to Aubrey, "She probably goes to pour out her sorrows to a bosom friend, bemoaning the tired old stiff her family has bound her to."

"Oh Jasper, you weren't?"

A wry smile pulled at Jasper's cheek as he nodded. "I suppose I was. No doubt there have been worse first meetings in all of history, but only a few in all truth. I'd think that half the cause of her sharp tongue if she hadn't lashed me with it before I spoke. Maybe the dance manager was right. Some are best appreciated from a distance. Only it's not my dancer from whom I need to stand separate, but my soon-to-be wife."

Aubrey only shook his head in response, falling silent as the carriage took them on a well-worn path to the theater.

DAPHNE THOUGHT HER MAD SCRAMBLE to change clothes, switch to the hackney, race to the theater, and change again into her costume would have been enough to wipe all memory of that infuriating man from her mind. Then, reflected in the dressing table mirror, she saw her finger lingering on the spot where he'd touched her cheek as if trying to recapture the caress. Even under the black satin of her mask, she could see the unfamiliar desire reflected in her eyes.

"He's no more than a rogue," she spat out, shoving back from the dressing table hard enough that her chair scraped against the wood floor.

Cynthia drifted by, waving a fan constructed of huge feathers, part of a new costume the dancer hoped to foist on Monsieur Henre. "A rogue? That certainly sounds interesting. I hear you had a visitor last night. A gentleman caller?"

The other dancers all turned to listen and Daphne found herself facing numerous curious looks. "What?" she stammered. "I had no visitor."

Even as the words left her lips, her eyes narrowed on Cynthia's smirk. Daphne pursed her lips and pretended to think. "Unless you mean Monsieur Henre's new sponsor," she bit out, emphasizing each word. "I guess our master knows you well enough to wait until you'd left for home before giving the man the tour. He came for the art and might have withdrawn his funding if you threw yourself at his feet."

Daphne stood with her pronouncement still hanging on the air, only grateful she'd been dressed before the confrontation.

"Well, I never," Cynthia said, advancing on Daphne.

Daphne ducked past the woman, heading for the door. Her hand on the doorknob, she echoed something she'd heard one of the other women use when Cynthia wasn't listening. "For one who hasn't, you sure act like it."

Cynthia gave a half-strangled yell and Daphne quickly stepped outside, closing the door behind her. A smile teased at her lips. Despite her sheltered upbringing, she understood enough to know she'd scored against the other dancer.

Exuberance at her victory gave an extra bounce to her step.

"You sure look excited. Found a new beau?"

Daphne stopped, turning to stare at one of the stagehands, a young man who she'd always thought of as friendly. She tried to smile, but the expression soured. She'd only found the courage to talk back to Cynthia because she'd been charged with energy from her run-in with her future husband. He'd mixed her up with anger and something that made her body both warm and shivery at the same time.

The bell rang, freeing her from the need to respond. She managed a twist of her mouth that he could interpret as a smile, and headed for the short stairs up to the wings.

Somehow, dancing seemed more important than ever tonight with her thoughts in a tangle. She wanted to lose herself in the perfection of the music, let her body take over and push aside the question of her husband to be, her future, and especially whether she'd be able to keep her passion.

The music started with her intro piece and she slipped between the curtains, crossing the stage in a quick, graceful stride. Already, she could feel her heart matching the beat, slow at first then increasing in tempo until her feet demanded to move and her arms rose above her head.

Her eyes drifted closed and her body started to sway, moving almost of its own accord through the motions. As always, she poured her frustration, her attraction, her whole being into the music, speaking with her body words she'd never had the gumption to speak on her own.

When the last note echoed across the suddenly quiet stage, Daphne collapsed, her pounding heart audible for a bare moment before thunderous applause drew her attention to the darkness beyond. She'd always known they were there, men and women staring at her, watching her, living through her, but tonight they seemed intrusive somehow, as if they wanted to strip bare her emotions and steal them from her.

The stagehands slipped out and doused the light, leaving Daphne to stumble off, drained more than she'd ever been. She couldn't even find the strength to react when Cynthia shot her an angry glare, their battle of wills a mere speck on Daphne's consciousness.

She made it to the dressing room, closing herself in, away from the prying eyes, but when she settled at her table, her hand tingled and the room seemed more dynamic, as if his presence still filled it. Daphne heaved a sigh that almost became a sob as she rested her head on her arms, giving in to the exhaustion pulling at her spirit.

In what felt like no time at all, the chime sounded a warning. Daphne jerked up, staring at her pale face and mussed hair as if the mirror condemned her. With a deep breath, she settled herself and started working on her hair. She managed to tame the wild mass and stripped quickly, having learned to be efficient. By the time the second bell rang, she was waiting, ready, in the wings.

The other dancers brushed past her, making little impression as she tried to find the mindset where the music took over.

"He's out there, you know. You may have fooled the others, but you're just a slut like the rest of us. Only your fellow has enough to get a box to watch from. He's out there tonight. I asked."

Daphne turned to stare after Cynthia as the other dancer swept away, not sparing Daphne another glance.

The music started, but Daphne barely heard it. He had come to the theater after all. He was watching her pour out her heart, pour out the emotions raised by his visit. Hadn't he done enough?

"You missed your cue," one of the stagehands whispered.

Daphne jerked and turned to stare out at the stage with her stomach churning.

The music stopped at the end of the measure, an uncomfortable silence replacing it for a heartbeat until the audience sounds reached her, shuffled papers, adjusted chairs, a cough, a sneeze.

The music started again, the same piece but with a more robust sound, bringing in the heavier instruments as though demanding she put foot on the stage, as though asking her if she really wanted to let that man take even this from her.

Daphne heard the message, felt it pounding through her feet as the stage vibrated with the drums. Her spine straightened and her arms went up over her head.

Returned for a moment to the ballroom when she studied purely for the joy of it, Daphne spun onto the stage, her pirouettes timed to turn her to face the darkness with every heavy beat. This time, she worked for her dance, unable to let the music in over the chaos in her mind. She thought through every move and, as the music reached a crescendo, sprang into the air, performing a complex leap as an offering, a request for forgiveness since she couldn't offer her soul, not knowing he was watching.

Her hands shot forward, intended for balance and grace, but she brushed against her cheek at the same spot he had touched, marked with his caress.

She stumbled, all thoughts of the landing lost in a bittersweet moment, hearing the echo of his voice.

Ice, he'd called her. If only he knew.

Daphne felt the bad landing even before she lurched out of position. Straightening, she tried to recover, but a sharp pain made her crumple. She twisted her knee as she fell.

The music stopped in a clatter of sound as if each musician stumbled with her, shock making the cymbals clash against each other, fingers drop to random keys on the pianoforte, and gasps setting the wind instruments to squeal for a heartbeat before they too dropped to silence.

She clutched her leg, wanting to tell them to keep playing, wanting to climb back up as if nothing had happened, but she couldn't move.

The curtain dropped down, only partially blocking out the sudden eruption of noises from the audience.

Daphne suffered the whispered questions, only half heard, the scrape of chairs and the heavy, pounding footsteps as people left the dance hall, disappointed.

One of the stagehands came and pulled her to her feet. "Are you all right?"

Daphne pulled free as soon as she could balance, sucking in a breath at the pain. "I'm fine." Her words came out harsher than she'd intended. She gave him a tight smile and limped off to the dressing room, trying to mask the injury even as fiery agony tore through her with each movement.

Once again, Cynthia was quick to step into Daphne's place, pushing by hard enough to knock Daphne against the wing support.

She stared after the other dancer and blinked back tears, unsure whether frustration or pain brought them to her eyes. Moving even slower, Daphne eased her way down the stairs and to the dressing room, pausing to pant when she reached the door before stumbling across the room to slump at her dressing table.

She wanted to forget the moment she fell, but she couldn't any more than she could push away the cause.

Him.

The mirror showed her pale face, strain visible around her mask and a sheen of sweat making her skin glow. She didn't look like herself, nor like the confident dancer. She didn't know who she was right then, but could not be happy with the results.

Forcing herself back to her feet, Daphne jerked the costume off and pulled her dress on, gasping as she leaned on her sore leg. None of the other dancers waiting their turn on the stage approached her, as though they feared her injury catching.

She had to get out of there before Monsieur Henre came to give her one of his speeches about professional dancers working through the pain or lambast her for trying such a difficult step when she hadn't been ready. Maybe he'd even give her a flash of sympathy, but she didn't want that either.

Daphne snatched her satchel and walked out, hearing the echo of what should have been her music as she moved down the corridor. No one tried to stop her, a fact that made her grateful even though the eerie quiet sent tension creeping up her spine.

"The walk will stretch my muscle," she muttered to herself, trying not to think about the difficulty in finding a hire coach in the dark. Usually, Monsieur Henre sent one of the stagehands or went himself to get her one. She didn't want to wait, nor to ask for any favors.

Chapter Twenty

$\mathcal{J}$asper stared blindly at the stage as another woman crossed the wooden floor, her gaudy movements a mockery of his dancer. How could she have fallen? She'd never stumbled in all the time he'd watched her. How could she fail him on this of all nights?

He clenched his fingers against the railing, shifting it in his anger.

Aubrey brushed the top of his knuckles, leaning over to whisper, "Go gentle on that banister if you don't want to spill down on those below."

Grimacing, Jasper forced his hands to release their hold on the wood, coiling them into fists in his lap. He tried to focus on the pageant in front of him, but the sight of his dancer falling repeated behind his eyes until he almost cried out with pain for her.

"I need some air," he said, standing up.

One of the four friends who had met them at the theater muttered for him to sit. Instead, Jasper bowed in their direction and swept out of the box. The stairs slowed him, pitch black in the unlit audience area, but he eventually made his way down to the bottom, no less distracted than he had been above.

An empty chair in the orchestra seats caught his attention, revealed by the stage glow. For a moment, he considered slipping into it and watching the rest of the show, seeing in his actions the obsession Aubrey had at first teased and now quietly questioned him about.

The sound of many footfalls made him glance toward the stage, a group of dancers replacing the stand-in, their movements more along the lines of what he'd come to expect. Still, he watched them with a jaundiced eye, feeling none of the surging emotions that drew him to this place night after night.

He blew out his breath in exasperation and got an annoyed look from the matron seated in front of where he stood. What he needed this theater could no longer provide this night. He might as well make good on his word and go for a stroll, maybe even take himself off to White's before the regular visitors forgot his face.

Though dissatisfied with this answer, he could provide no better one and so made his way toward the door, pushing it open by brute force.

"Here now, you can't be coming and going as you please. There ain't no readmits."

Jasper turned a twisted smile on the man responsible for corralling the customers and nodded. "I have no plans to return tonight," he said, keeping his voice soft and empty of anger. This man couldn't know what had occurred within. He'd been at his post the whole time.

"Would you like me to get you a coach then, sir? I can have one right quick."

Shaking his head, Jasper strode to the door. "No, my thanks, but I think the night air will do me some good," he said, not even turning to look at the man.

"Well enough, sir. Be careful out there. Not alls here for a fashionable evening you know."

Jasper raised one hand in acknowledgement as he shoved the door open, stepping into the chilly night air. There he paused, sucking in a deep breath and trying to push aside the strain he'd been under. It seemed all the women in his life were determined to disappoint him. His mother tied him first to a flighty girl who eloped and then to a shrew just released from the schoolroom. Even his dancer chose tonight to let slip her grace in favor of a clumsy tumble.

He stretched his fingers, deliberately forcing them to relax while he focused on letting a breeze caress his face and savored the crisp air. He had no need for this stress and would not let women drive him to a lunatic asylum. There was no need to give them that sort of power.

Revived by the fresh air, Jasper managed a smile. He couldn't really blame the dancer for her fall any more than he should have expected a warm welcome at his fiancée's home. After all, he'd dropped in unexpectedly. She'd most likely been unnerved by his presence.

Even knowing his thoughts a poor attempt at cheering himself up, he refused to let a bad mood spoil what remained of the night. Jasper half turned to go back in then remembered the warning. "White's it is," he declared with a shrug, stepping off the bottom step. "A good hand at cards will banish all women from my mind."

He made it almost to the other side of the building before some slight movement in the corner of his eye pulled his attention back. Jasper spun around, falling into a defensive pose he'd learned at Oxford. No footpad would make a victim out of him.

The empty street stretched before him.

Jasper laughed, relaxing his posture. "Must have been a rat."

Then a foot scraped against the pavement, and he jerked to attention, glancing in all directions before his gaze settled on a figure moving in the opposite direction.

He almost dismissed the stranger, but something about the movement pulled at him. Despite an odd limp, he realized this person was none other than his dancer. Jasper thought for a bare heartbeat before charging after her, struggling to catch up. She managed a quick pace even with her obvious injury, and he wondered why he'd ever considered himself fit as he panted from the effort.

DAPHNE'S LEG BURNED WITH EACH step, the tight muscle refusing her efforts to stretch it out. As much as she wanted to rail at the man who'd thrown her balance off, she couldn't keep her thoughts from tossing up images she hadn't known she'd seen. His face intrigued her, offering a wide variety of expressions despite their short conversation. She'd seen humor in his eyes, anger tightening his lip, frustration, and even disdain.

A smile pulled at the corners of her mouth as she wondered if he ever played cards. With such an expressive face, surely he wouldn't

have any success. She laughed, the sound pulling her back to her circumstances. The businesses along Drury Lane were busy with customers, but she didn't see any hackneys along the street, darkness
broken only by the light spilling out of the various venues.

Daphne slowed, reining in her thoughts to focus on getting a
conveyance. Should she move to another street, or continue along
this one?

The sound of feet hitting the pavement made her tense, and she
increased her pace, suddenly aware of her vulnerability. With the
noise gaining, Daphne forgot her injury and pushed for more speed.
A desperate desire to turn back time until she'd stayed to bear Monsieur Henre's lecture filled her. No matter how much his words
would have hurt, they'd serve her better than a footpad would.

Daphne pushed aside the possibility of someone other than a
simple footpad. She'd give up her purse without a qualm even if it
meant walking back home. Anything else—

She shuddered, refusing even to let the thought form as she
looked for the nearest opening. She'd prefer to stumble into a brothel
than be captured on the street by a villain.

Light shined above a door not so many paces in front of her.
Daphne pushed forward, using up the last of her energy. Her foot hit
the pavement harder than expected, twisting on an uneven paving
stone, and her bad leg crumpled. She fell with a shriek, anticipating
the hard ground beneath her.

Instead, her pursuer caught her arm in a bruising grip, jerking her
against his broad chest.

Daphne drew in a breath to scream, wondering if anyone would
hear her.

"Are you all right?"

Her mouth hanging open, she froze at the sound of a familiar
voice, though she couldn't place its soft tones.

Daphne tilted her head back to look at him, squinting in the dark
to make out his features.

"I'm sorry if I scared you," he said. "I'm Lord Pendleton, Jasper.
Your sponsor."

Her mouth opened again, a deep moan issuing from her throat. She pushed away from him, trying too late to protect her face before he could recognize her. What would her father say? And her mother? In this moment of weakness, she'd cost them everything.

He released her, but she could tell from his stare that he searched her features, the light from above the door that had signaled sanctuary now spelling the end of her family's hopes.

"Please," she whispered, not even sure what she asked of him.

He smiled, the expression startling.

She almost believed it would all be all right.

Then he reached up to touch her face, brushing his fingers down her cheek. "I'm not going to hurt you. I just want to know you."

His velvet voice sent shivers through her body and set her blood to pulsing, making her feel hot even in the chilly night. Daphne shook her head, whether to diffuse the tension that gripped her or to reveal her confusion she couldn't tell.

This tender man, with his soft voice and gentle touch marred only by the roughness of his fingertips, seemed as much unlike the man she'd met in her own parlor as night was from day. She licked her lips, struggling to understand her reactions even as she wanted to lean into his arms and rest herself against his broad chest.

He groaned, his gaze fixed on her mouth.

Unable to stop herself, Daphne wet her lips again, feeling his reaction as his hands tensed where they now rested on her shoulders. He pulled her toward him and she couldn't find the strength or desire to resist.

Her breasts touched his waistcoat, the movement shifting them against her stays until she felt dizzy with the surge of emotion racing through her. She clutched at him, the rough fabric abrading her fingers until every nerve seemed on fire.

A groan issued from her own lips, her body beset with unfamiliar but welcome emotions.

He laughed, the sound rumbling up from inside him, his chest moving against her hands.

Daphne pressed closer, knowing nothing but that she wanted to feel his warmth around her. After first the scare and then the power of his gaze, she'd lost the ability to think, wanting only to feel.

Lord Pendleton slipped a calloused finger under her chin and tilted her face up to look at him. Daphne tried to pull away, wanting to nuzzle against him, but he resisted her need, instead bringing his lips down to claim hers.

Daphne froze, the touch unexpected. A moment of clarity flared and then faded, leaving only the thought that this must be what the maids sometimes spoke of.

The pressure from his lips increased and his hand at her waist pulled her hips up to his. Daphne's satchel fell to the ground beside her, the quiet thump barely impinging on her consciousness. Her lips opened of their own accord and she sucked in his breath, hot and wet against her tongue.

Her knees buckled, but his arm held her up as he leaned in closer. When they moved, she didn't know, but suddenly her shoulders touched the rough brick of a wall.

His hands roamed up her back and down her sides, melting her with their caresses. They moved higher, stroking the curves of her breasts.

Daphne moaned, the sound swallowed by his lips as he feasted greedily on hers. Sensations swept over her, making her head spin when he traced the gently dip at the base of her throat, then rose to sketch her ears.

"We need no barriers between us," he murmured against her lips, pressing hard once then moving to trail kisses across her cheek and then down to her neck.

His words made no sense to Daphne. She let them slide away as her blood pounded in response to his gentle nibble on her ear. How could she worry about words when he touched her?

Daphne came awake as though someone dumped a bucket of water on her head when she felt his fingers trace the ribbon of her mask. Suddenly, his words made perfect sense. He didn't know her, could not know her, because she had forgotten to remove her mask.

She clapped her hands over her ears hard enough to make them ring and him to remove his hands with a startled cry. Twisting, she pulled almost out of his grasp before his hand gripped her shoulder, preventing her escape.

"Let me go," she cried, fighting him.

"Why? A moment ago, you were ripe for the taking. Why should I stop now?"

Daphne quailed from both the command and anger in his voice. With his words, she understood what she'd been feeling, what they'd been about to do. Shame filled her, and she barely managed to convince her fumbling hands to secure her mask again.

"I didn't mean—I didn't—I can't!" The panic in her voice came through clearly, and she saw him take a step back, giving her a leveling look.

"It's the mask, isn't it? What do you hide beneath there, dear heart? Whatever it may be, I swear to you no matter how marred your face is, nothing can diminish my regard."

He reached for her face again, and she turned away, desperate to protect her family's virtue when she'd been so careless with her own. "It's not that," she said, her voice an anguished whisper. "I don't want this." She added the last even though her still-heated cheeks and pounding heart made the words a lie, hoping only to quiet his ardor.

When he pulled away, she felt grateful until the light cast its glow on his haughty features, the softness of desire replaced by an aristocrat's mask, one her father wore more often than not. "I guess you're right," he said, his voice sharp. "A tumble in a darkened street is not much to my tastes either. What will it be? An apartment on Regent Street? A cottage on the outskirts? A carriage? What is the bargain you demand?"

She stared at him, unable to follow his mental paths at first until suddenly comprehension dawned. With a churning in her gut, Daphne faced the man who would be her husband and wanted nothing but to spit in his face.

Jasper looked down at his dancer, frustrated by the inability to see her features and the inability to curb his temper. Somehow, he'd never imagined her so mercenary. What harm would it have done to show him her face, to give him a hint of the delights he'd have to give over for?

Through the holes cut in her mask, her eyes widened then narrowed, a frown pulling at the mouth that showed beneath her covering. Jasper wanted to caress the expression away, to soothe whatever caused it.

She stepped back, rejecting his touch before he'd made more than a half movement to raise his hand. "I don't want your help," she said, her voice a study in resistance.

Jasper shook his head, a frown forming on his face as well. Had he misjudged her? Did she think he only wanted some quick tussle? "Wait. I didn't mean—"

"So your intentions are honorable?" she cut in, her inflection showing she'd spent time in the home of a noble, whether as a mistress or servant. "You mean to take me away from all this and make a real woman of me?" Her hand swept out to indicate the street with its subtle lighting and unsubtle establishments.

He laughed, the sound bursting free unexpectedly. "Surely you know that's not possible," he said, surprise stripping his words of kindness. "When I marry, it will be for my family, for my name, and my children. As much as you have entranced my soul, marriage has other purposes."

She froze, her pose almost birdlike as if an artist captured her at the moment before launching into flight. "And you see nothing wrong in this?" This time her voice came out an odd mix of contempt and hope.

Jasper stepped forward, pulling her into his arms despite a slight resistance. "Is there any marriage where the heart and mind meld? Is it not better to ease your emotions without the sanctity of the church than betray all for your selfish desires?"

Even as he asked the last question, his arms tensed around her, thinking of another who threw away her family's loyalty and expectations, making a mockery of his choices. Would he ever consider the same? Would he give up everything just to see this woman's face across the pillow?

She didn't pull away, and warmth poured from where her body connected with his. An odd sympathy for the woman who had thrown him over for another rose within him. He had an easy enough time, sharing his heart with a mistress while securing a wife to bear his progeny, but would he think the same if he had to choose between them?

Jasper pushed away his confusion and focused again on his purpose. Whispering into her ear, he repeated his offer without either the arrogance or anger of his earlier attempt. "I'll keep you safe in a nice apartment. You'll have everything you need, and I swear to be with you whenever I can. I need to know you'll wait for me, that you dance only for me. Don't deny me." He could feel her soften against him, his words of need striking some chord in her own heart. "Don't leave me to the cold mercies of the shrew my position requires I marry," he pleaded, desperate to secure her promise.

DAPHNE FELT ALMOST DRUGGED BY his warmth, the cool night air making her nuzzle closer. In his arms, everything else melted away, all her worries and strains. She'd never felt this way before with anyone, not even her father.

His last words filtered in through the sensation of warm, wet air caressing her earlobe and making her shiver. It took a moment for the meaning to penetrate her mind then she sucked in a breath on a gasp, pushing hard against his chest.

"How could you?" she demanded, stunned at the judgment he'd made with so little time to know her. "Do you think so little of me that you'd believe me willing to break some poor woman's heart? Is that all we are to you? Chess pieces to be arranged to suit your fancy?"

She slammed the flat of her hand against the very spot she'd found comforting only a heartbeat before. He'd taken no time to get to know his wife-to-be and yet found it easy to condemn her. Daphne, on the other hand, knew his thoughts only too well.

"I pity the poor woman condemned to keep your house," she bit out, remembering only after the words passed her lips that she was that very woman. Tears pricked at the corners of her eyes, but she blinked them away angrily as she met his stunned look.

Before he could muster a word, Daphne jerked free, grabbed her satchel, and marched off, calling over her shoulder, "I'll not be your whore for all the jewels in the King's treasury. I'd not sink so low."

Though her tone held anger, she couldn't quite convince herself the sheen of water blocking her vision came from pride as she marched off into the street. She'd find better protection at a seaside pub than in his arms.

He shouted something, but the sound barely penetrated her emotion-wrought mind before another took its place. Blinking, Daphne pulled out a handkerchief to signal the carriage she could hear coming her way, the firm clip-clop of hooves on cobblestone offering escape from the man who would have broken her heart if she'd ever been so foolish as to offer it.

Daphne cleared her vision in time to realize her mistake. Instead of halting to pick her up, the coachman seemed oblivious to her presence. She stared in horror as the horses bore down on her, moving at a fast clip.

Something hard and unyielding slammed into her side, shoving her out of the path. Before she could respond to the arms holding her, the carriage passed, its wood groaning and its speed generating a breeze.

Her savior grunted suddenly, and she twisted, jerked by his hold. Daphne felt herself fall, tensing against the expected crack of stone.

Instead, she hit hard on a yielding surface, lying splayed across the man who had saved her from the carriage. Her heart raced from the terror of the moment, and a sudden fear that he'd taken injury in rescuing her first from the carriage and then again as he took the impact of cobblestones to protect her from their fall.

"Kind sir," she said, her tone frantic, "have you injury?"

The gentleman moaned, and she ran her fingers through his hair, seeking a lump or cut.

"As much as your touch does my spirits good," a familiar voice murmured, "I think our position is far from seemly."

"You!" A blush heated Daphne's face as her fear faded. She became all too aware of their position. She could feel the pulse of his heart against her own and warmth invaded her body, making her limbs melt against him. A hard pressure against the join of her thighs made her gasp.

"Unless you wish to take back your worry about a public coupling, I'd suggest you move off me and give me the space to restore my dignity. I'll be happy to receive the full force of your gratitude in a more hospitable location."

Even sprawled on the road, Lord Pendleton maintained a commanding tone that at the same time seemed to be laughing at her. Anger returned, wiping out both her gratitude and any lingering fear for his health.

"You, sir, are a brute," she declared, slapping him across the face with enough force that her blow echoed between the nearby buildings. Daphne refused to let embarrassment at the sound deter her. "If not for you, I wouldn't have needed your tender mercies. You bring trouble upon your head and drag others with you. I'll thank you to mind your own business and leave me to see to my own."

She shoved off him, ignoring his oomph at the pressure, and stumbled to her feet to the sound of his fitful laughter. He hadn't even the decency to recognize his own boorish nature or apologize for dragging her down to his depths.

With a pause to check for oncoming carriages, Daphne marched off down the street, ignoring the twinge from her leg with every other step.

Much to her relief, a hire coach soon stopped to let off some passengers. Though she usually waited for a better specimen, right now, the most rickety coach in all of London would seem a grand transport.

She gathered her skirts in one fist and ran, raising her other hand to wave her now mud-stained handkerchief. Her satchel slid up to her shoulder, and Daphne jerked at the pressure, surprised but happy to find it still slung over her arm.

"You kin pay?" the coachman asked, his scraggily hat hanging off to one side.

Daphne stared into the unwashed face with distrust before re-membering just what she escaped from. Keeping her features in shadow to hide her mask, she nodded, reaching into her purse and finding a small coin by touch. Pulling it out, she raised the coin up to his lantern, ignoring the smell of lard, a poor man's lamp oil. She dropped the coin into his hand, careful not to touch the sweat-stained palm. "And another when we get there," she told him, keeping her tone firm.

The man tipped his hat to her, revealing strands of greasy hair that shone under the light. "Good 'nouf for me," he said, waving her to the door.

Suppressing a shudder, Daphne hoped the seats within held noth-ing more than straw cushioning. With her luck, she'd come from this night with fleabites decorating her body. She called up the address and ignored his grunt of surprise, trying to find a position where she touched as little as possible.

The coach started forward with a sharp jerk, sending Daphne tumbling full length onto the rough cushion. She dragged herself up-right using the length of rope bound to the door and prayed the squeak she'd heard came from poorly oiled wheels, not some four-footed creature sharing her transport. With a sigh, she pulled her mask free and tucked it into the satchel before giving in to the need to massage her sore leg. No one would recognize Daphne in her current state even if they could see her face.

Chapter Twenty-One

A glance out the window revealed familiar houses. Daphne tried to brush the straw from her skirt and calm down. Despite the long trip from Drury Lane, her pulse still raced and every other thought brought back not the stiff gentleman who'd introduced himself as her fiancé but the warm chest and deep laugh of the man who accosted her on the street.

"Miss, you sure this is the address?"

Daphne jerked out of her contemplation of the face that she alternately wanted to kiss or slap to discover they'd pulled to a halt in front of her home. "Yes. Yes, this is it," she said to the driver who peered through an opening behind his seat. She dug out the promised coin and handed it up.

He flipped the metal piece between his fingers, looking her over in the light shed by the lanterns at her door. "You want me to wait, missy? In case they don't be needing the likes of you?"

She felt the heat of a blush rise to color her neck and face. Just how did she look to this man? "No. You needn't wait. Thank you for offering," Daphne choked out, pushing the door wide and scrambling down to the street, her bag clutched in one hand.

The familiar hallway comforted her as she pushed open the door to let herself in. Heading down the corridor, she intended to let Willem know he wouldn't have to pick her up when the door to the front parlor opened.

"Daphne? I wasn't expecting you back—" Her mother's speech cut off as Lady Scarborough stopped to stare.

Glancing down to see what dress she had on, Daphne was grateful to see the nice one rather than the one she normally wore to catch a hire coach. She hadn't been able to change on her way back, but luck or fate had her too distracted when she changed at the theater.

"Oh, my poor dear. Just look at you. You're flushed," her mother said, grabbing one of Daphne's hands, "and your hands are trembling. This is not good. Not good at all. Come. Come."

Daphne let her mother pull her into the parlor and settle her into a chair with a knit blanket tucked around her. Lady Scarborough rang the bell for tea so at least Willem would get warning.

"No trips for you tomorrow, Daphne. No wonder Penelope sent you home earlier, looking as you do."

Daphne's flush deepened at the reminder of her deceit but she said nothing. Monsieur Henre would probably be happy not to see her, not to have her embarrass him once again. She'd just send word with Willem. Relief at avoiding that confrontation made her sigh out loud.

"Now, now, don't let it worry you. I can send word to your dear friend. Though I know how much she'll miss your presence, she can't want you becoming ill."

Rousing herself enough to sit straighter, Daphne caught her mother's hand before the older woman could rise to call another servant. "No Mother. Don't trouble yourself. I'll send her a note."

Lady Scarborough gave her a shaky smile. "Yes, you're probably right. A personal note would be better. We can't have rumors starting about your health now."

Though neither mentioned Grace, the specter of Daphne's sister hung between them for a moment, bringing tears to their eyes. Daphne vowed to find her sister as soon as she left her father's household, gossip or no. If her husband didn't like it, well, she'd learned deceit enough to manage around his wishes in this if not in something far more scandalous.

Lady Scarborough turned away abruptly, her hand rising to her cheek before she looked back. "Your health is of utmost concern now, dear. I've been working with Lady Pendleton—"

The door opened and one of the kitchen helpers backed in, pulling a cart with a pot of tea and small sandwiches. "Cook sent these right up, my lady," the young girl said. "Said you wanted something sustaining before you went out tonight." She stopped the cart in front of Daphne then glanced up and released her breath on an "Oh."

Lady Scarborough stared at the girl, clearly annoyed.

"Sorry, my lady," the girl muttered. "I'll be back with another cup quick as I can."

"You do that," Daphne's mother said, no sign of grief remaining on her face.

Daphne stood up and poured her mother a cup of tea, hoping to distract from whatever Lady Scarborough had been about to announce. Instinct warned her the news would not be welcome.

Lady Scarborough pushed Daphne's hands away. "You need to rest. I can serve myself well enough." She put a couple of sandwiches onto a plate and handed it to her daughter.

"Thank you." Daphne accepted the food and raised one sandwich to her mouth.

"At least you show better manners now from what I've heard."

Daphne choked on her bite, spraying crumbs down her front as she tried to imagine how her mother could have heard about the indecent proposal much less figured out Daphne's unsettling reactions.

Lady Scarborough shook her head. "I'd think you some urchin off the street from the way you act. Did you think I wouldn't learn with you raising your voice loud enough passing coaches could hear?" She approached Daphne, putting a hard hand on her daughter's shoulder.

"He's taken a lot already from this family. We need him so much more than he needs us." She continued, urgency audible in her tone, "If you spoil this marriage, don't think we'll still have the ability to fund your coming out. That will be the least of our necessities."

Daphne almost blurted that missing her coming out would be a blessing before she processed the rest of Lady Scarborough's words. Contrition filled her as she realized her mother spoke not of Lord Pendleton's proposition but of their meeting in this very room. "I'm sorry, Mother," she said, keeping her tone soft and her eyes down. "It just happened. I didn't mean to be so short."

Lady Scarborough shook her head again. "Really, I don't know what to do with you. I wish I could blame your obvious exhaustion, but to give Lord Pendleton that excuse would raise as many questions as it answers, especially since part of the problem seemed to be your urgency to be elsewhere. Is your friend as important as all that? Don't you know this man will soon be your husband? All others must pale before him."

Daphne flinched from her mother's assessment, struck harder by the harsh truth when it came from someone else's lips. Soon, she'd lose the passion of dance for a loveless marriage, and a sarcastic, unfaithful husband. What a waste to have squandered her few remaining hours because of his behavior. Even worse, she'd given up tomorrow as well. Her dream faded before her eyes, and she lacked the strength to catch hold and keep it with her.

"…unseemly haste but at the same time all the arrangements were already made." Lady Scarborough paused to stare at her intently.

Daphne tried to remember the import of what her mother had said. Only the last few words came back to her, distracted as she had been. "I'm sorry, Mother. I'm so tired…" She hated using the excuse but neither could she reveal how her mother's comment had cut her like a knife.

"You poor dear. You leave the comfort of your bosom friend because you can barely hold your head up and I'm running on, keeping you from your rest. I just want you ready for your engagement ball. It's only one week hence and there's still so much planning to do. I managed to pull in many favors to get you a moment with the Prince Regent in three days, enough to count as a formal introduction. You need only to look pretty and not offend."

Daphne stared at her mother, disbelief battling with horror. "One week? And the audience?" she managed, her words ending much higher than she'd begun. "Why such a rush? Won't it look wrong?"

"As I told you," Lady Scarborough replied, giving her a stern look, "the arrangements were already in place and too many would be inconvenienced by a delay. Both Lady Pendleton and myself feel the best way to get past the damaging gossip is to give people something else to talk about. Though I'd prefer it not be an argument between you and your soon-to-be husband. I would have thought we raised you better than that. See you get your attitude in order by then, or he'll lock you in a tower like some harridan and sell tickets to boys in knickers."

Neither tone nor words left any doubt as to her meaning. Daphne nodded meekly. "Yes, Mother. I promise to behave myself before the Prince Regent and at your party." Inside, she fumed both at having to perform in front of a critical audience like some puppet on a stick and the unseemly haste to wed her. In their efforts to placate the gossips, they stole from her the only thing that gave her life meaning.

The feel of Lord Pendleton's heat rose in her memory, mocking her total focus on the dance but she pushed it aside. He only wanted a frivolous affair with a woman he didn't know.

FOR THE SECOND TIME IN as many days, Jasper shoved to his feet during the first intermission and grabbed his coat. She wasn't going to show…again.

"From what you told me, she left you literally in the dirt, my friend. With a bruised elbow, even. Don't you think it's time to give up this obsession?"

Aubrey's soft voice did little to soothe and the hand on his arm sought to prevent his departure. Jasper shrugged his friend off and kept moving. "You can find me at White's when you're done here," he said, already at the door of their box. "My mind has had enough refining."

He growled in frustration as he heard Aubrey follow him out, increasing his pace in the hopes of losing his friend in the crush. The last thing Jasper needed was a lecture on giving up and letting go. His dancer plagued his every waking thought, the distraction greater now than when he first saw her dance.

If he closed his eyes, her soft form pressed against him while her ringing tones filled his ears. She had a strong bark, but her body had betrayed her. She felt the same draw he did, whether she'd admit to it or not.

Leaping down the last few steps, Jasper bullied his way through the crowd of those stretching their legs and buying refreshment. Frustration filled him as he thought of her. His dancer, unnamed, without even a face to remember her by and yet she lived in him as tenuous as a disease.

He grimaced. Jasper did not need his friend's worried looks or pointed lectures to know he was out of balance. Both hounded him as much as her memory. His eyes sank closed and he stood, one hand on the handle of the outside door, letting the memory of her lips fill his body with longing, his heart with…even in his mind, Jasper shied away from such thoughts. His heart belonged to no one and he did not believe that could ever change.

"Come on, old man. You're blocking the path." Aubrey closed his hand over Jasper's, pushing so the door opened onto the chilly night.

The cold breeze broke through as not even Aubrey's joking tone had. Jasper sighed, following his friend into the street. "You don't have to come," he said, still hoping to reclaim the private time to live in his memories since the present denied him such pleasures. Her injury must have been worse than it appeared and being thrown into the street couldn't have helped it.

"No, I don't have to come, but you're my friend. I can't very well see you wilt away, hiding off in the gentlemen's club simply because you can't see some light skirt you've set your heart on."

Jerking away from his friend, Jasper growled, "She's no light skirt, and my heart has nothing to do with this."

Aubrey laughed. "That you can say such in the same sentence only shows how far gone you are. Come." He clapped Jasper on the shoulder. "Let's take a coach ride down to some of your old haunts. Seeing Lady Mary will take your mind off even imminent disaster."

Jasper let his friend guide him into one of the hire coaches roaming Drury Lane, but called up to the driver to take them to White's before Aubrey could name a less respectable destination. "I don't need the attentions of a false lady when I just freed myself of Melissa and have another just waiting to bind me to her boudoir with marriage vows. I'll need as much time at the tables as I can get before the wedding."

He didn't mention that even as he contemplated his dancer's melodic voice, he remembered too her condemnation of his plans to pack away his new wife after securing the continuance of his line. He'd never thought of himself in such terms, but she'd made him feel the cad. Though he couldn't control the desire that drove him to find his dancer, at least he could make the appearance of respecting his new wife.

"And how go the preparations for that grand day? If she finds you at all, I'd hazard a guess it won't last past the honeymoon. Has she slapped you yet over how your eyes glaze over and your lips part with clear thoughts of another?"

Aubrey's words pulled Jasper from his contemplations with a jerk. Jasper shook his head, thinking of their only meeting. It was the one time he hadn't spared a thought for the dancer in many days. "She has a way about her that pushes all others from your mind," he murmured, not considering how his utterance might be taken.

The coach swayed as Aubrey jerked around to stare at his friend. "Have you changed your mind then? You think this marriage might provide for more than just a stronger title?"

Jasper stared at Aubrey, uncomprehending, until he heard his own words echoing back to him from his memory. He groaned, putting up a hand to stop Aubrey from any further speculations. "Not in the way you suppose, my dear friend. She frustrates and angers until you can't put any thought together besides the need to curl your fingers around her neck."

Aubrey settled back onto his seat, a faint look of disappointment visible on his features in the flickers from the coachman's lantern. "Now that's an idea I don't think you should spread around too much. If ever a footpad captures your bride, Heaven's forbid, you'd be the top of the suspect list. Maybe setting her down in the countryside would be best for all concerned."

"I've been rethinking that plan, actually," Jasper said, keeping his tone casual. "There's no reason we can't both go our own ways. London should be big enough." A glance out the window revealed the familiar buildings lining St James's Street, giving him hope the conversation would end shortly with their arrival at White's.

"You take your words and jumble them into conclusions that make no sense. You really think, with your mother and wife arrayed against you, you'll have a moment to yourself? Talk on this much further and *I'll* be the first to suspect you should harm come to the young girl."

A short laugh seemed all Aubrey's comment deserved, but as the coach rolled to a halt before their door, Jasper added, "Don't worry. With the engagement party coming up so soon, I'm sure to have my fill of her and any female company. Mayhap I'll choose myself a country estate in which to relive my bachelor life and let London have the run of them."

Aubrey laughed in turn as he swung down the short drop, not waiting to lower the steps. "After the engagement party your mother plans, probably all of London will be sick of the female voice."

Chapter Twenty-Two

Daphne groaned as her mother launched into another description of the flowers, having made changes for the fifth time. She stared down at the parlor's Persian carpet, trying to find patience in tracing the pattern with her gaze. Even her moment in the royal presence had offered little relief as it came after hours of primping and was followed by minute examination of every breath she took despite the whole event passing between one inhale and the next.

"Daphne," Lady Scarborough exclaimed, "this is all for you. You'd do well to take an interest in it."

Suddenly overwhelmed by several days filled with planning for a party she didn't want to attend and keeping her from the one thing she wanted to do, Daphne couldn't hold back a bitter laugh. "If I did, would you listen? You've got florists pulling their hair out and Cook threatens to quit with every change you call down. This isn't for me. It isn't even for the man you've sold me to. The party is for you and his mother, a blind attempt to quash whispers as if the world cares one whit about what my sister may or may not have done."

Lady Scarborough stared at Daphne, her face white with shock.

Daphne felt a twinge of guilt, but wouldn't withdraw her comment. She'd said nothing but the truth. The public's fickle nature preyed on her. Monsieur Henre had agreed to the time away, not that he'd had any choice especially with her injury, but maybe now she thought he'd seemed a little too eager. Did he plan to wean them of her then tell Daphne not to bother returning?

"You think we sold you?"

Her mother's tired question pulled Daphne out of her thoughts. Lady Scarborough's face showed lines her mother rarely allowed to crease her perfect skin.

"You have so little understanding of the world out there, my girl. If we didn't make sure you had a good match, you'd be thrown to the wolves with every title hunter ready to claim the prize. Do you think you could find a good match on your own? Do you think your sister will not sour on love when her hands are rubbed raw and smell of lye? I'd do anything to protect you from that life, even if it means casting aside Grace and pasting a smile on my features while the world laughs behind my back. Life is sacrifice, sacrifice for your family, for your husband, for your child. You make do with the choices offered and you work to better them. That's what a proper person does in this life."

Daphne stared at her mother, the shock she'd given delivered back four-fold. Though she could contest her mother's belief about her knowledge, she could not contest the devotion and care her mother showed no matter how misguided. Would she be happy, Daphne asked herself, living on what little pay Monsieur Henre scrounged for his dancers? She'd never really had to think that aspect through but knew she'd never manage the life shown by the dancer in her book.

She stood up and crossed to her mother's side, kneeling on the carpet with a contrite expression on her face. "I'm sorry, Mother. I know I'm not Grace. I know I have little patience for these things, but I do understand what you're doing and why. It's just hard sometimes when I gave everything up for this, something none of us intended for me or prepared me for." Only she knew the true meaning of her words, but Daphne felt them sincerely.

Lady Scarborough's face relaxed back into its normal, unlined state as she pressed a hand to the top of Daphne's head. "I know, my dear. We kept you in the schoolroom long past when we should, filling your head with nonsense like that dancing foolery instead of preparing you for the life all good young women desire. It has made this road a hard one for you to walk. I'm only grateful you found such a true friend in Penelope. Life is made bearable by those you share the journey with."

Daphne forced a smile on her features, but inside the knife of guilt dug deep.

"And I suppose I should have expected some sort of outburst," Lady Scarborough continued. "After sharing every moment together, you've not had the opportunity to see your friend for days. There's no need to distress yourself and end up tense and unhappy for your engagement. Why don't you go over to Penelope's tonight? Take a rest from all the planning and come back rejuvenated."

Staring at her mother, Daphne struggled to keep the frown from her face. In offering her greatest desire, Lady Scarborough had only twisted the knife of guilt in Daphne's breast. "Thank you, Mother," she whispered breathily. "It will be good to have a rest."

Lady Scarborough smiled indulgently. "Well? Why waste a moment? You can tell her all about the grand ball we're planning. A masquerade. You can thank Lady Pendleton for the idea. This late in the season, we'd be lucky to gather any of the ton to our door, but with a masquerade, who can resist?"

Nodding to her mother as she pushed to her feet, Daphne suppressed her true reaction. A masquerade. Somehow, it didn't hold as much pleasure as it once had. Now, her whole life had turned into a masquerade, and she only hoped it wouldn't become a morality play before she exchanged one existence for another.

Monsieur Henre's eyebrows rose when she slipped into his office much earlier than she'd ever come before, but then his mouth quirked into a smile. "Somehow I wasn't expecting you for this evening's performance," he said, waving her into the chair on the other side of his desk.

Daphne lowered herself onto the cushioned surface and raised a hand to check that her mask was in place for the hundredth time since putting it on. "Is that a problem?" She'd meant her voice to sound arrogant, but even she could hear the touch of desperation in her tone.

He shook his head, still smiling. "No, not at all. I'll have to re-arrange the schedule a bit, tell Cynthia to take a rest, but you're still the dandy of our audience. They've missed you, some more than others."

His words swallowed her up and threw her into the memory of her future husband pressed against her, whispering promises of jewels and clothing not to her, but to a body he'd only seen at a distance. Somehow, she had difficulty equating the passionate beau with the boorish snob who'd intruded on her home only hours before.

"Mistress Daphne? Are you sure you're ready to go on tonight?"

She jerked her gaze to Monsieur Henre, a flush heating her cheeks. "Yes. Yes, I'm sure. You said Cynthia had been taking my spot?" She'd started the last only to prove that she'd been listening, but all it showed was that she hadn't been, considering how long had passed since he mentioned the fact. Daphne shivered, wondering how the other dancer would take being pushed aside.

"Well enough then. You should go get ready. There's only a little time before the curtain rises."

Relieved to have gotten through the conversation without con-demnation or a lecture on commitment, Daphne rose and left, pausing at the doorway to wave goodbye.

She took a longer route through the behind stage areas, savoring the sound of instruments tuning and the scramble of those responsi-ble for the scenery she never noticed once the dance began. How many times more would she have a place back here? How long could she keep her parents in the dark and would she ever be able to escape the clutches of her new husband?

Breathing in the scent of sawdust and stage floor oils, tears pricked at her eyes. This could be her last dance, or close to it. Daphne frowned, determined to make the most of this chance. Just as her mother had said, they were given only so many choices and must work hard to succeed at them.

The dressing room, when she finally reached it, was already a bustle of activity. She moved toward the table she'd come to think of as hers then stopped. It had unfamiliar rouge pots and headdresses strewn all over it.

Daphne crossed the rest of the way, suddenly aware of the silence that had fallen as the dancers noticed her presence.

"You shouldn't touch those," one of the younger girls called out. "That's Cynthia's things."

Glancing around the room for Cynthia, Daphne tensed, waiting for the outpouring of venom she normally experienced when talking to the other dancer.

"She's talking with the master," another dancer chimed in. "Just sent for her."

Relief washed over Daphne as she realized her trip to capture memories had saved her from a vicious encounter in the hall. Still, the other dancer would return shortly and doubtless in a mood.

Her costumes had kept their place, though they'd been all piled together, and Daphne quickly changed into her favorite one. If she had to get all the enjoyment she could from this and a few other dances, she'd make it happen.

The noise returned slowly, helped by her lack of reaction to the status change. Daphne didn't really care about her standing; she only wanted the chance to perform. Somehow, others like Cynthia either never had or had lost that pure focus. A twist of pity made its way through Daphne, surprising her.

The other dancer had done nothing but cause trouble and yet, they shared something in common. Both had seen their dreams shattered, torn from between their grasping hands by fates beyond their control.

Daphne's mouth curled up into a mocking smile. At least the other girl was on the road to attaining her dreams now. Daphne had no such rosy ending before her. She'd gain nothing and lose everything tied to a man who despised her true self while entertaining randy thoughts about her masquerade persona.

She shuddered, suddenly wondering what would have happened if he'd succeeded in removing her mask. What would he do if he managed to expose her before the wedding? Would he destroy her family in retribution? And what if he discovered her after the wedding? How would he react then?

So caught up in her own fearful thoughts, Daphne didn't notice the silence that had taken over the room once again until a single dancer loudly cleared her throat.

Daphne tensed, unprepared in the aftermath of her worries to face Cynthia. She longed to stay behind the changing screen, but knew her delay would only make the retribution worse.

Squaring her shoulders, she pasted a gentle smile on her face and rounded the curtain as if she'd just finished changing, rather than lingering in the meager shelter, tortured by her thoughts.

Cynthia met Daphne's gaze with a smile of her own, startling Daphne and causing restless motions among the other dancers. Her smile growing, Cynthia turned and swept the room with her pointed stare. "I've just come from the master. As you probably guessed, he wanted to inform me that *she* would be dancing tonight."

Daphne saw her own tension mirrored in the faces of the others and wondered for a quick moment if Cynthia could be dangerous.

The other dancer winked, as if aware of Daphne's reaction, before continuing, "Though I'd prefer not to muddy the waters, the audience can build up a craving when denied. After this one does her *guest* appearance tonight, the center stage will be mine."

Daphne's fear melted into stunned horror. Though she'd known this could be her last, she never expected Monsieur Henre to cut the ties. Somehow, she'd thought she had some say in her performances, that her wishes had the weight of command. This, more than any other instruction, showed Monsieur Henre had left the position of teacher behind long ago.

Even as pain twisted her gut, a ringing started in her ears and Daphne grabbed for the nearest table, thinking she was going to faint.

Cynthia's smirk filled her whole vision as the other dancer moved close enough to push her shoulder. "Now run along, girl. You wouldn't want to miss your very last curtain."

Daphne stared at her without comprehension for a long while before she equated the bell sound with the call. Grimly, she grabbed her headdress, attached it with hard thrusts of the pins, and half-ran all the way to the stage. If this was to be her last dance, she'd make the most of it.

"LOOKS LIKE YOUR PERSISTENCE IS finally paying off," Aubrey said, slapping a hand on Jasper's shoulder to draw his attention to the stage. "They don't usually bring out the flutes for the new girl."

Jasper hesitated, wanting to look but fearing disappointment yet again. The whisper of her touch warmed his lips just as the musicians began a style of music so different from the tumbler who had replaced his dancer. Unable to resist the slow, erotic beat, he raised his head just as the curtain lifted and spread to expose a bare stage with only some props setting the mood in the back.

His heartbeat sped up, recognizing the slim body kneeling on the floor even before she raised her arms above her head and rose as if pulled upright from above. Her grace struck him as it always had. She'd be his no matter what her foolish protestations. He didn't care much for dissembling, and her reactions showed she desired him, but if any other infatuation, he would have moved on long ago. She flowed in his very blood, infected his every thought. He could no more walk away than separate his right arm from his body.

For once, her dance failed to absorb him though he watched every move. It left his mind free to plan his next step, to manipulate and twist the circumstances until she had no choice but to turn to him. Part of Jasper found his machinations disturbing, but the rest could not be swayed from the goal, willing to risk anything, to do anything, just to hold her in his arms once again.

The rustle of paper from a neighboring box brought Jasper back from his thoughts. The unexpected sound was overly loud in the silence that had always greeted her motions. It appeared others found her dance less compelling on this night as well.

With an odd reluctance, he forced his attention back to the stage. Any lust in his thoughts or loins curdled in the face of her frantic energy.

Instead of inspiring desire, her motions brought to mind the struggles of a pigeon clasped firmly in the claws of a hawk. What drove her so? What took from her the soul that normally filled her dance?

Though he kept his gaze pinned on the dancer, all enjoyment had fled, leaving behind a concern so deep that it soured his stomach. He couldn't quite restrain the thought that he might have caused some of her frenzy. He'd learned well enough this night what lengths he'd go to pressure her to become his mistress. He'd even planned to use his sponsorship against her. Had he caused this change? Had he torn her from the wild? Did she now batter herself against cage bars of his making?

The curtain fell down and Jasper pushed to his feet, needing to escape from his demons.

"What are you doing?" Aubrey asked, amazement in his voice.

He didn't know what he muttered in reply, so caught up in the urgent desire to leave that he would have said anything. Perhaps his friend thought him off to make another attempt to catch the dancer, but Jasper finally felt the truth of Aubrey's warnings. His dancer, still unknown and with her face barred to him, had laid claim to that small bit of property he'd thought unclaimable. His heart burned with the thought that his affections had harmed her in any way.

Both his heart and honor demanded he offer her something in apology, something more than the affair she'd thrown in his face, but he had no intention of following the steps of his first fiancée. Maybe the best he could do would be to stay out of her life, give her the chance to find another who was free to give his affections. Jasper grimaced at the thought, jealousy knotting his stomach.

He glanced around, surprised to find himself already outside of the performance hall. With a forceful wave of his hand, he called a coach over, unsure where he wanted to go or what could relieve his tangled feelings.

"Take me to where an honest man can drown his sorrows," he told the coachman. "Double your normal fare if you'll vouch for me."

"Aye, gov'ner, I'll set you right up."

The driver snapped the reins in the air above his horse and the coach started forward with a lurch. Jasper stared out the window, watching her performance hall dwindle in the distance, knowing he'd never return. If he couldn't have her, he'd deny himself the torturous pleasure of watching her dance as well. He had to learn both to accept and live his new life, no matter how he found his wife. He could not suffer the torment of seeing his dancer's movements transformed by another when she found love and fulfillment at last.

Chapter Twenty-Three

A bitter night of tossing and turning between bouts of tears made Daphne none so happy to greet the late morning sun now pouring in her windows. She groaned, cursing the helpful maid who had drawn the drapes. She dragged the coverlet over her head and tried to fall back asleep.

The distant chime of the longcase clock in the hall marked stroke after stroke, revealing the day well into the eleventh hour. Daphne groaned again and pushed her covers down, blinking in the sunlight. If she didn't rise soon, she'd hear no end of concerned statements. She barely found the strength to care.

If her mother chose to keep her back for her own health, what did it matter? She had no place to go.

Despair swept over her again, and she clutched the dancer's story to her chest, wondering if the other woman's sordid life was any worse than her own though she knew it to have been. To come so far and lose it all. To know Cynthia would stand in her place night after night. It burned Daphne, but what choice did she have?

Tears welled up in her eyes once again, but she forced them back, tucking the book away under her mattress. She rose and crossed to her mirror, hoping her fitful night didn't show on her face.

The expression that greeted her held little joy, but at least her eyes weren't red and puffy. She dampened her washcloth and pressed cold water against her cheeks and eyes, determined to meet her fate head on. She'd had her moment of joy on the stage. That time had passed. She had the rest of her life to find comfort and satisfaction, if not in her husband, then in her children.

A wisp of memory teased her, the heat of his body pressed against hers, his lips shedding their warmth onto her own. A delicious shiver shook her body and brought a curious spark to the eyes looking back at her from the reflection. The smile that curved her lips held a womanly knowing she lacked.

Maybe, she thought, maybe it wouldn't be so horrible.

Buoyed by this hope, and a return to her natural exuberance, Daphne rang the bell for a maid to help her dress. She'd make her mother happy and wear one of the more elaborate dresses and a normal corset, maybe even let the maid dress her hair in a fancy hairstyle as they always seemed to want to.

The sound of panting gave her warning even before the door opened after a short knock.

"My lady, you're finally awake. Your lady mother has arranged something special for you and was worried you'd be too late."

"Could you help with my dress and hair then, Betsy?"

Even before she spoke, the maid crossed the room and flipped through Daphne's gowns, finally pulling out one of the newer ones. "This will look right fine," she said with a grin. "And I'll get your hair set up too."

Daphne let the maid direct her through the motions, feeling like some kind of a manikin rather than a living, breathing person. Her heart thumped slow and heavy as she pondered what her mother would consider an appropriate surprise. None of the things her mind could offer provided any interest. How could her mother succeed when the woman knew nothing about her youngest daughter?

Again, depression threatened to overtake her, but Daphne would have none of that. She refused to spend the rest of her life moping. Maybe, in what little time she had left, she would try to cultivate Penelope's friendship in truth. If nothing else, they now had much more in common than before, both destined to become nothing more than vassals chained to husbands who had more desire for their mistresses than interest in the wives they'd left at home.

"There you go now, my lady. Don't you look a pretty penny," Betsy said, patting Daphne's hair one last time.

Jolted out of her thoughts, Daphne glanced at the mirror and paused, hardly recognizing the cultured woman portrayed there. Was this whom she would become? Would she lose all sense of herself in this marriage? She forced a smile onto her lips and turned away, trying to banish the image from her mind. "It looks lovely," she managed.

Betsy did not seem to find anything wrong in her tone, only shooing Daphne toward the door with both hands. "Lady Scarborough's waiting on you," she said. "Best you run along now."

Daphne felt transported back into her childhood, the echo of Nurse's voice in the maid's words. She longed for those times of freedom, riding horses across the fields and running with the stable hands when those responsible for her were distracted, usually by the perfect angel Grace had always been.

At the thought of her sister, Daphne sobered. If for no one else, she'd have to make the best of her future for her sister. Grace should never feel her choice had destroyed the family Daphne knew her sister still loved, though barred from it forever. "For you, Grace," Daphne whispered, heading down the stairs.

"Oh Lady Scarborough, when I received your invitation, I was beside myself in joy."

Daphne froze, her hand on the last banister, at the sound of a familiar voice. "Penelope?" The whispered question held a note of desperation even as she heard her mother's response.

"It's little enough we could do when she's spent practically every waking moment with you. I feel we should know you better anyway as our daughter's dearest friend. Come into the parlor. I'm sure Daphne will be right down."

Daphne raced down the stairs, forgetting any wish to appease her mother in the desperate need to stop the words sure to come out of Penelope's mouth next.

The girl she'd hoped to make a friend of glanced up in time to see Daphne scrambling down the last few steps, but not quick enough for Daphne's frantic hand signals to stop her words. "Oh, but I haven't seen Daphne since that first time. I was worried I, or my sister's friends, had offended her in some way until I got your invitation."

The last few words came out strangled as Penelope finally understood Daphne's message, too late to prevent the icy stare Lady Scarborough shot at her daughter. Daphne had to give her mother this though. The Lady Scarborough buried any sign of upset and grandly swept Penelope before her to where a fancy tea had been set up in the parlor.

Daphne went after, her stomach tied in such knots that she doubted she would ever eat again despite having missed breakfast all together.

THE VISIT ENDED WITH PENELOPE thrilled that she hadn't fallen out of favor and offering gushing invitations for Daphne to come over the next day. Under her mother's stern glare, Daphne agreed, hating the pressure even though it matched her own plans to make true friends with Penelope.

The main door had barely closed behind Penelope's back before Daphne felt her mother's hand clamp onto her shoulder.

"And you, young lady, will sit in your room and contemplate your behavior until your father gets back from the House of Lords. Isn't it enough that we've lost one daughter? Must you court disaster with lies and deceit as well?" Lady Scarborough shook her head when Daphne tried to answer, pivoting her daughter and pointing at the stairs.

Shoulders slumped, Daphne made her way back up the stairs to her room where she collapsed on her bed. She'd thought nothing worse than losing her dream and yet now she still felt the loss but would feel the brunt of her father's punishment as well. She pulled out the book and caressed its cover, a tear falling to make a dark spot on the worn leather.

She almost opened the book to read the words once again, but felt they'd offer no comfort. Instead, she clutched it to her breast and sat, cross-legged, her thoughts dwelling on what she'd done, determined, no matter what the cost, she'd know it had been worth what came after.

Some hours later, faint with hunger and wound tighter than the mantle clock in the front parlor, Daphne jumped half off her bed when a knock sounded at her door.

"My lady?" Betsy called in a faint voice. "Lady Daphne, your father is home."

Feeling much in common with a man walking to the gallows, Daphne hid her book and walked down the stairs again, neither delight nor panic propelling her steps. Despair had given away to a shocked numbness that seemed to absorb her whole being.

She mumbled a greeting as she entered the parlor and sat down in the nearest chair, wondering that her mother would choose such a pleasant place for her trial. The basement, since their house had no dungeon, seemed more appropriate.

"Daphne, what's this I hear about your doings? Don't you make the same mistakes your sister did." Her father's stern tone left little room for argument and sent a shiver down her back.

Then, her mother made a soft "oh" sound, pulling her father's attention away from her. "You haven't been meeting with your sister, have you?" Lady Scarborough asked, pain audible in her voice.

For a tiny moment, Daphne wanted to agree, to both use the excuse offered and soothe the wound her mother hid behind a regal demeanor. Then she sighed, knowing the lies had to stop. As much as she wished she had been seeing her sister or doing anything so noble, she'd known all along that the time would come for her to reveal her activities.

"No, Mother, I have not," she said instead, her tone firm. "I have been dancing."

Daphne glanced at her father then wished she hadn't when his brows drew together into as angry an expression she'd ever seen him wear.

"And what have you been using to pay that sniveling dance instructor. Have you given him baubles in turn for putting false dreams in your head? Does he even now believe your proper place is showing off your underclothes to randy men?"

Her mother gasped as he spoke of unmentionables, but Daphne ignored indignation in favor of anger. She rose out of her seat, meeting her father's glare with no thought to her own preservation. "I don't have to pay him anything. My dreams are no more false than your place in the House of Lords. I've been dancing at a professional dance theater for weeks now. Lords and ladies come to see me perform." She glowered at him. "And it isn't for the chance to see my under things either."

Lady Scarborough gasped again, sinking back onto the settee, one hand pressed to her throat.

"You did what?" Lord Scarborough shouted, his face purpled by anger with the veins standing out against his forehead.

He made such a frightful sight that Daphne shrank in fear, suddenly wishing she could pull back her words.

Her father stalked toward her, his measured steps more threatening than a furious run.

Daphne backed up once and then again until she pressed against the wall to one side of her chair. "I'm sorry, Father," she whispered, her words almost a whimper.

"Not sorry enough," he ground out between his teeth, grabbing hold of her upper arm in a tight grip. "You chanced the position of this family with your shenanigans. You think your sister's behavior somehow outweighs yours? That you no longer have to behave like a proper young lady?"

He shook her hard and Daphne's teeth slammed together. She trembled, but said nothing, hoping only for this wave of anger to pass. She'd known he wouldn't be happy, but this unrelenting anger terrified her.

"That's where you're wrong," he said, glaring down at Daphne. "More wrong than you'll ever know. If we hope to weather this storm, you have to behave better even than the angels in Heaven. There is no other choice if we are to be a family in truth and not hide away on one of our lesser properties until generations pass and memories finally grow faint."

He tossed her down into the chair, stalking away to pace the length of the parlor. His hands clenched into fists then relaxed only to clench again. He muttered under his breath, the fervent words too slurred to make any sense of them.

Daphne stayed where he'd put her, shrinking into the chair as best as she could in the hopes of escaping notice. A quick glance showed her mother doing the same even though Lady Scarborough had nothing to be blamed for.

"It's that dance instructor," he finally said out loud, shaking his fist toward the sky. "I should never have let him in the house for all that he came well recommended."

Daphne sat up straight and opened her mouth to defend her former instructor, only remembering at the last second that she'd make the situation worse not better.

"The guard will take care of him. Treat him as he deserves for leading young, impressionable noble women astray. I wonder how many others he has convinced to disobey their fathers and chance their family reputations. I'd guess a long string of broken lives stretches out behind him, hushed up to preserve a modicum of dignity."

"It's not like that at all," Daphne said, clenching her fingers against the upholstery. "He didn't want me to come." Though her voice shook, she wouldn't let her father blame Monsieur Henre for her own choice, not if he planned to act on that belief.

Lord Scarborough stopped in front of her, staring down with heated eyes. "And yet, he let you stay. He let you perform, did he not? A gentleman would have sent for me; a gentleman would have kept you safe then left me to school you in proper behavior. A proper gentleman does not let noble women parade bare in public."

Again, the blood pounded in his face, and Daphne swallowed heavily, her muscles tensed against a blow that never came. Instead, he turned and slammed his fist against the wall hard enough to send the lamp shuddering until she feared it would tip over and start a fire.

Lord Scarborough knelt at her side, the color now drained from his face entirely. He reached for one of her hands. She let it sit limp between his. "How could you do this, Daphne? Have you no sense at all? How many of our friends and neighbors are laughing now? How many wonder at the upbringing we must have given you? And how long do you think it will take for the Pendletons to hear about this and cancel the ill-fated joining of our two families?"

He slumped, his shoulders curving forward in a despair that rested awkwardly on his solid frame. Daphne had never seen her father look so defeated, not even when Grace had run away. She scrambled for something to say, something to make things better, and finally an answer came to her.

"Father, I danced masked," she declared, the joy in her voice hanging oddly in the still room.

Lord Scarborough raised his head to stare at her uncomprehending. "And how is this to make any difference?" he asked.

Before she could respond, Lady Scarborough sat up with all signs of a returning energy. "And no one knew?" she said.

Daphne nodded fervently. "Only Monsieur Henre," she responded, pushing aside thoughts of her close encounter with the one man who could have destroyed everything. "I was a bit of a mystery, but no one thought to pierce it."

"The masked dancer?" Lord Scarborough said, his voice stunned. "I've been to see her…see you…myself." He shuddered then brightened. "If I couldn't recognize my own daughter, we may yet be safe."

Daphne waited for some word of praise, some acknowledgement of her skill, but none came. Instead, her father pushed up, his stance once again commanding, and reached for the rope to call a servant.

"Wait, Father," she cried.

"Why," he asked, his lip curling back into a sneer. "You think to protect the man who thought so little of your virtue to use you so?"

Daphne shook her head mutely, catching his arm and pulling it down. "Just think for a moment. Right now, only Monsieur Henre knows who the masked dancer was. If you call the guard, you must charge him. Even if you lay false testimony against him, what cause would he have to hold his tongue?"

Lord Scarborough frowned, but he did not reach for the cord again. "If you have the brains to figure this out, daughter, pray tell me what led you to go to him in the first place?"

She kept her tone respectful, sharing the truth even though she knew her offering would be rejected. "I love to dance, Father. It's the only thing in the whole world that makes me happy and alive."

He snorted, pulling free of her grasp to cross the room and sink into a chair. Glancing over at his wife, he asked, "Where did we go wrong? What did we do to have this grievance weighed down on us?"

Lady Scarborough shrugged her shoulders in a delicate motion that drew attention to her ample breast and graceful neck. "We let them live as people. I cannot regret it entirely even as I have to live with the consequences." She turned to look at Daphne, sorrow clear on her face. "Most young girls know nothing but what fashions to wear and how to catch themselves a handsome beau. You think I didn't know how Grace chose to spend her afternoons? Helping the poor in those ways is not something for one of our class to do any more than dancing is, but it gave her a purpose and value. Little did I know she'd take to that life so strongly, or choose to stay with the man who worked at her side. But you, you had to choose something scandalous on more levels than my favorite tiara has gems. Promise me you'll never go back. Promise me you've learned from what you almost cost this family."

Daphne smiled, for once seeing some good in Monsieur Henre's decision. "I danced my last this night previous. I swear I'll not do anything to chance the Pendletons' regard. I swear."

Her father growled at the mention of her dancing, then subsided as he heard the rest. "You better keep to that promise or your last sight of freedom will be your teacher swinging from the gallows," he charged, his voice thick with unresolved anger. He didn't wait for a response, marching from the room and off to his library.

Daphne heard his gruff voice call out a command to one of the servants and she flinched, terrified by what had occurred, and what had almost happened.

Lady Scarborough came up and rested a hand on Daphne's shoulder. "Don't worry. Even when his anger burns so hot, it cools quickly. You came close to costing us everything. Count your blessings and say no more about this to anyone."

She waited for Daphne to nod before continuing.

"For now, I think it best if you stay in your room. You're promised to Penelope for tomorrow afternoon, but until then, I'll have your meals sent up. It'll do you good to spend some time on your knees giving thanks that you were never seen or recognized. And while you're there, renew your vows to the highest power. Then, maybe, you can be trusted to keep them."

Daphne flinched at the sudden hardening of her mother's voice, giving a meek "Yes, Mother," before slipping upstairs to the room that had become her prison, a welcome one. Here, she had only her conscience and memories of her parents' stricken faces to condemn her.

Chapter Twenty-Four

C ome, Aubrey. You look dashing as a highwayman. The ladies will be swooning at the sight of you. We've only to pick from among them and toss the lucky girl over your shoulder. We could have a double wedding, crossing the line into maturity and married life together as we once crossed the finish line neck and neck to become fast friends." Though he'd meant the words to be humorous, Jasper could help neither the bitter twist nor the almost longing that found its way into his tone.

Aubrey only shook his head, a serious cast to his face. "Neither beauty of face nor figure will capture my heart, good friend. I aim to hold out for that one special woman created solely to be my mate no matter how unfashionable that might make me."

Jasper tried to laugh, this time seeking out the mockery he would have found easily only weeks before. Now though, with his new understanding and the still raw wounds cut across his heart, he could little debate the dreams of his friend.

Instead, he sighed, clapping his hand on Aubrey's shoulder. "I truly wish you the luck of it, my friend. May you not only find your heart's desire, but find it packaged in one of blood and breeding to meet your mother's standards and your father's aims. And all this before your parents make the choice in your stead."

His face twisted into the semblance of a smile as he snatched up the billowing coat made to match his costume. Its ruffles barely covered his dignity while silk tights hugged his legs. What cloth should have made up his pants, instead dangled loosely from the shoulders, his arms freed to move by a slit cut from shoulder to well past where his wrist would have fallen.

Aubrey's smile had much more of his good nature in it. "You cut a rather dashing figure yourself. One can tell you keep yourself fit and the sleeves accentuate your broad shoulders."

Though he knew his friend tried only to help, Jasper shook his head. "My figure has little importance in this event. The only thing that frigid society girl I'm bound to is interested in is my wealth, and hardly even that from her reluctance."

"There's freedom in a masquerade found in no other place. You may find she learns to like you for more than the coins in her pocket if given half the chance. From your description, I think neither of you came off the best in that meeting. Would you ever judge a man on just one encounter?"

Jasper laughed, this time finding his bitterness again. "Sometimes one encounter is all it takes. Nor does it matter anymore. I'll do right by her and give her what she wants of me, both a flush allowance and children to swell her waist. She'll have nothing to mourn in this joining."

He turned away, heading out the door and to the carriage that waited beyond it. "We should be off now. I think the first satisfaction I should give my lady bride is to show up promptly to the event that announces our wedded bliss."

Aubrey caught up, matching his strides easily. "It doesn't have to be thus, Jasper. Given a little effort, your prison could become a blissful bower. Don't sell yourself short."

Swinging into the carriage with enough force to make the frame shudder, Jasper laughed again. His voice softened though when he tried to explain, "You were more right than you knew so long ago. I'd given my heart and wouldn't admit the gifting. I have none left to give and can't have the one I desire. I gave the dance hall owner a pretty penny to keep her safe, but it will never be enough. An affair with one such as me would only ruin her for a good life among her own. Me, I have my mate chosen and declared. I have only to accept the offering and make the best of it."

Aubrey said nothing more, only placed his hand on Jasper's shoulder and gave it a tight squeeze. The rest of the journey passed in silence, Jasper contemplating his barren future and Aubrey's thoughts on whatever a single gentleman might ponder.

Daphne took a deep breath, the smell of hothouse flowers almost overwhelming from her spot on the stair. Below, she could hear the murmur of first guests, and the occasional sharp commands from the staff involved in the final preparations. Her mother had excitedly announced the ball to be a crush based on the number of acceptances. Rumors had even gone around that the Prince Regent would grace their halls.

As much as she hoped to be able to lose herself in the press, Daphne wondered how they'd manage so many people. Both ballrooms were opened, as were the two parlors, the dining room and the music room. Even Father's library had been turned upside down, his desk pushed to one side in favor of tables for cards. Daphne felt as if her home had been transformed until she didn't even recognize it.

Some of her fear eased for a moment as a smile quirked up one side of her face, the beaded mask scratching against her cheek where it swept down in butterfly wings to almost her ears. She'd also been transformed, her costume that of a 15th-century noblewoman. The weighted skirt fell in pleats to the floor. A thick fur hem brushed the tops of her feet and trailed behind her not long enough to be considered a train but long enough to hint at a bridal gown, or so the seamstress stated many times.

Suddenly confident even Willem would not be able to recognize her, Daphne made her way down the staircase, stepping off just as the butler let in a new flood of guests. She joined them, making no attempt to reveal herself. Despite the tense occasion, she found herself enjoying the anonymity and her ability to listen to gossip without seeming an annoyance.

She drifted from group to group, lingering when words turned to dance in the hopes of hearing a true assessment of her skills, but if the guests had been to see her, they chose not to mention her by description or place. Disappointed, she reminded herself that life was now behind her.

A sharper reminder came when one of a group she passed leaned close and whispered in a carrying voice, "…the youngest only after the eldest ran away with a pauper. Can you imagine?"

Another hushed the speaker, but Daphne could not hide the flush that heated her cheeks or the heaving of her breast. It was one thing to know others spoke poorly of her sister and family, but quite another to hear the words herself.

Needing a refuge, she sought to escape by heading for one of the small, curtained enclosures to be found in the main ballroom. Though determined, her pace was slowed by the sheer mass of people and the need to be polite when asked a question. It seemed almost as if she'd never reach sanctuary.

Jasper accepted a drink from the masked servant, turning to look for Aubrey. He had little interest in communing with his fellow masqueraders. The game would have been to find his fiancée, but what then would he have done with her? He couldn't imagine anything less pleasant than spending the next few hours exchanging words with the woman he would spend the rest of his life with. Just the thought sent a wave of depression crashing over him.

Along with despair, images of the dancer he'd once held in his arms, confident in his ability to make her his, rose from his memory. He knew well enough who he should be spending his lifetime with, and yet the demands of wealth and name denied him such a simple happiness.

Suddenly, what little patience he'd managed to muster vanished. He pushed his way through the crowd, seeking out his host or hostess to demand they announce the engagement. Only then could he leave this place and find another seaside pub to drown his sorrows in tankard after tankard of vile ale.

His efforts came to an abrupt halt as he ran into a woman also working her way through the crowd. He opened his mouth to offer an apology, but no words issued forth. Her warmth pressed against him and those eyes looking up at him were hauntingly familiar even with the black satin replaced by beaded wings. "You," he whispered, seeing the impact of his words as her eyes widened and a rapid pulse showed at the base of her neck.

He took hold of her arm, forgetting his vow to let her escape him. The fates offered her to him in this place and time. They'd even matched their costumes in both color and period. He needed no bigger sign from on high of his destiny no matter what consequences this brought.

She seemed to feel much different as she jerked free, ducking between two broad-shouldered men whose thick waists made his own passage difficult. He craned his neck to follow her path and still almost missed when she ducked inside one of the curtained alcoves to hide.

He smiled, expecting the flurry of movement as she disrupted a lovers' cinch, but none came. Perhaps the party had not grown long enough, or the drinks plentiful enough, for the true value of a masquerade to make itself known. His smile twisted on one side as he recognized his mother's hand in this planning. She'd hoped to engage his interest by adding the intensity of a hunt. Little did she know he'd already engaged in, and lost, the game of love.

That his own love could find herself among this grand company garbed to match him seemed a gift from the Heavens until he thought through how she would come to be here. After all he'd given up for her, she'd offered her gifts to some other man, sharing that which he'd tried so hard to protect?

Anger welled up, washing away both his curiosity and the delight he'd felt with his discovery. Paying little heed to proper behavior, he shouldered his way through the crowd, leaving behind a path ringing with sharp exclamations in his effort to reach the alcove. He kept his gaze pinned on the gently swaying curtain, determined to trap her within and have this out once and for all.

DAPHNE PRESSED A HAND TO her chest, trying to still the pants that made her breasts rise and fall with their force. She had nothing more to hide and yet still she ran.

Even as she told herself that, she knew she lied. He'd known her. Somehow, even in a different dress, in a different mask, he'd known her. Just as she'd known him from the feel of his heat against her, from the sound of his voice whispered, from all that made him the man she could not forget though she'd tried to put him out of her mind in the days before this ball.

An exasperated sigh forced its way past her lips, carrying with it all the desires and wishes she could not articulate or even understand. What if she hadn't run? What if she'd stood her ground? What would he have done then?

As if to answer her question, the curtain sheltering her parted. Daphne glanced up, planning to persuade whoever approached that her need for peace and quiet was greater than theirs. Instead, her gaze fell on the one man she'd tried so hard to avoid.

She scrambled up, poised to run again, when he fell to his knees before her, burying his face in the pleats of her skirt and grasping the thick cloth with both hands.

"I've tried everything. I no longer go to see you dance; I have left your fate to God and he offers you up to me. I cannot deny myself any longer."

This speech, delivered muffled through the fabric, froze Daphne in place, a flush heating her neck and face at the embarrassment waiting for both of them.

He looked up, spearing her gaze with his own, giving her no opportunity to dissemble or look away. Rising to his feet, he clasped both her hands between his own, pressing their combined hold against his heart. "I love you, my dancer. I know not your name, or even your face, but your spirit calls to me like a siren on jagged rocks. I've tried to commit to this life I'm meant to live, to accept my fiancée though she means nothing. Still, you haunt me. I'm less of a man without you by my side."

The heat that surged even stronger through Daphne must have been rooted in embarrassment. Surely she could not feel a kindred spirit to the man who chose her own engagement party as the time and place to declare himself to one he must consider little more than a harlot.

Try as she might, she could not bring up indignation to counter the emotions broiling up in her chest.

Her fingers clutched the stiff brocade of his costume though when he'd freed them, she did not know. He held her tight against him, one side of her back pressing the wall while the cushioned bench met her knee. She couldn't move, couldn't escape, but neither did she want to.

His hands tangled in her hair, destroying a style Betsy had taken hours to concoct. Daphne didn't care, the feel of his warm fingers against her skin reducing her resistance to less than a moan. She wanted him to keep touching her from now until eternity. Then she realized his aim as his fingers snagged the ribbon holding her mask pressed to her face.

She gasped, jerking back in horror as the bow gave way. Before she could grab for the mask, it fell away, revealing her face. Daphne ducked, desperate to hide, to run from this confrontation. Even now, he could do irreparable damage to her father's reputation and her own. What hadn't mattered just a heartbeat ago suddenly rushed forward with her face exposed.

He captured her chin and raised it until the light shone bright across her face. A sharply indrawn breath revealed his reaction even as he stared down at her. "You," he whispered once again, but this time shock and horror had replaced desire.

She blushed, the heat burning against her cheeks with almost painful force. Daphne tried to duck her head, not wanting to see the condemnation and even hatred in his eyes, but he wouldn't let her escape. His grip tightened against her arm until she knew bruises would show his intensity come morning.

Almost against her will, Daphne raised her eyes to meet his as if she had to know his thoughts. What she saw caused her own tension to melt away, heat surging through her to replace it until she felt almost faint. Though she had been unaware of just how close he held her, suddenly, she felt every crease in his coat and every pleat of her skirt as the heavy clothes provided only a moderate barrier between them.

Once again, the present blended with the past as they touched, their reactions an echo of the time on Drury Lane when she still had a mask to protect her name, if not her virtue.

He released her chin, letting his fingers graze her features as if he were a blind man learning the shape of her face. Spirals of delight radiated through her flesh wherever his questing touched her and Daphne shivered, unable to contain her reaction.

A smile pulled at his mouth, revealing a dimple sunk into one cheek. Without thinking, Daphne pressed a finger into the indent, his skin rough against her fingertip.

He turned his head, brushing a kiss against her palm. The motion sent hot fire through her, and Daphne's hand dropped, the muscles gone limp. Having lost their prey, his lips met hers instead, crushing down until their hot, wet heat forced her lips apart and his tongue caressed the entry of her mouth.

Daphne shuddered, her body going limp with pleasure, held up only by the pressure of his body and the wall. Dizziness filled her and the world spun out of control until she thought she'd faint under the contact, but she never did, sensation after sensation flooding her body and pooling in spots she'd barely known her body had. She wanted the touch to go on forever.

Chapter Twenty-Five

A ny anger he might have felt, any betrayal at her unexpected presence and then the truth to her secret, melted as his body touched hers. Though he wanted to reject her, wanted to push her away, he could no more do that than cut out his own heart.

Deepening the kiss, he twisted the fingers of one hand through her elaborately dressed hair, wanting to stake his claim for all to see. By some miracle, the woman promised to his hand and the woman who had stolen his heart were one and the same. The fates might be laughing, but they did not deny him.

"He went this way?" a loud voice said from outside the curtain, breaking through his concentration on Daphne's lips, on the heat of her mouth, the taste of her breath.

Jasper pushed the distraction aside, knowing somehow that he had to capture her as completely as she'd taken over him. This time, there would be no denial, no accusations. When they stood before the massed ton, she would happily put her life, her future, and her heart in his hands.

"Lord Pendleton," a different voice called, sparking a growl of annoyance from him and a moan of regret from her.

He glanced down at the woman before him, drinking in her dark, swollen lips and the once glacial eyes that now swirled with confusion and hunger. He smiled, tracing her bruised lip with one finger, sorry for the discoloration but not for his kiss.

Her eyes slipped closed, and she shivered with pleasure, her body jerking tight against his until he could feel the heat pounding through her. His own emotions caused discomfort even in the relative freedom of his tights and a sudden desire to bury himself inside her coerced a growl from his throat.

The curtain pulled aside, revealing them to a crowd that first showed shock then tittered with delight.

Jasper grimaced, but turned to face them with the lopsided smile that had charmed many a reluctant mother to relinquish her daughter for a dance or stroll down the park. Now he used it to protect the only woman he'd be charming into one more kiss beneath vine-covered paths from this moment on.

He turned back to look at her, a startled laugh bursting free at her expression. Had he not been behind the curtain, he'd have thought her thoroughly loved rather than just introduced to the delights of passion.

Jasper's pleasure faded as he realized only his form masked her face from the crowd of interested onlookers. He shifted to block their full view, absorbing the moan of disappointment, and tucked some loose strands of hair behind her ear in a feeble attempt to restore order to what he'd deliberately sought to disarray.

"Love, there will be time for us later," he whispered, leaning close. "Now we have to announce our engagement, and before then, you need to regain your composure."

He leaned back to watch her face as she blinked, disoriented at first then with a growing embarrassment flooding her face. She peered around his shoulder only to duck back when she saw the expectant onlookers.

"Come," he murmured, offering his arm, "surely the woman who braved an audience can't find such things as these intimidating?"

His effort showed its success in her straightened shoulders. That chip of glacier in her eye returned, making him regret the loss of her more passionate face. He consoled himself with thoughts of many more chances as he turned her fully to face the crowd.

Though clearly rumpled, she wore her confidence like a royal robe and the watchers parted to make a path as if by instinct. Pride filled him as he stepped free of the alcove, the woman of his dreams at his side.

DAPHNE TIGHTENED HER GRIP ON his arm and stiffened her spine to hide the trembling that had overtaken her. A wisp of hair slipped down to bounce against her neck, reminding her that for all she tried to adopt her mother's arrogance, she still looked like she'd just tumbled out of a shared bed.

Her lips ached with the memory of his touch. She flicked her tongue out to stroke the bruised flesh, and his hand tensed into a fist. A delicious shudder ran over her, a movement she managed to cover by nodding a greeting to Penelope, who stood in the wall of people on one side.

Stop this, she told herself sternly. If she had any chance to repair her reputation, she had to stop acting like a light skirt no matter how she looked.

Another smiling nod and they'd made it half way down the impromptu corridor that ended in her parents and his mother, their stiff expressions boding poorly for kind conversations once they achieved the dais. Only the crowd surrounding the raised platform would protect them from the worst of the lecture.

Something about their expressions made Daphne want to rebel. She hadn't planned for Jasper to find her there. She hadn't planned for him to touch her.

Against her will, a new blush rose to heat her cheeks and neck. A wave of titters passed through the watching crowd and Daphne tensed against an even stronger blush.

Jasper glanced down at her, meeting her eyes with laughter dancing in his.

Daphne turned away, staring resolutely at the curtains hanging down from the ceiling in rose-colored washes. She might not have planned their meeting, but he'd known just who he expected to find behind that curtain, and it hadn't been her.

Anger boiled up, washing away the last of her tender feelings as she realized she'd been played the fool. First he'd planned to fix an assignation with a light skirt at her very own engagement party and then he'd behaved inappropriately, making her look the part of the one he'd lost.

Suddenly, the passionate tangling of his fingers through her elegant hairdo took a new meaning. He'd meant to pay her back for following her dreams, pay her back for his chasing after one who should have been beneath his interest but wasn't.

A wave of laughter passed through the guests as Daphne sped up, jerking against his arm to get free of him.

She overheard comments about how eager she was to wed then bed the handsome baron. Rather than making her blush again, this time the heat in her cheeks came from the flush of anger. She only wanted to get this over with so she could plan her own revenge.

THE IDEA CAME TO HER in the night and by the next morning had taken root. Guilt twinged her conscience but she pushed her promise to her parents back, knowing she had no other leverage over the man who had played such a cruel trick on her.

Unwilling to use Penelope as a cover anymore now that they had started to become friends in truth, she waited until her mother had left on one of her many visits. Daphne pleaded a headache as an excuse to stay home and spent the morning wrapped in her blankets, listening for the sound of the family coach.

When it returned, she leapt from her bed, already fully dressed, and grabbed the satchel she hadn't bothered to unpack though she'd thought never to use it again. Daphne caught Willem in the hall, giving him a significant look.

Willem shook his head, not in rejection, but in shock. She knew well enough the whole household had heard her father rage at her.

"I must," she whispered. "I must just this one last time and you have to help me."

He looked uncomfortable, but Daphne knew he would give in. His distance hadn't lasted past a few days, her unthinking words softened by her efforts to regain his trust. "Oh, my lady, do you even know what you're chancing in this? You're engaged now. You must behave with utmost decorum."

Daphne laughed at the incongruous words coming from the man who'd helped her perform many a scrape over the years. "I'm not shackled to him yet, Willem. Would you deny me this last moment of freedom?"

Though she'd concocted the idea for revenge, flaunting her other life before her fiancé if only through the prevalent gossips, it had become so much more than that. The previous time, she'd come to the theater full of hope and expectation only to leave crushed and thrown away as if scraps of garbage.

This time, she'd dance knowing it to be her last performance. She'd sink her heart into the motions, giving the audience something to talk about for years to come. When approached at parties and asked, had she been there? Had she seen the last performance? she'd be able to smile and nod her head, delighting that she stayed strong in memories usually so fickle.

Every motion took on new meaning, from the change of dress and securing her mask, to the switch of carriages, the happy goodbye to the hackney driver. A bounce in her step propelled her to the side door much faster than normal, and she offered only smiles to the dancers she passed, giving no pause to acknowledge their shocked faces. Like a ghost returned to familiar haunts, she belonged here just this once.

Monsieur Henre had other ideas.

The commotion in the hall drew him from his office, and he froze at the sight of her. Daphne flinched as his fingers wrapped around her upper arm in a match to her fiancé's bruises, and he jerked her into the small room, his glare boring into her.

"Are you mad? There is nothing worth the risks you take now that you are engaged formally to none other than our patron. You think I don't know what happens in your world that you're so willing to throw away mine?"

Daphne caught his arm and stared back at him, desire filling hers not for the man in front of her but for the time on stage, music filling her ears and lanterns heating the air around her. "Just one last dance," she begged. "One last time when I'm not full of confusion and despair. Let me make my final performance and I'll plague you no longer. I need to close this part of my life so I can begin my new one."

Though that hadn't been her initial purpose, her words resounded with truth and she could see him weakening. "You told Cynthia, but what about your audience?" she added, seeing how closure could be good for him as well. "Do you really want them restless and looking for me every time they arrive? Send runners out, play this up, get yourself a house stuffed to the wings and then make my farewell announcement. If nothing else, I'd think the fanfare would appeal." She pushed down guilt at how her father would receive the news. Perhaps he'd think Monsieur Henre substituted one masked dancer for another, but somehow she didn't think so.

A smile pulled at Monsieur Henre's mouth, softening his worried expression. "True enough. I'd always thought there was more to you than just a pretty face and some fancy moves. You have a merchant's head on your shoulders." He let the smile full out until it split his face. "I'll do it. I'll make this a grand extravaganza the like Drury Lane has never seen. Go, go, and get into your costumes. You'll have to get them out of the closet. I had them put away until a seamstress could alter them for one of the other dancers. Lucky now that I've been too busy."

He waved her out of the door, still muttering to himself.

She smiled, moving toward the costume closet with a firm step, happy in the knowledge that he'd make her leave taking just as splendid as she could ever have hoped.

An arm braced across the passageway brought Daphne up short, just a step away from the closet.

"And what do you think you're doing back here?" Cynthia asked, her superior tone grating against Daphne's nerves.

"Don't worry," Daphne said, holding her smile steady on lips suddenly rigid with tension. "I'll not steal your place. I only plan for a proper farewell."

The other dancer stared at her for a long moment, obviously hearing the implication that Daphne could take the spot if she wanted. Then Cynthia laughed, a full-throated sound that echoed in the tight space. "Fine," she said. "A passing of the baton like ancient Greeks. You hand over ownership of the stage to me, never to return and haunt these halls again."

Daphne stilled at the odd echo of her earlier thought then nodded. As long as she had her moment, why not let both of them excel. "You can tell Monsieur Henre about the idea. It has some merit. He's planning the performance as we speak."

Cynthia hesitated, perhaps having expected condemnation rather than support. "Don't think your pretty words can fool me," she bit out. "You're no better than the rest of us. Probably got caught with your skirts about your ears. The master's giving you this not as a privilege but only to protect his investment."

She stomped off toward the office, choosing not to accept the laurel Daphne had offered. With a shrug, Daphne opened the closet and fished around, seeking the costume she wanted to wear in this, her last performance ever.

Chapter Twenty-Six

asper lowered the papers he'd been reading, surprised to see Aubrey entering the library, a place he rarely shared with guests. His friend must have persuaded the butler of some great need, most likely a restless hunger for activity despite how few hours sleep must have claimed. The sun had just begun to sink below the horizon.

They'd been at his engagement party late into the night, so late dawn had touched the sky before his carriage brought them both home. Satisfaction filled Jasper at the thought of his bride, something he'd never dreamed of experiencing. He closed his eyes, the memory of her lips beneath his making heat rise and pool within him. He couldn't wait to see her again and had to suppress the need to call on her this very afternoon.

"I thought as much," Aubrey said, settling into a chair at his side. "Even politics or farm work can't keep her from your mind, can they?"

Jasper smiled. "No, I doubt anything will succeed for long. She's no further than my thoughts, though our bodies are some distance."

Instead of congratulating him, Aubrey frowned. "Giving up your heart is a noble step, but not if it wounds you so deep that you lose the joys of life. I never thought I'd be one to encourage your notion of confining your lady wife to a distant property, but I wonder if it might be better for the two of you if you don't give up the dancer."

Jasper opened his mouth to reveal his delicious secret then shut it again. He could no more share her past with his best friend than offer up Aubrey's secrets against her soft breast. "I've made my decision, and I'll stand by it," he said instead, placing the pile of tallies on a side table before pushing to his feet. "Though I enjoy your company, my friend, I have much to do before the wedding. I'm afraid you'll have to find pleasures on your own for the day at least."

Aubrey rose as well, sending Jasper a dubious look. "So you are decided? Nothing can sway you?"

Aware of things beyond the ken of his friend, Jasper replaced his smile with a serious nod. "Nothing."

Turning, Aubrey stepped to the library door where he paused, swiveling back to look at his friend. "Not even the chance to see your dancer perform? To test your resolve and secure your decision?"

Jasper stared at him, trying to pretend he hadn't heard what he thought he had. "She's performing tonight? You know this for sure?" he ground out, ignoring his friend's look of surprise.

Aubrey slipped back into the room. "I guess you haven't quite managed the separation you'd hoped for. Runners are out in all the right places calling the news. A grand extravaganza they claim, featuring none other than the one who holds your heart." He put a hand on Jasper's arm. "Come with me. What harm can it do that's not already done? If you can watch her unmoved, then carry on with your plan. If not, better you learn now then become embittered as the years pass and your only chance vanished long ago."

Jasper jerked from under the touch, struggling for control when anger whipped through him at her audacity. Did she think he wouldn't find out? Did she think she could parade herself before the crowds, and he would only sit back and smile? He'd thought they'd found an understanding the night before, but she'd played him the fool. All that maidenly shrinking and embarrassment had covered up a mercenary heart that he'd have to tame.

"We're going, all right," he declared, reaching for his coat. "I'm putting a stop to this once and for all."

Pulling Aubrey in his wake, he shouted for the carriage, his gruff tone making his butler frown.

Aubrey stopped in the front hall, jerking Jasper as well. "Put a stop to what? Your heart? And it's early yet. Let's have a civilized meal or we'll be at the door well before it opens."

Jasper turned to stare at his friend for a long moment then realized he could offer no explanation, no reason for his need to capture the dancer before she set foot on the stage. Running a hand through his hair in frustration, he signaled his agreement with a tight nod.

She'd won this round. He had no way to prevent her performance without creating just the stir he had to avoid at all costs. No matter what she'd been in the past, he refused to give up his heart twice No breath of scandal would touch her name. His mother would not have the slightest reason to cancel their wedding. He meant to have this woman and none other if he had to lock her in a cage to make it happen. Not that he planned to keep her in one any longer than it took to overcome her stubborn nature.

THE THEATER SEEMED UNUSUALLY CROWDED when they arrived a few long hours later. Jasper swung down from the carriage, a heavy frown pulling at his cheeks as he contemplated the mix of society matrons, young bucks, and the scattering of tradesfolk all waiting for the doors to open. He couldn't help but think they'd come to see *his* bride, come to ogle what no properly brought up young woman would ever display.

"And more the fool I, who hopes to get through this without a whisper of gossip that could threaten the ties to bind her to my side," he muttered to himself.

"What was that?" Aubrey asked, speaking louder than usual over the crowd.

Jasper only shook his head, moving forward with the rest as they surged through the now open doors. At least the effort to move without crushing this young lady or tromping on that man's toes kept his mind from dwelling on what they sought so eagerly.

He breathed a sigh of relief when he was able to peel away from the crowd and enter the relative quiet of his box, but before he could even settle into his seat, the questions began again, and not those dissecting her motives. Was it this part of her that he'd come to love?

He planned to take it from her, confine her to the limitations society imposed on one of her status to protect her family and his own. Would she wilt, or would she thrive? Was he the one to crush her soul in the name of propriety? Could he give her enough to make up for losing the adoration of so many?

The thrill of notes from flutes followed by a heavy drum strike pulled Jasper from his thoughts. He leaned on the balcony, no less eager for the first sight of her than the randy bachelors lining the other boxes.

Men he'd named friend not so long ago now irritated him as they stared down at his fiancée, undressing her with their eyes, feasting on her form and lusting after her. His stomach churned with anger and an odd envy for their easy emotions. Fingers clenched on the balcony rail, Jasper forced his attention to stay on her, trying to find something soothing in her motions where he knew a glance around would only send flaming heat through his body.

Instead of relaxation, a different heat rose to fill him, and Jasper vowed she'd still dance for him at least. He could not take the movements from her, the clear expression of her deepest emotions. Still, he planned to shield her from other eyes if he had to lock her in a tower to which only he held the key. Again, anger pushed away everything else, feeding on his desire and returning a deep rage that had him fighting the need to challenge each and every one of the men watching her perform.

Finally the curtain sank to the stage from each side and the lights came up, revealing an intermission after a much longer than usual routine.

Jasper shoved to his feet.

"Bring me something?" Aubrey asked.

Jasper only shook his head, knowing he needed to step outside and cool his head.

Aubrey rose to come with him, pausing at the door to whisper, "You're not planning trouble with her again?"

Jasper gave him a grim smile. "Stay and enjoy the rest. I'm planning to avoid what trouble would erupt if I were to stay here even a moment longer. The chill air should do much to cool my temper."

His friend stepped aside to let Jasper pass, giving him an odd look, but said nothing further.

Jasper struggled with his temper as every group he passed offered up yet another comment doomed to inflame his blood.

"She's a ripe one," a young dandy offered to his crowd.

"I'd not mind one like her to bury my sorrows," from an older man.

A matron raised her spectacles to peer toward the stage even though the dancer had long left. "Some randy lord'll snap her right up, leaving broken hearts in his wake, I'd wager," she offered to her friend, apparently unaware of his presence as he sought to pass them.

The comments continued, both appreciative and bawdry, but none that served to calm him. By the time he burst through the door into the cool night air, he almost panted with aggravation. He wanted to march back in and press a knife to first one throat and then another, discovering a violent streak in himself where before he'd been the first to mock those who chose duels as any form of a solution. They could not know how they offended, nor could he tell them.

He turned at the corner and paced down to the doorway he knew she'd use to leave once the performance ended. Another minute inside with her admirers, and he could not be held responsible for the destruction he would wreck in his haste to protect her virtue. Better he shiver here and wait her out, letting the cold calm him where her motions within would only inflame.

After pacing the length of the alley once, twice, and then again, his speed finally slowed along with his thoughts until all he cared was that it end here and now. She had to listen. Whatever she hoped to gain in this display, he'd convince her, somehow, to see it brought only risk and danger of ruin.

ONCE EVERYONE RETURNED TO THEIR seats and the lights came down, Daphne handed over the baton, passing her life to another as Cynthia had planned. The audience reacted to the moment with a variety of dismayed sounds, but no anger. As she'd hoped, they only wanted a grand farewell.

Turning to face them for the last time, she made an elegant curtsy, ignoring shouted requests to unmask and reveal the mystery. She pressed both hands to her cheeks and shook her head in mock horror, drawing spontaneous laughter from many of the vague shadows hovering beyond the stage lights.

A gut-wrenching pain filled her as she stared out at those faces she could see no more than they could see hers. She'd miss these moments with the audience holding her in its palm, following her emotions along with her movements.

Almost against her will, she looked toward the boxes. Was he up there in the shadows? She forgot her attempt to lash back and wanted only for him to have enjoyed her final performance. If a hint of understanding crept in for what she'd have to give up, she wouldn't complain.

Her body moved automatically through the familiar steps of changing out of her costume and restoring the low-level maid she pretended to be when traveling. If her hand lingered on the costume or her fingers trailed along the screen, no one said anything, the other dancers all busy preparing for their last sets of the night. She envied them this life even though she'd guess any one of them would happily switch places if given the choice.

Finally ready, Daphne moved to leave the room only to stop when Cynthia blocked her way, sweat shining on her cheeks and forehead. Daphne flinched, waiting for the latest spew of vile hate. This was one part of her hidden life she would never miss. As much as she longed for female companionship, she had not found it here.

"Thanks for that," Cynthia said, breaking through her thoughts. "After all done between us, you didn't owe me anything. Still, you acted right fine."

Daphne stared at her in shock then smiled. "Make Monsieur Henre proud, Cynthia. And love every minute that you're on the stage. Love it enough for the both of us."

The other dancer smiled back, her expression growing slowly until it covered her face. "I will. Never fear I don't know exactly what I've won in this. The center stage gets in your heart and…I guess you know all about that."

Daphne nodded, her gaze pinned to the floor because she could not face the desire and joy in the other woman's eyes. Without another word, she turned away, leaving the changing room, and soon the performance hall, for the last time. She'd never come here as part of the audience. The change in position would tear her apart.

Natural enthusiasm struggled with her morose mood all the way down the corridor, and by the time she reached the end of the passage, her thoughts dwelled not on the final moments but on her dynamic performance before then. She'd danced with more energy, more heart, than ever before, outstripping herself by a wide margin.

"They'll think of me," she whispered to the dark hall. "They'll think of me long after I've become no more than one of the matrons who gather in my mother's parlor to discuss the failings of the latest run of girls coming out."

The energy of her performance and a grand sense of moving on to another life, one filled with new experiences, made her feel like she floated along. She laughed as she stepped through the open door, tugging her mask off for the final time.

The sound choked off as a squeak when a hand appeared from the darkness, clamping down on her arm.

Before Daphne could react, she was pulled against a hard chest. Terror filled her, blocking out all senses as her mind demanded that she run or fight or do something but her body stayed limp. "Don't hurt me," she whimpered, wondering how long before more dancers spilled out and scared off her assailant.

"Don't tempt me," a gruff but familiar voice ground out beside her ear. "Any punishment I could concoct would be a mere shadow of what you truly deserve."

"Jasper?" The name slipped from her mouth, her body's relaxation suddenly making sense. She swiveled in his arms, wanting to share the experience with one she knew appreciated her skill. "Didn't it go splendidly tonight? It felt almost as if I soared a foot off the stage and angels guided every moment."

He pulled her down the alleyway toward the street beyond, his grip rough. "More like devils. Have you no pride? Have you no care for what your family would suffer should more than just I discover what you do with your time? Did you whip off your mask and display your features to the crowd, offering me that final humiliation? Do you consider me so little?"

Daphne jerked out of his hold, ignoring the ache where his fingers had bit deep, all fellow feeling vanishing under his accusations. Rounding on him, she slammed both hands against his chest hard enough to make him back up a step. "Humiliation? You have the gall to speak to me of humiliation when you branded me like a common harlot before my family and the assembled ton." She smacked his chest again, her words drying up with the heat of her anger.

Jasper grabbed her hands, pinning them to him as he stared at her, anger heaving his chest under her palms. He shifted so only one hand held both of hers, and before she realized what he'd intended, he'd pulled her toward him, his arm wrapped around her shoulders to hold her tight.

"You think I held you thus out of an attempt to injure?" he asked, his tone incredulous. "You think I could fake how my body comes alive to your slightest touch?"

She gazed up into his passion-dark eyes and struggled to swallow against a suddenly dry throat. "You had just discovered my secret," she murmured, trying to explain but finding her thoughts disordered both by memories of the previous night and by sensations flooding her now.

He laughed, a sharp bark of sound, and thrust the hand no longer needed to confine her wrists through her hair, his broad palm stretching back far enough to tilt her head a little further. "You have much to learn about men, my dear heart. You'd answered all my prayers. I'd thought to give up my honor or my heart then found both held in your keeping."

As if driven by forces he could no longer combat, he bent toward her, his lips capturing hers with dizzying passion.

Daphne swayed under the onslaught, her body sagging against his supporting arm as weakness invaded her limbs and stars danced behind her eyelids.

Then he dragged his lips from hers, his frown visible in the vague moonlight. "And yet, for all that you give, you take away," he growled, his hand in her hair tightening into a fist and pulling against the strands. "If you think to continue such activities now, when I've claimed you as my own, you're gravely mistaken. I'll not tolerate such foolishness. You'll find yourself sequestered as tight as any nun if you try to make the fool of me."

Daphne stiffened at his tone, remembering her first reaction to his demands and how he'd seemed like nothing more than a condemning bore. She went to push him away, but glanced up at the last moment and felt her resistance melt. His face held not condemnation, but rather a jealous passion that brought a slow smile to her lips for all it worked against her.

Reaching up to brush his cheek, she let her smile broaden. "My fierce protector. You need not worry for my own virtue or your reputation. Had you but stayed for the whole, as you obviously did not, you'd know your worries hold no ground. I never meant to continue my performances. This was to say goodbye to that life."

Confusion filled his expression, then the anger subsided and something deeper took its place. "I swear I'll let you have this part in some fashion. I won't ask you to lock yourself away. I swear this."

Daphne only smiled, unsure what he meant but loving that he thought to try. He had understood her passion after all, but had yet to realize he now drew her with the same strength.

As if he'd read her thoughts, Jasper pulled her against him even more and gave her a long, deep kiss that she thought would never end. Passion rode over her, leaving Daphne ragged and a puddle of desire in his arms. She'd felt nothing like it before, only adding to her growing happiness. She'd have him for her own until the grains of time washed away from their shore, time enough to explore every new emotion he provoked.

Chapter Twenty-Seven

Daphne stepped down from Jasper's carriage before the coachman could open the door for her, turning back to smile at the man who could melt her bones and still seemed to see her as a person rather than a fancy decoration for his arm. "You're sure your friend will figure out that you went ahead?" she asked, a twinge of guilt at having taken him away pricking her conscience.

Jasper smiled, his expression so relaxed and open that she wondered how she'd ever thought him a bore. "Aubrey's a big boy, Daphne." The way he said her name sent shivers down her back. "Better he take a hire coach than you anyway."

She frowned, unsure about his comment. "I've been taking them by myself for longer than you've known I exist," Daphne said, trying to keep anger from her voice.

He jumped down beside the carriage and pulled her close. "Now don't frown at me, darling. I shudder to think of the risks you've taken."

Giving up the effort to control her temper, Daphne shoved against his chest. "And now you're here to protect me? Keep me locked away to shelter me from danger?"

Jasper stepped back to look at her, a frown pulling at his face as well. "You really think I'd want that? I finally have someone who makes my heart pound and can carry a conversation. You think I'm going to cage you?" He shook his head. "Maybe once I wanted to when I feared you would run from me, but not now. I'll happily show you anything you desire. Then maybe you'll understand my fears. It's not whether you are capable, dear, but rather knowing what the others around you are capable of. You could have been taken for ransom or sold for worse. I shudder to think of all the things that could have happened. But by the grace of God, they did not. And now you have me."

At first, she tried to rebel against his words, but then memory of the moment he caught her in the alleyway returned with startling clarity. She wasn't as innocent of the ways of the lowlifes around Monsieur Henre's theater as Jasper thought. Her former teacher gave her warnings often enough.

Unwilling to give in entirely, Daphne only smiled. "And now I have you," she whispered, promising nothing about his desire to escort her everywhere, but affirming the most important part of all.

Whether he understood her message or was just relieved the conversation had ended without another fight, Jasper returned her smile. He reached out and jerked her close so quickly, she let out a surprised gasp.

"Unhand her," a sharp voice demanded.

Daphne gasped again, huddling closer to Jasper as she raised her head to peep over his shoulder. She blinked twice before she accepted what she saw approaching rather than the thief she'd expected. After pushing free, she put her hands on her hips and stamped one foot. "Willem, I don't need another protector. Jasper's not harming me one whit."

Willem shook his head, only half lowering the whip he held in his hand. "Lady Daphne, I agreed to help you dance. This isn't in the bargain. I thought you held yourself as better than the likes of him."

Restraining Jasper with a hand on his arm, Daphne sighed, recognizing the betrayal in the coachman's voice better for understanding its cause. "It's not what you think, Willem. Look on the carriage and you'll see it is no hackney. This is Lord Pendleton. The man I'm to marry."

Willem stared at her without comprehension for a long while before taking a menacing step toward Jasper, who stood a good half foot taller and was much broader in the shoulders. "And what's he going to do now?" the younger man growled. "Now that he knows and all, he'll just make trouble."

Daphne stepped between them, covering her worry with a gentle smile. "He won't make trouble. Not for me or for you." She nudged Jasper, who nodded slowly. "See, you have nothing to worry about."

Willem moved closer and caught her arm with one hand. "Well enough, but we should be getting back. Your lady mother will be none too pleased to find you gone, after all. The later you wait, the harder to explain."

Catching the hand that Jasper put out to remove the inappropriate touch, she shook Willem's hold off. "I'm returning with Jasper, Willem. You'll just have to say truthfully that I didn't require your services on the return."

He leaned close. "My lady, he's only trying to get from you what he should wait for until the wedding night. He has no more wish to be seen with the upstairs maid you resemble than you'd choose the coachman."

Daphne pressed a hand to his chest, sympathetic to the bitter twist in his tone. "I'd have no concern at all in spending time with a good friend," she said, emphasizing her point with a light tap on his coat. "But I can't chance Mother or Father seeing me like this." She pulled at the skirt she'd chosen, this night's clothing much too worn to pass her mother's inspection. "That's why we came back here— other than to tell you, of course—to change my clothing. I do appreciate your care, Willem, but you have no say in this."

He stared at her for a long moment before shifting to give Jasper a pointed look. "As you wish, my lady. The gentleman and I will wait here until you're ready."

Daphne smothered a smile, slipping past him with her satchel. The sooner she got changed, the faster they'd get her home and the greater chance of escaping detection.

"You truly inspire loyalty, don't you?"

Daphne blushed in response to Jasper's question, settling onto the opposite bench. Her proper dress crinkled as she tried to tuck it out of the way, giving her an excuse not to answer while she considered what best to say. Finally, she glanced up. "He's been a friend since childhood. I'm sorry if his attitude offended you."

Jasper laughed, rocking forward with the carriage motion until she could feel the rush of air from his breath. "And I'd guess this is not the first trial you've put him through either. I see we're soon to have much in common."

She didn't know how to respond and so sank into silence, letting the exhaustion from her eventful night wash over her.

The carriage jerked to a halt and Jasper caught her as she surged forward. Daphne savored the touch. How wonderful to know he'd be there to catch her for the rest of her life. To catch if she fell, not restrain.

"Your parents may have heard the carriage, my dear. We shouldn't keep them waiting."

As his murmured words brushed against her ear, Daphne realized she lay half over him, hugging tight to his chest, and had made no protest. She pulled back, feeling the heat of a blush coloring her cheeks. "True enough," she whispered back, trying to regain control of tangled emotions when all she really wanted was to cling to his warmth and feel the pressure of his lips against hers.

Instead, the door swung open and the coachman lowered the step for her. Daphne sighed inwardly, grabbed her satchel, and stepped from the carriage, allowing the coachman to assist her balance. Jasper descended behind her, tucking her hand under his arm before they mounted the steps.

At the door, Daphne paused, suddenly wondering how it would look to her parents for them to arrive together. Had Willem been right after all?

Before she could resolve her doubts, Jasper pushed the door open, not ringing the bell or waiting for the butler. Daphne had no choice but to follow him in.

The door closed behind them with a loud thump, the sound ominous. Proving her instincts true, her father stomped out of the front parlor, her mother right behind. He waved a piece of paper and

Daphne had to fight the urge to cower behind Jasper, having forgotten in her joy how her father would have seen the announcement as well.

Instead, she stood tall, ready to face the consequences.

"Do you have any idea what I have in my hand, young lady?" Lord Scarborough fumed. He never gave her a chance to answer before he continued. "It's a leaflet handed to me in White's."

Gut churning, Daphne tried to make out the lettering even as it jerked around her, but she could guess its meaning from her father's expression.

"I-I—" she stammered.

Jasper stepped forward, snatching the paper from Lord Scarborough with a quick movement. "A dancer performing? Is that what you were supposed to be attending?" he asked Daphne, turned so only she could see the mischief in his eyes.

So cued, she struggled to come up with a response, but could think of nothing.

Jasper looked first at her father then her mother, shaking his head. "I must apologize, Lord and Lady Scarborough, for absconding with your daughter in this way. It's only that we had such a close moment the previous night and I could not wait any longer to see her again. I never expected to find my fiancée so enticing."

Only when she saw the shocked expressions on her parents' faces did she remember to school her own into an easily found guilty expression.

"You-you spent the evening together?" her father asked, his tone unsure.

"Yes, my lord, we did. There are parts of Vauxhall gardens that can only be appreciated under the glow cast by lanterns. I hope my actions didn't cause undue concern. Daphne resisted at first, claiming another engagement but,"—he smiled a beguiling smile—"I convinced her I would waste away if kept any longer from her sunlight."

If the blush that rose to Daphne's cheek had more to do with the lies they told than wandering in a garden under fairy lights, her parents wouldn't be able to tell.

Lady Scarborough tried for a reproving look, but a smile teased the corners of her mouth. "I cannot say I approve of such behavior, young man," she said to Jasper. "It will do no one any good if you destroy her reputation."

Jasper hung his head, mostly to hide the dimple Daphne could see peeking out on his cheek. "You're right, of course. I'd thought since I was her fiancé, no harm would come of it, but it was not responsible. I apologize again for the worry I've caused you. If any question her presence, I will be sure to respond appropriately."

Lord Scarborough cleared his throat loudly then clapped Jasper on the shoulder. "Now, now, no harm done. We should have known better than to expect you could resist the beauty of our daughter. Come, join me in my study for a nightcap."

Daphne couldn't believe she'd survived the confrontation and with so little admonishment. She almost missed Jasper's demur in her shock.

Then he turned to face her, sweeping one of her hands up in his own to lay a decorous kiss on the back of it. "And you should go and take to your room so you'll be well-rested for our curricle ride tomorrow," he said as she stared up at him, dazed. "If that's all right with you, Lord Scarborough?"

"Hmm. A ride should be well done. Show all of London how well the two of you suit." Her father smiled broadly at both of them.

"Run along now, dear," her mother said, waving Daphne toward the stair.

Daphne obeyed by instinct, only turning to say goodbye when her foot lifted onto the first step.

Jasper smiled back at her, his expression making her heart pound once again. Tomorrow could not come soon enough.

"And then Aubrey grabbed the reins and hauled back..." Jasper clucked under his breath as he encouraged the horses into a faster pace once they passed the carriage that had half-blocked the way. After these many weeks, and as many curricle rides, he knew Daphne preferred speed over the meandering pace a chaperone would have required. He glanced at the woman he planned to wed, grateful for her father's indulgence, but mostly for her presence in his life.

Instead of watching him intently as she had been, her gaze stretched the length of the road as if caught by the horizon. He shifted the reins to one hand, frowning when he saw how her fingers tensed in her lap, creasing the material of her skirt. Leaning toward her, he placed his free hand over her fingers, squeezing gently.

She jerked as he surprised her out of deep thoughts.

"What is troubling you?" he asked with little hope of a true answer. He'd come to know her moods, if not the cause for them. Even as she seemed to return his regard, he often felt a tinge of sadness within her when she would stare off into the air, distracted.

"Nothing really," Daphne answered, her mouth stretching in an obviously forced smile. "I just have a lot on my mind from helping Mother with the wedding and everything. What were you saying about Aubrey?"

Jasper shrugged, not sure if she had been listening after all or only made a good guess. He didn't want to force her to confide in him, but still, he wanted to make her happy.

His mind only half on the tale, another of the escapades she seemed to enjoy so much, Jasper probed the problem, contemplating how he could make this transition better for her.

Her laugh when he finished off the story pulled his focus back, and he reached out a hand to brush a wind-tossed curl behind her ear. She turned into his touch, leaning her cheek against his palm and closing her eyes for a long moment.

Jasper gazed down at her. Whatever troubled her, she told him in words and motions that he held as important a spot in her life as she'd taken over in his own. No matter what it took, he'd find a way to free her of the cobwebs that threatened her happiness.

"And I know just the place to start," he muttered, shaking his head when she looked a question at him. He wouldn't mention anything to her until he'd arranged things, but he needed to talk to her father about Willem first thing tomorrow morning.

Chapter Twenty-Eight

Daphne woke on the morning of her final fitting having made a decision. She waited until the maid left after dressing her, then strode to her bedside. The worn leather of the book cover caressed her fingers. She felt in the touch all her impossible dreams and desires.

Where once that thought would have brought with it a welling up of despair, instead, a smile tweaked the corners of her mouth. "For you, Jasper," she whispered, picking up the book and tucking it into her small hand satchel.

She never would have believed it possible, but the man chosen to be her husband filled up the emptiness in her heart. Though Daphne still desired the sheer joy of dance, she no longer needed the audience to make her happy. She planned to ask Jasper for a practice room and saw no reason for him to deny her request as long as she promised to confine herself to that space alone. If ever she needed a performance again, he would be the only audience she desired.

"Daphne, we do have an appointment," her mother said, standing in the doorway to the room.

Daphne jerked a hand to her satchel, feeling exposed in a moment of peace between her past and present. She had only to do one more task and she could advance into her future unfettered by what she had been.

"Stop here," she commanded a short while later, slapping a hand against the paneling separating Willem from the coach. "I'll only be a moment," Daphne told her mother as she slipped out the door before Lady Scarborough could complain.

Another coach squeezed past them, coming near enough to Daphne to make her heart pound and remind her of when Jasper made his desires known, even though he remained unaware of her identity. Peering out to check the distance, she smiled, thinking about how shallow she'd thought him when, in truth, he'd only listened to his heart.

Finding a clear space, she skipped across the street, unable to restrain her happiness. The bell over the door jangled as she entered the bookshop, taking in the scents of so many tomes filled with wonders.

The shopkeeper came forward, staring at her intently over his eyeglasses. "I've not seen you in here for some time," he said, crossing to stand behind his desk.

"I had all I needed in the one book I borrowed," she answered with a smile.

"And what frippery was that, may I ask?" he said, an answering smile taking the bite from his words.

Without speaking, Daphne removed the dancer's diary and placed it on the counter.

The shopkeeper stared at it, glanced at her, and frowned. "I'd forgotten about this. Not frippery after all. I'm surprised such a book could entertain a fine lady as yourself."

She reached out to brush the cover one last time, feeling as if she abandoned a good friend, then straightened. "I found her story powerful and moving, but I need it no longer. Maybe it will fuel another's dreams."

He nodded, still looking uncertain as he calculated the charge.

Daphne paid from the coins she'd brought, unsurprised to find her supply much diminished. That book had been worth every penny spent for its keeping. It had given her dreams meaning, and ultimately, brought Jasper to her. She'd listened enough to his stories to suspect his plans for whatever wife his mother foisted on him. If not for dancing, she'd have hardly known, and certainly not already loved, the man she planned to pledge her heart and life to.

"Imagine. Running off to a bookshop today of all days," her mother exclaimed when Daphne slipped back into the coach.

"It was something I had to do, Mother," was all Daphne offered aloud. Inside, she knew herself ready to start her new life with Jasper, rather than dance, at the center.

"Lady Daphne, a note for you," Betsy whispered, caught up in the moment as much as everyone else.

Daphne took the thick paper, her wedding gown rustling as she moved. They prepared in the small parlor in the back, the little used space perfect for where the wedding ceremony had been planned. She shifted her feet, already tired from standing still, but unable to sit comfortably in the skirt.

"Aren't you going to read it, my lady?"

Laughing at her wandering thoughts, Daphne unfolded the paper and forced herself to concentrate. Since the morning of her wedding dawned, she'd been hard pressed to think of anything but Jasper.

Her gaze drifted to the paper. She smiled at his strong, dark strokes against the page. She treasured the notes he sent her, but never expected to receive one today. She looked again to see what words he'd formed, her heart softening as he began with a greeting.

My Dear Heart,

While I hope your thoughts are full only of me, I know there is one other you would want to share this day who cannot. As you trust me with your life, know that I hold your heart as sacred. Look on the back corner to the left when you turn to face me and you'll see the one fates denied you.

Yours,

Jasper

Daphne stared at the paper, reading the words again before she dared to let herself guess at the meaning. The corner he'd described would hold the household, those servants who had either watched her grow up or grown up beside her. And yet, from this missive, it would hold one more: her sister.

She crushed the paper against her breast, her heart bursting with love for the man who had invaded her life and demanded his place there.

Betsy reached out to pluck the paper away, and Daphne released it only so it wouldn't tear.

"I'll find a place for this in your packages, my lady. We wouldn't want the wrong eyes to fall on it." The maid jerked her head to indicate Lady Scarborough, even now preparing her own appearance.

Daphne took the maid's hands between her own, the paper crinkling much like her skirt. "Thank you, Betsy. And to all those who made this possible."

Betsy winked as she dropped into a curtsy. "I'll see that those who did get your thanks, my lady. I best be on about it."

Staring after the maid, Daphne felt as if she could drift on clouds for the rest of her wedding day.

"Come along, Daphne. Don't you hear the music? You wouldn't want to be late on today of all days."

Lady Scarborough took her arm then handed Daphne to her father just outside the room. He beamed a smile down to her, and they walked toward the raised dais and her future husband.

Her feet sped up, almost pulling her father's arm in her eagerness to reach the front. Though she felt the back corner burned into her consciousness, that wasn't why she sought the raised place. That Jasper had done this despite her father's choice, that he understood her so well, filled Daphne with joy and hope for their future.

When she reached Jasper's side, she gave him a long look from beneath her veil. He reached out to take her hand, and she returned the gesture with a gentle squeeze. Only then did she glance toward the corner.

Hidden by her veil, she mouthed her sister's name, a broad smile lifting her lips. As if knowing her feelings, Jasper smiled as well. Together, they turned to face the minister and vowed to share the remainder of their lives.

THE REST OF THE WEDDING passed in a blur. The dancing, eating, drinking and toasts all only served to keep her from her husband. Though she'd hoped for a moment alone with her sister as well, by the time the ceremony had ended, Grace had vanished.

"Has something upset you?"

Daphne smiled, throwing herself into Jasper's arms just to feel arms around her. "I'd hoped to see more of my sister," she whispered into his ear, "but there'll be time enough for that later, won't there?"

Hugging her tight against him, Jasper replied, "Of course there will. I'll do what I must to make you happy, my love. I swear to it."

He pulled away only far enough to touch his lips to hers, giving her a kiss so strong she went weak at the knees and would have fallen but for his arm across her back. "What say you we leave this place?" he asked after a moment to catch his breath.

"But we're supposed to leave next morning," Daphne said with only the barest of protests.

"They won't even notice our absence. Once the toasts have been said, we're merely the excuse."

She glanced around the room, finding her mother holding court with a group of older women. Her father had retired to his study for a game of cards some time ago. Daphne put her hand against Jasper's cheek, thrilling to the faint roughness she found there. "You're right. They'll only notice long after the guests are gone."

Like mischievous children, they stole out of the house and to Jasper's carriage, already waiting for them with Daphne's belongings heaped on the back.

"At your service," a familiar voice intoned with rigid formality.

"Willem?" Daphne asked, confused. "Won't Lord Scarborough have need of you?"

Jasper nudged the other man aside and handed her into the carriage. "Your bridal gift," he murmured once they'd settled onto a bench and the horses started forward. "I asked your father if he could part with Willem. If you're to have secrets, you should keep them close and I will keep them closer." He winked. "This way, at least I know who to go to if I suspect you're up to something."

Daphne made a half-hearted attempt to slap him, and he caught her hand, drawing it up to his mouth so he could kiss her palm. She shivered at the hot, moist heat of his breath.

"I plan to be in the thick of any shenanigans you come up with from now on, my lady love," Jasper added, tugging her against him so he could move his lips from her hand to her mouth.

After that, Daphne couldn't have said whether the journey took an hour or a day. Her husband had her full concentration.

THE CARRIAGE CAME TO A stop sometime later, and Daphne waved a hand before her face to calm the flush that heated her features.

"We're here," Jasper declared, his voice rough with passion.

Daphne glanced out the window and saw a large mansion with rolling fields off to one side. "Where are we?" she asked, unfamiliar with Jasper's properties.

Willem opened the carriage door and Jasper stepped down before the coachman could lower the step. "We're not far from London. I thought to start our life together here. It's close enough should we want to go back for an engagement but far enough to give us some distance from our interfering parents…and some privacy."

Her spine tingled at the way he said the last. She gasped when, instead of letting Willem help her down the step, Jasper swung her into his arms so he could carry her up to the mansion. He reached the top with no apparent strain.

Willem rushed forward to open the door, and Jasper crossed the threshold, Daphne clinging around his neck. "Mrs. Withers," he called, slowly lowering Daphne to the floor. "Mrs. Withers, we're home."

Daphne put a hand on Willem's arm, halting him when Jasper strode deeper into the house. "Are you good with this? Will it not hurt to be here?" She'd seen too much to consider her needs any greater than those of lower society.

Her childhood friend and confidant gave her a wink rather than a formal response. "I am good, Lady Daphne. I needed to see you happy, and I can see you are. I'm freed now to seek my own happiness."

She had to be satisfied with that answer as they had no more time for private conversation.

Jasper returned just then with a stout woman, a smile on her face despite the sweat on her brow most likely from working in the hot kitchen.

"Welcome, my lady." She bobbed into a quick curtsy. "We weren't expecting you until the morrow."

Daphne smiled at the woman, hoping to dispel some of the worry marking Mrs. Withers' forehead.

"And we're not here for all anyone knows," Jasper broke in, his voice low as if they were conspirators. "We can introduce my lady tomorrow. Is my room prepared?"

Mrs. Withers' gaze moved between Jasper and Daphne, and a broad smile split her features. "Of course it is, Master Jasper. Do you want me to have tea sent up?"

Daphne shook her head even as Jasper said, "No. We had our fill at the wedding ceremonies."

"You go right on up then, master, and I'll see nothing disturbs you."

Jasper took her at her word, pulling Daphne along beside him. As they climbed the steps, she heard Willem introduce himself and half turned back.

"He'll manage fine. My staff is a friendly lot," Jasper said. "Let us sate the fire we lit one night on Drury Lane."

A shiver overtook her, but when concern wiped the heat from his expression, Daphne smiled and laced her fingers with his. She might have little knowledge of what went on behind closed doors, but she knew he loved her. That confidence calmed any fears and left her brimming with expectation.

Chapter Twenty-Nine

aphne woke the next morning disoriented. Her whole body ached as if from a vigorous dance session and yet she'd given up that part of her life. The thought restored her memory, and she stroked a hand down her bare side, reliving the sensations of the night before along with the gentle care Jasper had taken to introduce her to this new world.

"Good morning," a deep voice rumbled next to her ear.

She shifted, realizing her head lay pillowed on Jasper's chest.

He leaned down and dropped a short kiss on her lips before pulling away. "It's past time to rise, my love. Mrs. Withers will be champing at the bit to introduce the new lady of the house around."

Daphne froze, suddenly overwhelmed by the thought of meeting all the servants. She'd known her father's staff her whole life, and he'd rarely added anyone new. Every one of the servants here would be strangers.

"Now don't forget about Willem so soon," her husband said with a laugh, revealing she'd spoken her worry out loud. "And the rest are good people as well. Besides, they won't expect you to be a strict and proper lady after a night and morning spent teasing tales out of your man. I'm sure Willem has spread enough of your past to remove any mystery."

Daphne blushed, worried now about what they'd think of her. Still, knowing they wouldn't expect a paragon, and that Willem would be standing with them, helped reassure her.

"You'll do fine, love. If you could storm the barriers around my heart, they will be sure to love you too." He rolled away and crossed the room, his naked form a delight for her eyes even as her cheeks warmed to see him. "Shall I send up a maid to tend you?"

Daphne shook her head then spoke when she realized he couldn't see. "No, I'll do for myself this morning."

He came back with a washcloth in his hand. "There's one thing I'll do for you," he whispered, stripping the bedclothes to expose her nakedness.

She reached for the covers, unnerved, but he caught her hand, using the other to stroke her lower body with the damp material.

"You'll be sore for a bit, or so I've heard," Jasper said, his matter-of-fact tone calming her. "No horseback riding today at least, but I hope you'll have the energy to receive the rest of your bridal gift," he added, stepping away after he finished.

"Another gift?" she asked. "You'll spoil me. I have given you nothing in return."

He dropped to his knees beside the bed and caught her hand in his. "Before finding you, the future stretched out as an endless round of barren obligation interrupted only by momentary pleasure. I'd thought myself broken, heartless." He dropped a kiss on her palm. "Now, I can look forward to endless mischief broken only by the peace to be found in your arms."

She frowned at him for a heartbeat before joining in with the laughter. "Come, my husband. Help me up so I can begin this peaceful life you foresee for us."

Daphne groaned as her muscles protested the movement, but her efforts were rewarded when Jasper pressed her against his length, replacing the morning chill with his own heat.

"As much as I wish I could take advantage of you one more time," Jasper said, stepping away, "the household is waiting."

As he had the night before, Jasper acted her lady's maid. He paused on occasion to brush his lips lightly against her neck, shoulders, and mid-back, until she could barely stand for the desire coursing through her.

She pulled away and turned to face him, doing up her last tie. "Stop now, if you want to parade me before your household as a respectable lady."

He gave her an innocent look then laughed. "I only want you to feel half the way I do," he whispered, his throaty tones caressing her skin as his lips had only moments before.

Daphne shook her head, feeling a strand of hair fall free from the clasp.

Jasper stepped forward and tucked it away behind her ear. "You look a splendor, my very own Lady Pendleton. Come, let me share you with my staff before I fail to control my desire to keep you all to myself."

With her arm tucked securely in his, the row of servants waiting at the foot of the stairs did not intimidate her. Daphne nodded and smiled and whispered names she knew she'd have to practice as she made her way down the line.

Willem gave her a wink before his more solemn bow when she stood across from him.

Daphne giggled, happy to hear no sign of her earlier fear in the sound.

"And now that you've met your staff," Jasper said, clasping his free hand over hers. "Let me give you a tour of the house."

Daphne stared at him for a long moment, having expected anything but for him to show her around the endless rooms this mansion contained. Her stomach rumbled with hunger, but she ignored it in favor of the curiosity his odd command provoked.

Instead of starting with the front rooms as might be expected, Jasper swept her along, passing opening after opening to stop before a large, double door with a flourish. "Of all of my home, I think you'll find this the most welcoming," he said, pushing the doors at the center so they swung open together.

He stepped aside, but rather than entering, she just stood and stared. "I'd meant to ask for a room," she whispered, her gaze taking in the huge stretch of wood floor and areas set up much like her practice room at home, mirrors lining one wall. "But this is too much. You may need this ballroom and I don't need all this space just for me."

Jasper laughed, turning her to face him. "If *we* have need of a large ballroom, this house comes with another for that purpose. You will need this much space and maybe more."

Daphne shook her head, overwhelmed with the bounty and confused by his words.

"My love, I bound my life to you, the woman I have come to know in all her facets. How could I then crush you into a box where you'll never be happy? This is for you to dance. I know it's not the same as the roar of a full audience, but perhaps you can put on small performances to share your love beyond the rigid forms of society…properly dressed of course to protect your mother's sensibilities. The fates put my boyhood dreams of being a naval officer out of reach. I would not do the same to you and yours, not when it was in my power to change."

Love swelled through her for a man who saw so much more than the conventions. "My mother and yours would faint at the sight of this," she told him with a grin, still taking in the wonder of how he loved all of her. But the very size of this space overwhelmed her, and she demurred. "This room is larger even than my piece of the stage, Jasper. It's a waste."

"What? You think to offer no crumb of floor to your students?"

Daphne pivoted at the sound of a familiar, but unexpected, voice. "Grace?" Her voice wavered as she spoke her sister's name.

Grace ran the rest of the way across the room to hug Daphne to her breast. "Yes, little sister. I'm here thanks to the generosity of your husband. If I'd known what type of man he was, maybe I'd not have left him for my Richard."

Daphne glanced between them, but Jasper had only attention for her while the suppressed laughter in her sister's face showed Grace had truly found happiness with her minister.

"When Jasper found us to request I appear at your wedding ceremony, he learned Richard had lost his position due to our elopement. My new brother offered Richard a position in the chapel tied to this property."

Dizzy with emotion, Daphne reached for Jasper's arm. "Here? You're living here?" she managed.

"Not but a quick walk down the lane." She waved toward the back of the house. "And between my work at the chapel, I can help you school other highbred girls who share your love of dance and even performance. Not," she added, "that I have any skills besides the ability to herd children, but they can get the training from you."

Unable to restrain herself, Daphne leapt into Jasper's arms, tugging his shirt collar until he bent far enough for her to press a kiss to his lips. "This morning, I'd thought nothing could make me love you more, my husband, but you've shown me the error of my ways."

His mouth curled into a perfect smile for a brief moment before his lips sank onto hers, reviving all the sensations she'd forgotten in the parade of staff. From behind her, she heard her sister murmur some excuse then heard the doors close, leaving them in privacy.

She had her whole life to enjoy being with Jasper and planned to make the most of every minute.

Thank You for Reading

I hope you enjoyed spending time with Daphne and Jasper as much as I did. I'd appreciate an honest review at your favorite store and/or wherever you go to learn about books. Your feedback can help the Uncommon Lords and Ladies series find the right audience.

I'd love to hear what you think of my stories, so feel free to drop me a line in email to:

* author@margaretmcgaffeyfisk.com

or use the contact form on:

* margaretmcgaffeyfisk.com

And while you are there, if you sign up for my monthly newsletter, I'll share a bit of my writing and publishing journey, fun events, and even snippets or pre-publication stories as a thank you for letting me into your inbox. You can also choose to receive just release announcements, which are split into genre and go out only when a new title is available in that genre. Feel free to select as many options as you'd like.

If you'd like to read an excerpt from *A Country Masquerade* (Book Two), please turn the page.

A Country Masquerade

Book Two of Uncommon Lords And Ladies

Unthinking criticism, bad timing, and a young lady's stubborn nature turn the
perfect match into a recipe for disaster.

Lady Barbara Whitfeld stood still as Sarah helped her out of the simple, but elegant, white gown she'd worn to the poetry reading.

She hardly noticed Sarah's efforts, her mind still caught up in the rich tones and lovely words Aubrey St. Vincent had offered in his reading. He'd put the rest of the gentlemen to shame.

"Your mother should not be having you out so late every night," Sarah scolded. "You'll have to sleep well past noon to keep from getting dark circles beneath your eyes, and what then will the young gentlemen say."

Barbara laughed as cloth pooled about her feet. "Sarah, you sound like a woman twice your age. You know full well you'd have been happy at my side. You're just jealous." She stepped free and sat at the dressing table.

Her best friend and maid softened enough to smile. "Jealous of what? Listening to conceited men talking about lines on paper? I think you're mistaken."

"Ah, but what lines. To hear them read aloud makes such a difference. Resonate tones, elocution…it makes the poems come alive, I tell you."

Sarah released the last of the pins holding back Barbara's riot of dark brown curls and ran her fingers through to loosen them further. "He was there, then, was he?"

Barbara raised both hands to cover her cheeks, but from Sarah's knowing glance reflected in the mirror, she knew she'd failed to hide her response. She shrugged as though it were of no consequence, then a grin burst out across her lips. "Aubrey St. Vincent. A better specimen of the male breed I've yet to see. Handsome, reasoned, and kind. The perfect gentleman."

"You'd have me believe him a paragon of virtues. The only man to meet such a standard is one still in the cradle, and even then they're all about demanding attention." Sarah laid a heavy stroke through Barbara's hair, and it caught on a tangle.

"Not so rough," Barbara cried. "And he is all that and more." She raised a hand to count off on her fingers. "He escorts his youngest sister to all manner of gatherings when other young men are off seeking their own pleasures. He doesn't retire to the card room the moment they arrive at an event. He's willing to participate when asked like tonight, though he had no plans to read. One of the readers fell ill and could not attend. Then there's how he considers education in philosophy something even women should be able to strive for."

"Enough, enough," Sarah wailed, both hands pressed to her ears though the twinkle in her eyes belied her protests. "You've made quite a study of the man, but I've heard it all before. You marked him as your interest at the very start of the season. So tell me, did you speak with him this time?"

All confidence drained from Barbara as she stared at her twisting fingers, no longer raised to count his worth. She'd encountered Aubrey on her first outing when, sitting against the wall unnoticed, she'd overheard him discussing how unsettled the Continent was. His conversation attracted her attention when the other young men spoke only of fashion and horses.

Since then, his presence acted like a beacon, calling out to her. She did what she could to be within earshot, and if she succeeded, almost every time she learned something new or had a thought to ponder. Still, she'd never spoken a single word to the man.

Sarah tucked a curl back behind Barbara's ear. "Your mother would be happy to arrange an introduction, I'm sure. He's a man of good standing, from a good family, and with a title of his own free and clear since he has only sisters. An earl, he'll be."

Barbara pulled away and rose, though what she intended once upright, she had no idea. "I've seen the way mothers bring their daughters up to meet him. He's surrounded by them too often for me to miss. I can't come to him as just another young lady in white and expect him to notice."

"Don't you think that way," Sarah said, rushing to catch her arm "You meet with him proper, Barbara, or you'll do nothing but make yourself out to be a fool, especially when the man in question shows no sign of returning your regard. But then, how could he share your interest when you've avoided the chance for an introduction. You want to stand out from the rest. That's how to do it. Get your introduction and show Lord Aubrey you can put more than two sentences together without dissolving into cloying giggles."

They shared a significant look, remembering the afternoon party Lady Whitfeld had arranged shortly after Barbara's presentation. Sarah had assisted the staff and so suffered the same babble and attempts to preen Barbara had. A bunch of ninnies with nothing of consequence between their ears, and her mother wanted her to find bosom friends among them.

Barbara had Sarah for her companion. None of them had offered an adequate substitute.

Her mirth faded as she addressed the flaw in her approach. "But what if I do? What if, when faced with none other than the most perfect Aubrey St. Vincent, my tongue curls up in my mouth and my mind vanishes into the clouds. Sarah, how can I be sure of the impression I'll give. You've heard my mother often enough. She says first impressions are the most important as they form the foundation of everything going forward. I cannot chance this going astray."

Sarah shook her head, but when she met Barbara's gaze, her own held sympathy. "Better to take that risk than never to chance it all. Trust yourself enough. You've certainly studied his habits, read whatever you heard him mention, and even plagued your father about the questions you didn't understand. You've prepared for this moment better than most gentleman study for their examinations. Besides, how could he not be taken in by your combination of beauty and thought? If he isn't, then he's not the paragon you seem to think him either."

Barbara laughed at Sarah's stout support, but knew she'd be hard pressed to put her friend's advice into effect when faced with the gentleman in question.

"Just promise me you'll try nothing foolish. Tradition has set these ways for presentation to society, and it's because they prove worthwhile. Hatching some crazy plan will only bring you trouble."

Barbara turned away more to hide her smile than because she disagreed. "You're sounding old enough to be my mother again, Sarah. Not so long ago, you were happy to join me in whatever adventures I could concoct."

She climbed into bed, pulling the covers up under her chin so she could peek out at her friend.

Sarah paused in collecting the discarded clothing. "Fair enough," she said, her gaze on a distance place, "But that was when you were at your father's country estate, or your uncle's farm, not here in London. You're not to run wild. It will do you a disservice and break your mother's heart. If sounding old is how I must be to keep you from trouble, then I'll turn the hag rather than see you receive a reputation you cannot recover from."

Barbara sank lower, no longer playing as she accepted the somber warning. London did have its own standards, and gossip ran rampant. She'd taken many months to adjust when brought up from the country a few years ago, and even now found its strictures confining.

"Besides," Sarah added with a rich chuckle, "If you fail to catch in your season, you'll be left to live out your days under your mother's thumb, which means I will too. That's a sorry end neither of us would prefer."

Though her mother little deserved such a slight, and well Sarah knew it, Barbara appreciated the effort to lighten her mood. She waved her friend off with a smile. "Then I'd best catch some sleep or those black circles will come whether you will them or not."

Arms full with soiled clothing, Sarah paused in the doorway. "I'll bring you a cup of chamomile tea. That will send you into a deep, soothing rest."

Her friend didn't wait for Barbara to answer, and from the yawn that split Barbara's face, she suspected sleep would overtake her long before Sarah returned. At least the tea would not go to waste, and Sarah needed the rest as much as any what with having to manage Barbara's complicated wardrobe now that she'd been presented.

Thoughts full of balls, readings, and theater, Barbara sank into oblivion. At least in her dreams, she could amaze Aubrey with her wit and wisdom.

Available in eBook and print.
Purchase a copy at your local bookstore or preferred online vendor.

About the Author

Margaret McGaffey Fisk is a storyteller who explores tales across genres and worlds. Raised in the Foreign Service where she developed a love for anthropology, she has been a data entry clerk, veterinary tech, editor, support engineer, and programmer, among other roles. She pulls on her studies and experiences to give depth to the cultures and people that form the heart of her stories. As her website is titled, she offers tales to tide you over.

She'd love to hear from you through any of the contact points or social media accounts listed on her website, or you can subscribe to one of her newsletters for release announcements, snippets, and other news:

margaretmcgaffeyfisk.com/subscribe-to-my-newsletter/

Website

MargaretMcGaffeyFisk.com

Acknowledgments

There have been many who've helped me on the path to this moment. I would like to thank each and every one of you who encouraged me in my writing, took a moment to listen to my mad blathering when stuck on a plot point (especially my sons), or offered a suggestion, a critique, or a shoulder to cry on.

I thank my husband, Colin, for bearing with me; the band of writing friends I've collected, especially Erin Hartshorn, Valerie Comer, Dawn Hebein, and Lazette Gifford, all of whom helped with this particular novel; and my parents and sisters who, while questioning other decisions as family does, never once pushed me to put down my metaphorical pen.

www.ingramcontent.com/pod-product-compliance
Lightning Source LLC
Chambersburg PA
CBHW030616120726
47904CB00006B/1923